WAHIDA CLARK PRESENTS INNOVATIVE PUBLISHING

LONERS

D.B. Bray
with Wahida Clark

Wahida Clark Presents Publishing
60 Evergreen Place
Suite 904A
East Orange, New Jersey 07018
1(866) 910-6920
www.wclarkpublishing.com

Library of Congress Cataloging-In-Publication Data:

Loners
ISBN 978-1-947732-87-2 Hardback
978-1-947732-90-2 ebook
978-1-954161-06-1 paperback
978-1-954161-07-8 Audiobook
978-1-954161-08-5 special edition ebook

1.   Dark fantasy dwarves 2. Adventure Grimdark   3. Sword and sorcery 4. Epic fantasy   5.   Minotaur goblins orcs

Cover design and layout by Nuance Art, LLC
Book design by www.artdiggs.com
Editorial Team: Natalie Sade and Phillip Smith
Printed in United States

Dedication for those lost

To my mother, Patty who passed from this world years ago who bought me my first King Arthur book and sparked my imagination.

My father-in-law, Bray who's name I have taken in his honor after he has left the Earth.

And to my Uncle, Eugene (The Gov) Mack for keeping me entertained with stories of the mighty King Brian Baru and why I should be proud of being Irish.

Acknowledgement

I just want to take a second and thank everyone who made this book possible. 2020 was a pretty tough year for everyone around the world. COVID did a ton of damage and wiped out so many of our loved ones that we didn't know where to turn.

My uncle died from COVID just before I started writing this book with Wahida Clark, The Official Queen of Street Lit and who now is looking to get back in the ring for the Queen of Dwarven Fantasy or as we say here at TEAM WCP (DWA). Dwarves With Attitude.

So, this is how I met Wahida Clark. I founded my show The OooWeee Chronicles during COVID on IG and after interviewing her (with a really janky flyer), I am now sitting on this cover with her.

Many of you have never heard of me, and that's not a problem. I'm just the proof you need to know that with a pen and a legal pad anything is possible in this field. Anything!

So, I'll take a quick minute and start with thanking my wife, Dolores. My rock in an otherwise unpredictable and harsh world.

A special heartfelt thanks to Barry Benham and my father Brad. K'wan (The Biggie of Literature), Stanley James II, Val King, Shannon Green, Karl Haycock, Walt Allen, Chase Bolling, Baby Chaos, Kelly and Chaim Holtjer, Mursit Catal, and our ever faithful steeds, The Fjord Horses who we ride as The Queens Vanguard.

And lastly and most certainly not least, Queen Wahida Clark and Nuance Art who gave this writer a shot that would have faded from the pages of literature without their belief in me.

So, enjoy The Loners. And remember, no matter how dark the day begins, the sun will rise again, the moon will shine ever so brightly, and you'll make it another day! Just keep writing, hell, it's what we do. Writers bring the torches to light your cavern. With the Queens compliments, the woman who they told, "It cant be done"

Bleed The Pen- K'wan Foye

-DB Bray

LONERS

Chapter 1

Bounty hunting is a complicated job; some love you, most despise you. But if Jari Rockjaw showed up with a poster, it was your final day on Labrys.

Goblins always attack when the dew still clings to the long, green grass. They are easy quarry . . . too easy. With a loud rip, Jari sliced off another ear, then touched his temple and winced. One of the goblins clubbed him in the head as he was engaged with two other brutish ones. After all three had been dispatched, he cursed himself for not paying closer attention to his surroundings.

I hate these shitty goblins.

The battlefield in front of him was slick with blood. With a sigh, he spat a large wad of phlegm from his parched throat. The field was not only choked with scores of goblins, but most of his mercenary company lay dead or dying around him.

A large minotaur approached him through the grey mist. "Betha," Jari said in greeting.

She growled a greeting in return and dropped her bag of ears. Gently, she slid her fingers across the deep gashes peppering her chiseled body.

"Couple more scars to add to your collection?" Jari asked with a wink.

"Don't need armor," she growled and with a grunt, hacking off an ear of another goblin nearby. "Shitty goblins."

Jari chuckled. The thing about Betha was she didn't like her own kind, often preferring the company of dwarves as companions (they were the most loyal). The two of them were allies, well, for the most part anyway. Wherever Jari went, Betha was always close behind.

Jari and other hunters like him really didn't care what race of beings they hunted—just the prices for their ears or scalps. They frequently hunted rogue dwarves, goblins, orcs, minotaurs, elves, centaurs, harpies, and any other group that raided the kingdom. This week, it was a pesky group of goblins raiding the settlements closest to the city of Port Agu.

There wasn't much money in goblin ears, but plenty of money in other groups like elves and dwarves, who sometimes put aside ancient feuds to pillage the lands around them . . . most no better than brigands and highwaymen. Jari had recently heard a rumor that a leader had started organizing the rabble into an army, far-fetched as it may have seemed.

The other members of their small group struggled in with their own spoils of war. A young dwarf with a hook for one hand gave a mock salute to Jari and smiled wide.

"Surprised you lived, Toli Hookhand. How many ears have you claimed?" Jari asked.

"Not enough to retire, but enough for a few mugs of gut-rot," he said.

Jari shrugged. "Always thinking about a drink, aren't you?" he asked.

"Or lasses. Large dwarven asses," Toli said, grabbing his crotch.

Toli was short, even for a dwarf. He stood two and a half feet tall, closer to a goblin in stature than his own kind. His black braided beard hung to his waist, knotted by silver beads, and the hair on top of his head was shaved on the sides and dyed bright blond.

Toli whistled a melody and started to sing. *"Oh, the beautiful dwarven lasses' asses make me so eager for a drink, but Jari likes . . ."*

Jari frowned. Toli smiled and sang, *"A big fat stink!"*

Jari shook his head and went back to scalping. Toli jiggled his open canteen over his mouth. "Not even a drip," he muttered.

A goblin lying nearby tried to crawl away from the group. Betha spotted it edging his way out, his entrails dragging along with him. She snorted, rattling the bronze septum ring in her muzzle. The goblin made a quick glance over its shoulder and crawled faster. She took two giant leaps, landed on the goblin's back, and pulled its head back in one motion. Jari heard the sickening tear as she cut its ears off. The goblin screeched until Betha cut its throat with a knife fastened to her hoof.

Jari glanced at her and swallowed the lump in his throat. In all the years he had known her, he never dared to ask why she was missing one horn, or why the other was broken in half. Grizzled and hardened, she was a true warrior, keen on killing everything that wasn't on her side.

I'm glad she's on my side, he thought, inspecting the bloody ears clutched in one paw and a blood-drenched, large, double-sided battle-ax in the other.

He glanced around at the latest group he led, at least, those who were left. Most were exiled dwarves from the Blue Mountains, a three-day ride to the northwest.

Toli walked up to him and hissed, "I never liked the Yellow Dwarves. They stink of fear."

Jari smiled at him. "Maybe, but these bunches weren't

cowards," he said.

"Says you."

"Is it just me, or did one of them save your life toda—"

"I didn't need any help," Toli snapped.

Jari stared at the dwarf a few feet away who took the sword blow meant for Toli. "I beg to differ. Now, bury him." He motioned to Betha, who was looting corpses. "Betha, let's ride out," Jari said, pushing past Toli.

The dwarves waited for Toli to bury the dead dwarf, then mounted their ponies and rode off. Betha kept pace with them as they rode toward Port Agu in the Kingdom of Ekepia. The lush, rolling meadows they rode through gave way to Volcano Valley, a place full of black, white, and red volcanoes with rivers of lava meandering through the countryside.

Labrys was a small world, full of humans, dwarves, elves, orcs, lizardfolk, lionfolk, and any other number of races. Yellow and black icebergs floated around every coast, making a natural harbor defense. An open desert in the middle called The Expanse stretched for hundreds of miles in every direction, and several different mountain ranges on the upper crust led to the mercenary city of Anak'anor.

Jari rode at the head of the column and tugged on his bloodred beard. He was tall for a dwarf, standing nearly five feet. He was missing his right eye and had a long scar running over the socket. He glanced at the volcanoes looming overhead, casting shadows across the land. He twitched in the saddle when he saw a band of raiders watching them from the cliffs above. Without incident, they soon reached the gates of Port Agu and rode through the front entrance.

Jari led them to The Scalp, a tavern for hunters. He dismounted, walked up to the doors, and flung them open. The floor creaked as he crossed. To him, the tavern was home, the only place a dwarf could be at peace.

He walked up to the table where some scalp hunters sat. A familiar face greeted him and pulled out his ledger as Jari approached. Kala Silverbeard was a closer ally than most, but Jari didn't completely trust him, even after all the years he had known him. Kala raised an eyebrow and nodded in Jari's direction.

"Jari, I didn't expect you back so soon," Kala said.

"Not much of a fight," he said, dropping his blood-soaked bag on the table.

Kala glanced behind Jari and said, "If I recall, you left with fifteen and returned with seven. I'd venture to say it was a little more resistance than you expected."

Jari smiled and sighed. "Every battle is costly, Kala. I'm here for my coin, not your observations."

"Fair enough," Kala said, pulling a pouch full of coins out of a box on the table.

Goblin ears were only really worth a mug of gut-rot, a brew made from fermented potatoes and juniper leaves. It was a highly potent alcoholic beverage that usually burned going down and when it came back up or went out the other end.

Kala counted out fifteen ears from Jari's bag and then handed him thirty coins. The Yellow Dwarves followed his lead, got their pay, and walked out of the tavern without saying a word to Jari. It always went that way. They were work associates, never friends.

Jari, Betha, and Toli sat in a shady part of the tavern by the door. Jari never kept his back to anything. It was too easy for someone to slip a knife in between his ribs. He glanced at the door and then swung his chair around for a better angle.

Betha was already on her second mug of gut-rot before he started his first. She always did everything in excess, without a care in the world. In part, Jari envied her. She never spoke about her past unless she drank herself into a blind drunk.

"Betha, don't you miss seeing your tribe?" Jari asked.

He thought he noticed a slight smile on her lips, but it could have been a sneer. "No, they're probably all dead by now," she said.

"So, you don't—" Betha cut her eyes at him, ending his sentence.

Jari knew better than to press the issue. It could have negative consequences. One night, he had been brazen enough to press the question he asked when the mood struck him. A thump on the noggin from the flat of her ax was enough to still his thoughts for the rest of the evening.

"Kala told me there was a group of female dwarven belly dancers performing tonight," Toli said, trying to lighten the mood.

Jari snickered and took another long pull from his mug. "Dwarven belly dancers? Do you only think of half-naked lasses?"

"Have to create little dwarves, don't we?" Toli said, elbowing Jari in the ribs.

Betha roared with laughter and slammed her paw on the table. Toli and Jari stared at her as she pointed across the room. Belly dancers were weaving in and out of the crowd in front of them, making their way to the table.

One of them danced by Toli, her lips moist with saliva. He jumped up on the table in front of the dancer and started singing, his feet moving swiftly for one so short with his hands on his hips. Betha glanced up at him with a drunken chuckle until he accidentally kicked her mug off the table.

With catlike reflexes, she grabbed his ankles and threw him onto the dancer. Jari laughed so hard, gut-rot poured out of his nostrils. He slapped Betha on the back and clapped his hands as Toli helped the dancer up.

The belly dancer straightened her short skirt and slapped Toli across the face. He stumbled back and fell onto Betha's lap. Jari kept laughing until tears rolled down his cheeks. Betha, not amused, pushed Toli off her and took his mug from the table.

"The dancer hits better than you do," Jari shouted above the laughter from the other dwarves in the tavern.

Toli rolled his sleeves up and gave him a drunken smile. The other dwarves watching him roared with laughter as Toli licked his lips.

He watched the dancer walk away, staring at her succulent hips swaying back and forth. "Don't wait up, lads."

Chapter 2

Jari opened his eye and winced. The night had ended like every other he spent in Port Agu. Hungover and feeling like fire ants were parading around his mouth and throat, he got out of bed. Betha snored in the next bed over. A herd of Loxodons could have stampeded through their tent, and she wouldn't have blinked an eye. He didn't see Toli anywhere in the room, and that meant he was only in one likely place . . . a fair dwarven lass's bed.

As he washed his face in the bowl of water in the middle of the tent, Toli burst in with a smile that only a well laid dwarf could, or would, make.

"Good morning, Jari."

Jari nodded in his direction and went back to washing his face.

"It's an absolutely lovely morning, isn't it?" Toli pressed.

Jari shook his head and wiped his face. "Do you have any news, other than the good time you had last night?"

"Actually . . ." He pulled a piece of parchment from his pocket. "New bounties posted this morning. Seems like a group of Dark Elves raided a settlement and destroyed it. Thirty coins a scalp," Toli said.

"That a fact?" Jari asked, snatching the paper out of his hand.

They heard a loud groan behind them, and without turning around, they both said, "Good morning, Betha."

Jari went back to studying the bounty poster and muttered under his breath. He looked over the rim of the paper and said, "Toli, put the word out. I'm forming a new company. We leave at first light to search for this group. It says there should be at least twenty, so I'll need at least fifteen more hunters."

Toli saluted and ran out.

Betha walked up behind him. "Another contract?"

"Seems so." Jari walked over to his armor, and as he put it on, he said, "Group of Dark Elves causing some sort of ruckus. We find them and exterminate them," he said, pulling his dented helmet on.

"How much per scalp?" she asked.

"Thirty."

She ran her paw across the edge of her battle-ax and said, "For thirty a scalp, I'll stuff the bodies as proof."

"Easy, Betha, these are Dark Elves, not shitty little goblins. You know they have talent and are slippery as mercury. Don't rush in headlong like the last battle, or you won't live long enough to spend the scalp money," he said.

Betha snorted. "Don't tell me business, Jari Rockjaw. I've saved your worthless hide in more battles than I care to count. Now, do you want to go and collect our coins or join the Yellow Dwarves?"

Jari's face flushed.

"That's what I thought. Now make yourself useful while I get my beauty sleep," she said.

"The Dwarven Lords will retake Labrys before that happens," Jari muttered under his breath.

"What was that?"

"Nothing," he said, picking up some bacon and a cast-iron skillet.

Several hours later, they walked over to The Scalp. There were only a few dwarves in the bar drinking by themselves. Toli sat at the bar, chatting with the old dwarven barkeep.

"Where is everybody?" Jari asked.

"They heard it was Dark Elves, and the other hunters wanted no part of it," Toli said with a shrug.

"We can't kill twenty Dark Elves by ourselves," Jari said.

"Speak for yourself, Jari," Betha said after ordering a drink.

He shot her an evil glance. The saloon doors opened behind them, and a few different races walked in.

In the lead was a dwarf from the Blue Mountains flanked by two others. The dwarf walked over to the bar and stood nose to nose with Jari.

"Jari Rockjaw, heard you needed some mercs," the dwarf said.

"Gnok the Rock, I heard you were dead," Jari said, referring to his cousin by his nickname.

Gnok raised an eyebrow. "Warm blood still courses through these veins, at least for the moment."

Gnok was twice as wide as Jari. His black beard was tied in three separate braids, each with a large silver ball tied at the end. The two embraced for a few moments, and the pats on Jari's back brought an instant feeling of ease and comfort.

"I see you brought killers," Jari said.

"Indeed, I have," he replied.

"That's Sinda Rockgut," he said, pointing at a female dwarf ordering a drink.

Sinda was beautiful. Her long, red hair was tied in a thick french braid. Toli stared at her, his mouth agape. Betha reached over and closed it for him.

"You have no chance. Now, keep it in your pants," she said.

Gnok pointed at the tortle behind him. "This is Arnak. He's the best Hah-Nu-Nah I've ever served with," he said.

Hah-Nu-Nahs were large, quiet, tortle humanoids who spoke

with their weapons instead of their mouths. He had a scar that ran across his face from just above his left eye to his jawline, and he carried the largest spiked club Jari had ever seen. Arnak nodded a greeting as he stood silently against the bar.

"A Hah-Nu-Nah? Never seen one up close," Jari said.

Toli gave Jari a buzzed smile from the gut-rot he was drinking and pushed on Arnak's green scales with his stubby index finger. Arnak looked down with a growl and pushed him away.

"He killed four orcs the other day single-handedly," Gnok said.

Jari nodded and stared at him in wonder. "I wouldn't stare if I was you. He hates that," Gnok said as Arnak looked over at him.

Jari made eye contact.

"Help you with something, Dwarf?" Arnak asked in a gravelly voice.

"Nope. Just counting the new company members," he said.

Jari continued counting the faces. "That makes six. Still not enough to hunt Dark Elves," he said.

A few soldiers from the King's Guard walked in, arrogant smiles across their faces. Their leader, a human, walked over and shook Jari's hand.

"King Zista bids you blessings, Jari Rockjaw," the man said with a bow.

Jari sighed. "Lord Polis Silverwell, what brings you here?" he asked.

Polis shrugged, inspected a dirty shot glass, and then sniffed the contents with disdain. "The king heard you were forming a company to go after some Dark Elves. He wants to see if you will bring him a scouting report on the countryside instead. We have good intelligence that a leader who calls himself Boro Spiderbinder, a dwarf from the Silver Peaks, is organizing the raiders."

"Boro Spiderbinder? Figures," Gnok said with a sigh.

Polis raised an eyebrow. "You know him?"

Gnok spit. "Yeah, we all do. I've been in a few raiding companies with him when we were young."

"Is that the same guy who burned all those villages on the western plains?" Jari asked.

Gnok nodded and watched Sinda walk over to them. "Uh-oh, here comes trouble."

Sinda ran her finger across her knife blade. "If I see him again, I'll kill him, so I'm going with you," she said, and then walked over to the table with her drink.

"What was that about?" Polis asked.

Gnok frowned and tugged at his beard. "Boro is... Nevermind. He burned down their village and killed her family," he said.

"Oh, so she is single?" Toli prodded.

Gnok was not amused. "What did you say, Pint Size?"

Betha knocked Toli to the ground, lifted him up by the pants, and dropped him behind the bar. "Apologies. He's had too much gut-rot," Betha said.

Gnok nodded.

Jari gave Toli a look of disgust and then made eye contact with Gnok. "So, what's in it for us, Polis?"

"King Zista is prepared to offer you an extra hundred coins," Polis said.

Jari scoffed. "We're mercenaries, not scouts. Warriors fight, scouts report. I won't risk my company on a mission that will probably entail much more than you're saying," Jari informed him.

Polis chuckled. "Then what do you want?" he asked.

"I think it's time for you to be honest with me. What is this job really for?" Jari asked.

Polis smirked and said, "We need to ascertain the situation, and if need be, kill Boro if he has the power we think he has."

Jari looked around. "Out comes the truth. Well, then, I think my warriors would like to retire," he said.

Polis laughed. "You won't retire on this mission alone," he said.

"That may be so, but it's obvious you fear him, or you wouldn't be here aski—"

Polis made to interrupt him, but Jari held his hand up. "You're asking for intel, fine. But you have no other choice because we fit the criteria of his warriors. And you know you can't infiltrate their camp."

Polis shrugged. "Jari, you're right. If it were possible for us, I wouldn't be here."

"Then if you want him dead, we retire."

Polis smirked and tapped his fingers on the bar, then winked. "I'll have an answer for you in the morning. I don't speak for the king, only deliver his messages. No promises."

Jari looked at the faces of his little company, most of them drinking from their mugs and minding their own business.

Betha leaned her battle-ax against the bar. "I'm in," she said.

Jari glanced at Toli, who nodded with a smile from behind the bar. "My new hammer needs some breaking in, and retirement sounds mighty good to me."

He turned to Gnok. "What about you, Gnok?" Jari asked.

Gnok glanced at Sinda and Arnak, who were sitting at the table in a hushed conversation. Arnak looked up and nodded. Sinda was busy sharpening her knives.

"We're with you," Gnok said quietly.

"Looks like we're all in, Polis. Meet us back here at first light with more men and an answer from the king," he said after taking a sip from his mug.

Polis smiled at him and left with his men. Jari and the others went to sit at the table with Sinda and Arnak. Sinda waved the barman over and ordered another drink.

"So, we go," Jari said, staring into his mug.

This is not the plan I had in mind, he thought.

"It will be difficult to get into his camp. We will have to kill a patrol and take their uniforms. If we manage to do that, it will be even harder to get into Boro's tent."

"So, what do you suggest?" Jari asked.

"Pray to the gods for luck, because ours will run out," Gnok said and then paused. "We're dwarves, Jari. We're always doomed."

Chapter 3

The next morning, Jari sat in front of their tent as the sun rose on the horizon. Leaving Port Agu was never hard. He preferred to sleep under the stars.

He heard Betha's snores from behind the tent flap and shook his head. *That snore will give us away when we get there.*

He chuckled to himself and took a bite of his dried salt beef.

Toli came out of the tent with a deep yawn and raised his hook over his head. He touched his toes and adjusted his hammer when he stood back up.

"Morning," Toli said.

Jari nodded a greeting and took another bite of beef. Toli walked over and stood in front of him.

"We ready to go?" he asked.

Jari pushed him aside with his hand. "You're spoiling my view."

Toli glanced over his shoulder. "Oh, sorry."

Toli moved out of the way just as the sun peeked through the grey clouds. The rays of sun touched Jari's cheeks and moved up his face. He closed his eye and warmed his only eyelid.

The sunrises in Labrys were beautiful . . . breathtaking, even. Jari stared straight ahead as they watched the sunrise a little further in the sky. It soon blanketed them. Jari yawned and took another bite of beef.

"Shit don't get no better than this. By this time, the next moon, we'll be retired with enough coin to watch this every morning," Toli said.

Jari scoffed. "You think this is a milk run we're going on?"

"No, I—"

Jari cut him off. "—am being an idiot, like usual. You know this may be the death of you."

Toli smiled. "Gotta die someday, may as well be for retirement. I'll get Betha. It's getting late."

The trio walked into The Scalp and found Gnok, Sinda, and Arnak sitting at a table sipping stew from their wooden bowls. Jari walked over and pulled up a chair.

"Morning, Gnok," he said.

"Morning."

"You ready to go?" Jari asked.

"We are, but we need to set a few ground rules for this venture," Gnok said.

Jari raised an eyebrow and took the warm cup of tea from the bar Toli gave him. "And that is?" he asked.

"First, my warriors are worth more than yours, so they get the first choice of loot. Second, if I think your friend Polis isn't shooting straight dice, I'll kill him. Finally, if we get close to Boro, Sinda has the right to kill him."

"I agree, except for the loot. Whoever kills their opponent is entitled to the loot." He waved Betha over to the table. "Unless you want to tell *her* that she can't have *her* loot," Jari said.

Betha snorted at Gnok and leaned against her ax. "You want to fight me for it, Gnok?"

Arnak stood up, walked over to her, and put his club over his shoulder. "You will go through me first, Taur. Do you want that?"

Jari stepped between the two as Betha tapped her hoof on the floor. "Easy now. There will be plenty of loot for everyone."

Polis walked in with several men and watched the situation unfold. Gnok looked at him with disdain and sipped more of his stew. Jari glanced over his shoulder and waved him over.

"Greetings, Jari Rockjaw," Polis said.

"Enough with the pleasantries, Polis. What did King Zista say?"

"The king says if you are successful in your mission, he will retire you and the rest of your company," Polis said.

"Why don't I believe you, Polis?" Betha asked, still eyeing Arnak.

"I'm not asking you too, Betha. I've been instructed to take you near Boro's camp north of here and await your return," he said.

Jari chuckled. "Polis, this smells like a trap."

"You have my word; this is no trap. Why would I do that? King Zista is a man of his word. Has he ever been known for breaking it?" Polis asked.

Jari shrugged. "If you screw u—"

Polis butted in. "Or what?"

Jari paused and looked at his companions. "We'll kill you *and* your men."

Kala, the scalp master, walked in the tavern. Jari glanced at him and turned around with a smile. Kala was dressed in his ancient armor, some pieces so tight they looked like they were cutting off his circulation. He wore a thick silver breastplate, and his silver hair ran in two plaits over both shoulders. His shield hit his back as he approached, making the sound of nails hitting a tin roof.

"Kala, you look like you're heading to war," Jari said with a laugh.

"Overheard you talking about your mission, and these bones of mine are tired. I want to retire too," he said.

Jari looked at the large warhammer in his hand and nodded.

"That what I think it is?" he asked.

Kala hoisted it up and took a practice swing. "It is."

Jari had heard of Kala's exploits as a child. He was the only warrior who took the time to train young dwarves like him, who had been orphaned from the constant wars.

Kala was a kind soul, but his warhammer had claimed many scalps in his one hundred years of fighting. Approaching two hundred and twenty, he knew he wasn't long for the world. But at one point, he was one of the best mercenaries in Labrys, a worthy addition to the band of warriors.

"You want to go, Kala? This is not going to be in and out. Our odds are slim this will even go well. All of us want to retire. You sure about this?" Jari asked.

Kala walked up to Jari face-to-face and said, "If you ever question one of my decisions again, Jari, I'll make sure you never see another sunrise."

Jari smiled and looked at Polis. "Seems like we're ready and all here," he said, stepping out of Kala's way.

Polis closed his fist, placed it over his heart, and said, "And so it begins."

Chapter 4

The small group made their way out of Port Agu, and Jari breathed a sigh of relief as the clean air hit his face. He preferred the cool air of the mountains to the polluted air of the cities. The oxygen levels were higher near the frozen oceans, and as they passed, Jari got a little light-headed.

"You all right over there?" Betha asked.

Jari nodded with a smile and kept riding. They rode in relative silence until Polis held his hand up a few miles down the road. Standing in their way was a massive orc with a bloody club in his hand, and several bodies laid out in front of him.

"None pass," the orc said with a gruff voice, its incisors jutting out from the bottom of his lip.

"By order of King Zista, move!" Polis said.

The orc laughed.

Jari glanced at Betha and nodded. She stared at the orc for a long moment before moving.

"Is that you, Zog?" she bellowed.

The orc stood silently as if he didn't hear her. "If that's you, Zog. Stand—"

Zog slammed his club into the ground. "Betha, you want to be first Zog kills?"

Betha shook her head and looked at Jari. "He's drunk."

"Well, then, move him," Polis said, moving his horse aside.

"Have to kill him to move him," she said.

Polis shrugged. "And?"

"That's one of the best orc mercs on Labrys still alive, anyway. I've seen him kill scores of men and beasts," she said, shouldering her ax.

"Are you scared?" Polis asked.

Staring straight ahead, she said, "Human, don't tempt me. I would love nothing more than to kill you and say you fell on your own sword. If you want him dead, ride to meet him."

Polis glared at her. "I'm the leader of this party. Kill him, or—"

Jari's eye opened wide at the statement. "Lea—"

Betha swung her fist up at Polis and knocked him out of the saddle. His men rushed to his side and leveled their swords at her. She unslung her ax and stretched. "Who's first?"

Zog's laughter carried high in the sky. Betha watched him take a swig from the cow's liver he carried.

"Shit, he's drinking cow's blood mixed with gut-rot. He's *beyond* drunk," she muttered.

Polis's men took one look at the orc and then at Betha. They sheathed their swords, picked up Polis, and carried him to the rear.

Betha turned back and stared at Zog. She tapped her hoof against the ground as she thought. Then she opened Jari's saddlebag and pulled out a pouch.

"I'd like to know where you think you're going with my coins," Jari said.

"I'm buying help," Betha said.

"We already have enough warriors in our company," he protested.

"Jari, we have weak humans with us. If someone watches our backs, it will be the best. I just got to sober him up."

Jari tugged on his bloodred beard. "Good luck."

Jari and the others watched Betha approach Zog. He swayed unsteadily on his legs. With a loud belch, he lifted his club. Betha stopped a few feet out of his kill radius and threw the pouch at his feet.

Zog glanced at his feet and kicked the pouch back over. He raised both arms and roared, his double chin jiggling.

"Come, Betha, see you can beat the Mighty Zog."

Betha stayed still. "I won't fight you, Zog. I want to pay for your services."

"And you think this will help you?" he asked, spitting on the pouch.

Betha snorted, her hoof tapping the ground. "Zog, don't make me kill you."

It was Zog's turn to chuckle. "You and the little people?" he said with a hiccup. "Taur?"

Betha never even heard him call her a minotaur before she had her battle-ax swinging at his head. Zog ducked and slammed the end of his stone club in her stomach. Betha roared and hit him with an uppercut. He staggered back and then kicked Betha in the chest. As he gripped his club to launch a counterattack, Arnak leaped past Betha, spun in midair, and slammed his shell into Zog's face, knocking him out. Then Arnak held his hand out and helped Betha up. She shook him off.

"Didn't need help," she snorted.

"Yes, you did," Arnak grumbled before walking back to stand by Sinda.

Betha picked Zog up and threw him over her shoulder. She walked back over to Jari and shrugged.

"He's worth it, believe me," she said, lifting him onto the wagon Polis brought along.

The group moved past the bodies in the road, stripped them bare, and kept riding.

A few hours later when they were making camp, they heard Zog growling as he woke up.

"Betha," he roared.

Betha walked to the side of the wagon and double-checked the ropes holding Zog's charcoal-colored arms and legs.

"You ready to play nice, Zog?" she asked.

"No, get me out of wagon."

"Tsk tsk tsk." She stepped in front of him. "You should be grateful I didn't kill you. If you calm down, I'll tell you why we need you," she said.

"If you didn't have turtle, I would rip the last horn from your head!" Zog shouted.

He struggled with his bindings for a few more minutes and then lay still, his breathing labored. Betha waved the others away as they walked up behind her.

"I'm going to untie your bindings, Zog. If you attack, the king's guard will kill you," she said, pointing at the men with their crossbows raised a few feet away.

Polis walked up, rubbing his jaw. "I ought to kill you for that, Betha," he hissed.

She snarled at him and yanked her battle-ax free. "Fine, let's finish what we started."

Polis's men took a step back and lowered their crossbows. Polis sagged his shoulders in defeat and muttered, "Another time then."

Betha slit Zog's bindings with her knife, and he jumped to his feet. He frantically felt around his waist. Betha held up his cow skin and shook it.

"Are you looking for this?"

He reached for his cow skin and almost fell out of the cart.

Betha uncapped the top with her teeth and poured the contents onto the road. Zog roared and reached for his club. He felt around his back for a few moments and then saw it underneath Betha's hoof.

He pointed at her. "Give me club, Minotaur."

"Not until you agree to help," she said.

"I want to kill in the open, not in a group," he said, clenching his fists.

"You've fought with me enough to know what I can do. We'll pay you with all the scalps and ears you can carry and any loot you take off your dead. Are you with us?" she asked.

Zog let out a grumbling laugh and vaulted from the cart with catlike reflexes. "The Mighty Zog with you," he said.

With a snort, Betha flipped him his club and walked toward the fire.

"Great, now we have a drunk orc, Jari. Can it get any worse?" Toli asked after taking a sip from his full canteen of gut-rot.

"That's enough out of you, Toli," Jari hissed, following Betha to the fire with Toli right on his heels.

Polis patted one of his men on the back and said, "Scout ahead and let me know what's in front of us."

The man placed his fist over his heart and mounted his horse. He dug his heels into its flanks and rode off.

"Why are you sending a human scout into Spiderbinder territory? He's probably not coming back," Gnok said, pulling his blanket out of his saddlebag.

Polis shrugged. "Wasn't going to ask a group of dwarves to ride their ponies around in the dark."

Gnok shouldered Polis aside with a grunt and walked to the fire. Then he turned around after a few feet and said, "Careful, human." He glanced into the forest around them. "People end up in holes 'round here all the time. Tell me I ride my pony in the dark like some kind of simpleton, and you'll find yourself in a hole with your asshole sewn shut."

"My ass—"

Polis reddened as Zog pushed him into the cart as he walked by. "The one I pull out if you don't pay Mighty Zog."

Jari and Toli joined the others by the fire while Arnak prepared the stew for the night. He unfolded some papers that were filled with powder and then poured them into the cauldron.

"What's that you're putting in there?" Betha asked.

"Food," Arnak grumbled.

"All I see is a powder," she said.

Arnak smirked as the powder solidified in the stew and gave a very earthy aroma. He fished a large piece of grey matter from the pot and offered it to Betha.

Betha shook her head and took a sip from her canteen. "Don't think I want any of that stuff. I'll stick to my liquid diet of gut-rot mixed with cow's blood."

"Suit yourself," Arnak muttered before turning his shell to her.

Zog walked up to Betha from behind and slapped her on the back. Her canteen hit her septum ring and splashed down her chest. She growled as he sat down.

"You owe me drink," Zog said.

Betha handed him the canteen she was drinking from. "If you get shitfaced, I won't warn you before I kill you."

Zog roared with laughter. "Kill me? How you plan on mi—"

Zog felt the blade press against his upper rib cage, close to his heart. Betha snorted. "I won't warn you, *understand?*"

Zog nodded, stared her in the eyes, and winked. "Zog understand."

"Good, now where is the rest of your band of killers? Off fighting in the southern deserts again?" Betha asked, withdrawing her knife.

Zog was quiet for a moment, long enough for Betha to get the hint. "How many died?" she asked softly.

Zog grumbled and took a drink. "All."

Betha took a sharp breath and then stared at Zog in the firelight. "When?"

"Don't matter," he muttered.

"It matters. What happened, Zog?" she asked.

Jari and the others overheard their conversation across the fire and moved their eyes to Zog. Seeing their expressions, he took a long pull from his flask and then spat into the fire.

"Zog not far from here waiting on caravan to pass from Port Agu. The caravan was carr—"

"Weapons and gold," Polis said, cutting him off.

Zog growled and looked up. "So, Zog thought, human." His bottom incisors slid further from his jawline, and his brow furrowed. "The wagons covered. We charged out of tree line to rob, but different group attacked us." He pointed to the west. "They came from there." He took another sip. "Killed all traveling with Zog. I hit in head and woke up later. The wagons gone."

Betha shook her head. "Who was it?"

"Ask human," Zog said, pointing at Polis.

Everyone turned their gaze to him.

"How'd I guess he'd know," Gnok said, sliding his hand to his belt.

"Care to explain, Lord Polis?" Jari asked.

"No."

Jari stood up and walked over to him. He stuck his finger in Polis's face. "Speak! Is this why we're out here, to find lost weapons and gold?"

Polis ignored him.

Jari smiled. "Betha!"

Before his men could defend him, Betha hoisted Polis off the ground and dangled him six feet in the air by his neck. He sputtered and tried to free himself from her iron grip, but all he managed to accomplish was swinging in place. His men quickly drew their weapons and approached her.

"Put him down, Taur," one of Polis's braver men said, raising a crossbow to his shoulder.

"Taur, is it?" She squeezed Polis's throat until he started turning blue. "Back up, or he's dead."

Polis's men stepped back and lowered their weapons. With a final squeeze, she dropped him back to the ground. Polis gasped and then rubbed his throat for a few seconds as he coughed.

Jari knelt next to him, and after he finished coughing, he snatched him by the collar. "I think you were going to tell us about those wagons."

Chapter 5

"So, Lord Polis, I won't ask you again. Why are we out here?" Jari asked, sliding his hand to the ax hanging from his belt.

"Aghh—" Polis spat and wiped his tunic sleeve across his lips. "Damn. All right, I'll tell you. Boro Spiderbinder is in the southern mountains forming an army."

"That much you've told us," Jari said. "Tell us something I don't know."

Polis cracked a smile. "The king doesn't know we're out here," he said, barely above a whisper.

"*What* did you just say?" Toli asked, joining the conversation.

"I said the king doesn't know—"

Before he could finish, Gnok had him by the throat. "So, where's *our* money?"

Polis's smile gave way to a pathetic look. "My son has disappeared, and the princess has been taken captive. I couldn't tell the king. He would have killed me if he—"

Toli moved his hook closer to Polis's throat. "Not our problem. Now, where's the gold?"

"Release him, Gnok," Jari said.

Gnok released his grip. Polis pushed Toli's hook away with his finger, stood up, and brushed himself off. "I planned to pay you with the wagons that would find themselves lost in transit, but now they're gone."

"Zog made that clear," Gnok said, pushing Polis out of his way. "Then my team and I are done here."

Gnok readied to leave. Sinda held up her hand, Arnak by her side. "You can leave if you want, but I'm going after that slimy shit, Boro," she said. "And when I'm done with him, I'll cut his ears off and sell them in Port Agu."

"I'm staying with Sinda," Arnak grumbled.

Gnok gave an exasperated sigh, then moaned. "You know there's no coin in this, right, Sinda?"

Sinda nodded. "Some things are worth more than coins."

Gnok ran his hands through his hair and lowered his head. "This is a bad move, but I'll stay with Sinda too. So, what's the plan, Cousin Jari?"

Jari grabbed Polis by the scruff of the neck and pushed him into Betha. She pushed him into Toli, knocking the smaller dwarf onto the ground with a grunt.

"First, we're going to find out *everything* he knows, then I'll decide if we need him further, or to send him back to the king tied to a horse," Jari said, nudging him toward the others.

The soldiers nodded at Jari and helped Polis back to the fire. Betha walked over to Jari and snorted.

"I don't like it, Jari." She sniffed the air. "It smells like a trap."

"Tell me something I don't know, old friend," Jari said, adjusting his armor.

"I'm with Betha," Kala said, his voice raspy.

Betha glanced at him. "Kala, do you have a frog in your throat?"

Kala spat and took a long pull off of his canteen and then sighed. "Ach, that's better. This looks like a setup, Jari. How do you want to do this?"

Jari stared at Polis as he sat by the fire drinking gut-rot. "Watch my back. Take up the rear and when we stop for breaks, send word that all is clear. Take Toli with you."

The group broke camp the next morning and mounted their horses. Zog and Betha walked together at the front of the column. Arnak walked beside Sinda and Gnok. Kala and Toli took up the rear with Polis and his men.

Some would say that this group of bounty hunters were normally races that wouldn't mix, but gold is a powerful motivator, and no one wants to follow bounties until they're buried in a shallow grave in a field no one cares about. (At least that's how Jari felt about it.)

"Bring Polis up here," Jari shouted over his shoulder. "I need directions."

As the column rode over the next hill, they saw a small snow-white horse covered in blood. Betha walked up to it and tried to soothe it. The smaller horse neighed and reared up on its hind legs. Betha took a step back and snorted, her hoof tapping the black soil.

"Easy, Betha. It's scared is all," Kala hissed from behind her. "Now, step back and let me take care of it."

"Old Dwarf," Betha said as she slid her battle-ax into her left palm. "You can carve up the meat after I'm done cutting."

Kala slipped behind her, slammed the butt of his ax shaft into the back of her knee, and then pushed her to her knees. He held his hands up as he slipped around her and advanced.

"I may be old, but I'm still quick, Taur. Remember that."

Betha went to say something, but a look from Jari silenced her.

Kala started humming a soft melody and then eased a little farther forward. "Easy, girl, easy." He made soft kissing sounds until he stood directly under its neck. The horse snorted and pawed the earth, its eyes darting around in their sockets. Kala slid his fingers through its bloody mane to soothe it.

He lifted the bridle, turned the underfed horse around, and walked past Jari and the others without a word. As he reached the back of the column, he began to wash the blood from its silky coat.

Polis picked up a sword with a hand strapped to it. "Well, now, I know what happened to my scout."

Jari stared at the hand for a moment and then glanced over his shoulders. "Where's the rest of him?"

Zog shook his head. Jari couldn't tell, but he thought it sounded like a chuckle. "I say all over place," he said, flicking a piece of flesh off his foot.

Polis bent down and picked up a head with its tongue cut out. He muttered something under his breath. Jari tried to read his lips, but Polis held his hand over his mouth as he spoke.

"What was that, Polis?" he asked.

Polis glanced up and then lowered his head. Jari took a step forward.

"Polis, I asked—"

Polis stood up, his hands shaking. "This was my brother-in-law. My wife will kill me—"

Jari barked out a laugh. "Lord Silverwell, you probably won't live long enough for her to kill you in Port Agu." He pointed at their company standing by the side of the road. "They'll kill you faster than it will take you to blink." Jari patted him on the shoulder. "I'd bet my life on it."

Jari left Polis to bury what was left of his brother-in-law and walked back over to the group.

"So, what, now?" Toli asked, swinging his hammer over his shoulder.

"I say we kill him," Betha muttered, much to Arnak's enjoyment.

"We agree on something," Arnak grumbled with a hint of a

smile.

Jari held his hand up. "No, we need him to lead us to the gold."

Zog grunted, lifted his club, and pointed north. "Follow Zog."

"What about Polis?" Kala asked.

Jari smiled. "We wait, then follow Zog."

Zog paused and turned around. "You call me Mighty Zog."

Toli tapped Zog's side with his shiny hook. "Mighty? Then you can call me, Toli, king of the dwarven lasses' asses."

Zog glared at Toli. "Zog don't understand."

Betha pushed Toli. "Move."

Toli rolled to the ground with a dramatized high-pitched laugh. He rolled into Sinda's feet, startling her. She snatched him by the back of his collar and lifted him to his feet.

Toli straightened up. "Easy on the goods, darling. I'm Toli Hookhand," he said, brushing himself off.

Sinda stared through him. "What goods? All I see is a sawed-off dwarf that's the size of one of Arnak's turds."

Arnak turned his head at the mention of his name as he rooted through his bag. He shook his head at the statement and went back to pillaging.

"I take offense to that," Toli said. "I am no tortle turd."

Sinda grinned, her braid swaying in front of her face. "Toli? That's what you said your name was, right?"

Toli nodded. "Hookhand."

"Well, unless you want to be Hook*hands*, I suggest you never bump into me again," Sinda said as she checked her gear. She pushed Toli an arm's length away and mounted her pony.

The rest of the team mounted and waited for Polis to finish. After ten minutes, Gnok lost his patience. "Polis," he shouted.

Polis glanced up. "What?"

Gnok scanned the grey clouds moving in and held his hand out. A few droplets of rain hit his grimy palm. He took a deep breath. "Unless you are bringing him with us," he looked over his shoulder and grimaced, "we should be going, but he seems to be a little bit of—"

"Everywhere," Zog bellowed and then roared with laughter.

Jari glared at Zog, and the laughter faded. "Enough, Gnok. Follow Zog and Betha. I'll wait for Polis and his men."

The others followed Zog as he took the lead. Kala cantered over to Jari on his new mount and smiled.

"What do you want, Kala Silverbeard?" Jari asked, a hint of frustration in his voice.

Kala stared at Polis's men and gave a head nod at two of them standing away from the rest of the group.

He whispered, "I trust them less than Zog. And you know how much I hate orcs. I'll stay with you. But we need to dismount if they attack. We're vulnerable up here."

Jari gave a sign of approval.

They both dismounted. Jari eyed Polis and slid one of his hands to his shield. Kala backed up a few paces and then sniffed the air.

"You smell that?" Kala asked.

Jari gave a slight nod. "Troll."

Polis and his men knelt by the grave, chanting, their heads bowed. Jari and Kala were a moment too late. As they attempted to warn Polis and his men, a gigantic troll covered in boils and wearing a dirty loincloth burst from the trees behind them.

The troll picked up two of Polis's men and bit their heads off. It tossed the bodies onto the other men and then lunged for Polis, who was attempting to pull his sword from its scabbard. As the claw reached Polis's throat, he tripped and rolled away.

"For the Dwarven Lords," Kala roared as he slammed headfirst into the troll's stomach.

The troll bellowed and kicked Kala in the face. He landed a few feet away on his back as Jari engaged. For every cut he inflicted, the troll would roar, and the wound would close.

The troll bashed Jari on the side of the head, denting his helmet further. With a grunt, Jari tried to pull it off using both hands. As his back was turned, the troll attempted to finish him. The last of Polis's men joined the fray, interrupting the attack. The troll dodged and lunged with deadly efficiency. Jari couldn't see, but he could hear the sickening crunches of men's heads, arms and legs being torn off, and their pitiful dying screams. In short order, all of the humans lay in strewn pieces.

The troll pressed its advantage and knocked Jari to the ground, and then kicked Kala as he charged forward again. To Kala's credit, he regained his feet, but the triumph was short-lived. He flew through the air and landed at his horse's hooves with a grunt.

Standing over Jari, the troll snarled and glanced down, spit dripping from its jawline. It reached down and snatched Jari by the throat and then lifted him seven feet in the air. Jari's tongue was sticking out, and his face was turning blueberry in color as the seconds ticked by.

Jari struggled against its hands, but the harder he fought, the weaker he became. He heard the troll bellow and felt it let go. He crashed to the ground, gasping, holding his throat.

Betha ran by Jari, pulled her broad ax, and growled, her lips turned into a sneer. Now, the troll turned its attention toward her. Kala stepped up beside her and swung a large tree branch that he had set on fire, burning the troll's upper body as he drew closer.

"Back, beast, back," Kala shouted.

Polis lay unconscious nearby. As Betha and the troll squared off for the second time, Jari finally managed to push himself to his knees. He heard a war cry behind him as he desperately pulled at his dented helmet. The rest of their company stood in a line side by side, and then sprinted past Jari and engaged the troll. Moving as one, Betha would take a chunk out of its body, followed by Arnak's and Zog's clubs to its throat. Lastly, Zog and Kala burned every wound that their companions created.

"Toli," Betha roared.

Toli ran as fast as his little legs would carry him. He leaped into Betha's clasped paws, and she launched him into the air. He landed on the troll's head and then dug his spiked heels into each side of its neck. "I got something for you, you smelly bastard."

He drove his hook into one of the troll's eyes and pushed down, ripping it from the socket. The troll screeched and thrashed as it tried to break Toli into a thousand pieces.

Without the slightest hindrance, Toli pulled his hook free, with the eyeball attached, and somersaulted toward his group. Betha caught him like she always did and dropped him as she reengaged the one-eyed troll.

Kala yanked Jari's helmet off and threw it aside.

"You good, lad?" he asked.

Jari spat, and they rejoined the fray with the others. After a few final minutes and numerous wounds, the troll fell to its knees. Betha kicked it onto its stomach and then gave it a coup de grâce, her razor-sharp battle-ax separating its head from its shoulders (after three hearty strokes). Its head slowly rolled into the fire.

Betha's septum ring rattled as she slowed her breathing. Toli took a long sip from his canteen and handed it to Kala, who was busy wiping the blood from his white beard.

"Disgusting creatures," Kala hissed.

"You look like hell," Toli said.

"Watch your tongue, Little One, or I'll cut your head off. We had that troll under control," Kala spat before walking off.

Toli laughed as he walked away. "Sure you did, Old Dwarf."

"Shut it, Toli. No one likes a smart-ass," Jari said, bumping forearms with Betha. "Thanks for the help."

Betha snorted in response and thrust her ax into Jari's hands. "You know the rules."

Jari bristled, but he knew she was right. Whenever they saved each other in battle, the individual who was saved cleaned, sharpened, and repaired the other's weapons and armor for a week as a customary thanks. They also had to buy their savior whatever they wanted from the bar. (Something Jari never liked because she could drink her ass off.)

Arnak and Zog stared at each other for a moment and then gave each other a slight recognition before sheathing their weapons. Tortles and orcs never got along. Their races were sworn enemies on Labrys. Tortles were quiet, rarely out of each other's company. Orcs, although loud and crude, were essentially the same in regard to who they fought with, but the few who ventured into mixed company and became mercs never gave it much thought. They worshipped coins, not the gods of their respective races.

Jari walked over to Polis and nudged him with his foot. Polis groaned and tried to open his eyes. He rolled onto his back and coughed for a few seconds.

"What the hell happened?" he managed to croak.

Jari held his hand out as Polis's eyes refocused. "You got your ass kicked by a troll." He glanced over his shoulder. "And it killed the rest of your men."

Polis blinked. "Damn."

Jari helped him to his feet and pushed his sword into his hands. "Now, I think you should head back to Port Agu and let us get our gold and retire."

"I have to find my son," he whispered.

"I don't care about your problems. I want that gold," Jari barked.

As Jari and Polis went back and forth, Zog approached Toli. "Zog want the troll eye."

Toli grimaced and held his bloody hook out. "Be my guest."

Zog removed the eyeball, licked his lips, and then ate it with a broad smile, his teeth stained red. Toli gagged and covered his mouth.

"Zog like eyeballs."

Toli pointed to the head in the fire and walked away, a little greener than he was before. Zog walked over to the head, cut its ears off, and pulled the other eyeball out.

Betha snarled and pushed Zog. "My kill, Zog. Those are *my* ears."

Zog roared, and before she knew it, he had a knife at her throat. "Zog got to ears first."

"Betha, enough," Jari shouted.

Zog pulled the blade from her throat and sheathed it. He popped the other eye into his mouth and ground it between his teeth as she stormed off.

Zog handed Kala, who was standing nearby, one of the ears. "Good fight, Dwarf. Zog like you."

Kala didn't attempt to hide his distaste of Zog. "And why's that?"

He laughed. "Zog saw the headbutt." He tapped Kala's helmet. "Strong dwarf."

Kala smirked and then inspected the near-perfect ear. He dropped it in his scalp pouch. "Thank you."

Zog shrugged and walked away.

Gnok walked over to Kala. "Making friends with orcs now?"

Kala gave him an icy stare. "I don't know you well enough to enjoy your candor, Gnok. Remember, you're Jari's family, *not* mine."

Gnok ignored the insult. "So, how much is the ear worth?"

"It's good quality and large. Probably worth at least twenty coins. It's worth less than a minotaur horn, but more than a vial of elf blood," Kala said.

"Ah, elf blood. Love to mix it with gut-rot," Gnok said with a smile.

"You're disgusting, Gnok," Sinda said, walking by.

Gnok chuckled, walked over to his pony, and mounted. The

rest of the group mounted after him.

"Zog, if you'd be so kind," Jari said, pointing north.

The band followed Zog and Betha as they led the way into the forest to make camp.

Chapter 6

Jari, Gnok, and Betha peered over the escarpment at the figures below them. The dwarven raiding party below them sat drinking around a campfire, their sentries asleep.

"Who's raiding party is this?" Gnok muttered.

Jari glanced at him. "I'll give you two guess—"

"But I'll only need one, right?" Gnok said.

"Why are Boro's troops this far south?" Betha hissed, her septum ring rattling.

"How the hell should I know?" Jari hissed back, motioning for her to hold the ring.

"Why the hell does it matter? Let's kill 'em and be done with it," Gnok said.

"What's the call, Jari?" Betha asked, holding her septum ring as she spoke, giving her a nasal tone.

Jari chuckled. "Something funny?" she asked.

"No, nothing at all," he quickly said.

Betha snorted in reply.

Gnok lay between them and farted. Jari wrinkled his nose. "C'mon, Gnok!"

"Sorry, getting excited," he said.

"Must play hell with the belly dancers," Betha said as her body shook with muffled laughter.

Jari pushed her shoulder and shushed her.

"This is the plan. Kala, Toli, and Betha will flank the east side of the camp, Gnok and Sinda will attack from the west, and the rest of us will start the fight from here. Everyone have their crossbows and slings ready?"

Betha shrugged, and Gnok nodded his head. "Mine do."

"I'll wait here for Zog, Arnak, and Polis," Jari said.

"The human? Why in Labrys should we trust him?" Gnok asked, not trying to hide the rancor in his voice.

"Because he has a sword. There are twenty Red Dwarves down there. Do you have any better ideas?" Jari hissed.

"Yeah, move around them," Betha said. "Their ears and scalps ain't worth the trouble, Jari."

"Too late, old girl. We need those uniforms," Jari said, sliding backward down the hill.

The group split into their separate parties. Arnak and Zog snuck up the hill overlooking the dwarves. Kala and his team flanked to the east, Gnok and Sinda, to the west. Jari slid his way back up between Zog and Arnak, who were readying themselves. He felt like a fresh pup as he lay next to two different races who took immense pride in their work: *collecting scalps.*

Before Jari could blink, a stone the size of a small fist soared through the air and smacked one of the dwarves in the center of his forehead, knocking him into the fire.

Betha.

Arnak and Zog roared and then leaped off the overhang.

Ah, shit!

Jari yanked his bolas from his belt loop. He twirled them above his head, the six solid steel balls whirling at a constant velocity.

With a flick of his finger, each separate rope holding a ball screamed downrange, hitting each dwarf he aimed at. In a matter of seconds, all six balls had been released, wounding some, killing others. Betha waved him down as she decapitated another dwarf and then kicked the body forward, knocking Toli over.

"Gods dammit, Betha!" Toli shouted as he hit the ground and rolled with the spasming corpse.

Jari jumped, nimbly landed on Betha's shoulders, and then ran forward. Betha bowed her head, and Jari's feet touched the ground. He pushed a dwarf in front of him off balance and sprinted past. Betha gored the dwarf with a deep roar, shook him like a rag doll, and then tossed him to the side.

Jari scanned the remaining dwarves.

Ten left.

Zog roared, ripped the arms off one dwarf, rotated his right ankle, and then slammed the arms down on another dwarf nearby. The bloodied dwarf staggered back, dazed, then pitched forward as Kala's warhammer caved in his skull.

Eight.

Arnak hoisted a dwarf above his head, snapped his neck, and then threw him at the other seven. Toli managed to push off the body lying on him, then rejoined the fray. "For the dwarven lasses' asses," he shouted, drenched in blood.

He leaped into Betha's paws and vaulted over her head. He landed on a fleeing dwarf, hook-first, piercing the back of his neck. Savagely, he withdrew his hook with a flourish and eyed Sinda as she killed two dwarves, one in front and one behind her. Sinda's knives danced like a weaver in a tapestry, cutting the dwarves, over and over again, until they were leaking blood like fountains. A moment later, both bodies collapsed at her feet, and before their souls were released, her knives were back in their scabbards by her side.

"Damn, she's ice-cold," Toli muttered, staring at her ass as she walked away.

Polis yanked his blade from the stomach of another dwarf and returned to a defensive position behind his shield. The last dwarf ran as fast as he could to get clear of the kill zone. Betha pawed the dirt and leaned forward. Kala stepped up and restrained her. He put a long, thin, wooden reed to his lips.

"Now's no time for practice, Old Man," Toli chided him. "If he escapes, we're dead."

Kala stomped on Toli's foot. Then he took a deep breath, his cheeks bulging out. He exhaled, and multiple darts flew from the blowgun. They hit the dwarf in succession and sent him crashing into a tree. Zog growled his approval and elbowed Kala.

"Good kill, Dwarf."

Kala allowed himself a slight chuckle. "Yeah, not too shabby."

"Can I have eyes of your prize?" Zog asked.

Kala groaned in disgust. "Any enemy I kill, you can keep the eyes. Just don't eat them around me."

Zog's eyes lit up as he went to collect the eyes like a giddy schoolboy.

"The orc desecrates the dead, Gnok," Arnak rumbled.

"Yes, yes, he does." He patted Arnak's arm. "Don't die," Gnok said.

Arnak took a step forward and swung his club over his shoulder. Gnok raised his arm across his midsection and shook his head. "Not what I meant, Arnak."

Arnak growled and walked over to the dwarves he had killed and started scalping. Betha packed her ears and scalps into a scalp pouch as Jari approached.

"You hurt?" he asked.

Betha snorted and calculated how much she made. She shook her head no, blood dripping off her horn. She unslung her battle-ax and thrust it into his hands. "You know the deal, Jari."

He groaned and dragged her battle-ax to the fire. Kala and the others pulled the bodies closer to them.

Polis sniffed the air. "What is that smell?"

Zog roared with laughter. "Crispy dwarf." He sniffed again. "Well done." The comment had Arnak give a half smile, but it was gone as fast as it appeared.

Jari, unamused by the banter, said, "While you crack jokes, can one of you help strip the armor off the dead. Only dwarves can infiltrate Boro's camp, so it's me, Sinda, Toli, Gnok, and Kala. The rest of you will stay here until we get back."

"And if you don't come back?" Betha asked, glancing at Jari.

"Move on," he muttered.

"Your idea won't work, Jari. Either we all go, or we head back to Port Agu," Polis said, sitting alone by the fire, the flames casting shadows over his face.

"You have no say," Gnok said, picking his teeth. "You have a vote among humans, but among us, you're as worthless as a three-legged minotaur."

Betha cut her eyes at Gnok and growled. "No disrespect, Betha. A figure of speech is all." He swallowed the lump in his throat and watched Sinda sharpen her bloody knives. "What about you, Sinda?"

Sinda kept sharpening her knives, not paying them any attention.

"Sinda," Gnok said again.

Sinda flicked one of her blades between Gnok's legs and into the log he was sitting on. Gnok fell back. "What the hell has gotten into you?" he shouted.

"This will never work. The only way we win is if we get more mercs and attack him wherever he camps for the winter." She pulled her blanket closer around her shoulders. "It's suicide if we try to sneak in." She pointed at Polis. "Probably what this one wants anyway. A large dwarven diversion."

Polis cleared his throat. "Listen, She-Dwarf—"

Toli pressed his hook against Polis's throat, the hook making a curved shadow. "Watch your mouth, human."

Jari smiled. "Better listen to him, Polis, or we'll bury you with the Red Dwarves."

Toli chimed in again. "It's *Sinda*, by the way."

Sinda gave him a coy smile and a head nod.

"I didn't plan this out. I just want my son and the princess back. If you won't go with me, I'll go alone," Polis said.

"No argument here," Kala muttered, gliding a whetstone over his bone-handled knife.

"You got a problem, Master Dwarf?" Polis asked, reaching for his knife.

Kala glanced up at him. "Don't tempt me, Human. I'll gut you and let the Mighty Zog fuck you."

Zog licked his lips and popped another juicy eyeball into his mouth. "Any hole will do."

Polis frowned at both of them. He stood up and walked into the wilderness.

"Jari, why do I care about the human's son again?" Gnok asked, without looking up.

"His name is Lord Polis Silverwell, and you don't have to care, but we gave our word, and dwarves keep their word, right, Scalp Master Kala Silverbeard?" Jari asked.

"To other dwarves, Jari—other dwarves," Kala said, swallowing a piece of dried meat.

"I don't trust the human, Jari," Toli added. "He seems off."

Betha sat on her log and watched the others debate. She cleared her throat. "I want to retire. There is more than enough treasure Boro's been hoarding all these years. I don't know about the rest of you, but I'm riding with Polis. I'm done scalp collecting."

Kala nodded sagely. "All right, then, I'm with Betha. I'm getting too old for this shit."

"The Mighty Zog needs revenge. I go."

"I wish you would stop referring to yourself in the third

person," Arnak growled. "Wherever Sinda goes, I follow."

"I still think you guys are all bat shit crazy . . . but one way or another, I'm killing that bastard if it's my last act on Labrys." She touched the ring that hung around her neck. "Bondur will be avenged."

All grew quiet, remembering why she had come in the first place. Her voice was soft at first, the pain still present. "Bondur was a special dwarf, cheery and vicious, a true master with a warhammer in battle. He died protecting my parents and me. The only reason I survived is because he knocked me unconscious while I readied my weapons. He shoved me into the secret room we cut into the floor to keep our potatoes cold." She paused and then spat. "I found my mother first, her head cleaved open like a broken piece of pottery. My father was kidnapped. I never saw him again. Boro probably sold him to the humans who travel Labrys performing for the masses. I found Bondur last." Toli handed her his gut-rot. She took it with a smile, a sad, distant smile. "Well, all that was left of him, anyway. They had tied him to five ponies and then ripped off his arms, legs, and head. All I found was his wedding ring on his chest."

"Why would he have that on his chest?" Toli asked.

"A gift from Boro Spiderbinder. Bondur had defected from his army. He wanted a quiet life with me. So, when Boro finally caught up to him—" She spat again. "He paid for it. So that's *why* I'm going to find him, kill him, and force-feed him his cock." She shoved the gut-rot flask back into Toli's palm, stood up, and walked away.

"Where is she going?" Jari asked, glancing over his shoulder.

"To pray for her death," Gnok said.

Chapter 7

Jari rose from under his bearskin blanket and walked over to the fire where Arnak was sitting with his grey meat.

Jari gagged. *God, that stinks.*

Arnak attempted to hand him a piece, but Jari waved him off. "Upset stomach, maybe later."

Arnak shrugged and swallowed the offered piece.

"Can I ask you a question?" Jari asked.

Arnak nodded as he poked the fire. Jari could hear the crickets chirping, the only noise in the dark night.

"Why do you follow Sinda without question?"

Arnak made a noise, which could have been a chuckle of amusement or a chuckle of insanity. Jari scooched over a few inches in the opposite direction just to be on the safe side.

Arnak sighed. "She saved my life."

Jari raised an eyebrow. "Really?"

"I was captured in the north corner of Labrys on a hunting expedition. They wiped out my company of tortles. The slavers brought me south and sold me on an auction block in Port Agu. I found myself in a gladiator pit, fighting everyone and everything. The part Sinda left out of her story was how she found me and bought my freedom. I've been her escort ever since," Arnak said, his voice raspy and gravelly.

Jari smiled at him. "Always fascinated by your kind, Arnak. Never met a Ha-Nuh-Nah up close, but the stories of your race's battle prowesses are correct."

Arnak grunted. "Can I tell you something, Jari Rockjaw?"

"Sure."

"If one hair on my Sinda's head is touched, I . . . will . . . kill . . . you." Arnak stood up, handed Jari the poker, and walked over to Sinda. After adjusting her blanket, he lay down beside her.

Jari rubbed his eyes. *What have I gotten myself into?*

Morning came like any other, only this time, not a sound was heard. Betha, Arnak, and Zog sniffed the air around them, turning their backs to one another.

Betha snorted. "Something doesn't smell right."

Gnok walked out of the forest. "Bet they could smell that for miles."

The group groaned. "Dammit, Gnok."

"What did I say?" he asked, packing his saddlebag. He groaned as he swung his leg over the pony. "I hate getting old."

Jari smirked and mounted. "Imagine how Kala—"

Jari fell from his pony. Everyone roared with laughter as Kala rode off. The others followed him, leaving Jari in the dirt. Jari dusted himself off, remounted, and then rode behind them, Betha keeping pace the whole way.

"Be quicker on your feet, Old Dwarf," she muttered.

Kala held his hand up when they reached a fork in the road. Jari rode to the front of the column. "Why are we stopped, Kala?"

"What fork do you want to take?" Kala huffed, touching his upper arm.

"You all right over there?" Jari asked, studying the paths.

"Yea, my arm aches is all. I'll be fine," Kala said.

Jari nodded and glanced over at Betha. "What do you think?"

Betha tapped her hoof into the wet soil and sniffed for a few seconds. "The mountains lay to the west; the other path lies to the south away from Boro. As I said, I'm getting my gold and retiring. If you're coming, follow me."

Jari moved his pony in front of her. "You know you can't sneak into that camp. Only dwarves will make it. And like Sinda said, we are few. We need other mercs to help us kill Boro."

"May I make a suggestion?" Polis asked, interrupting them. "We could find minotaurs in Wolfwalker Valley."

Jari smirked and winked at Polis. "That's the best idea you've come up with, Polis."

Betha snorted, gripping her battle-ax tighter. "Are you suggesting what I *think* you're suggesting, Dwarf?"

"Easy, Beth—"

Before Jari could finish, Betha swung the handle of the ax up and caught him under the chin with a solid whack. He flipped off the back of his pony and landed in the dirt. Betha shoved his pony aside and reached for him. Jari rolled back over his shoulder and dove for her ankles. Taken aback by the move, she stumbled backward and fell to the ground.

Jari shimmied up her body and wrapped his meaty hands around her throat. Toli moved to break them up, but Kala held him back. "Let them solve this, Toli. They need to clear the air."

Betha managed to break his grip and then threw him back a few feet. Jari struggled to his feet and charged her, leaping past her outstretched arms.

Betha let out a bellow. Jari had her by the septum ring and was pulling it with all his might. He grunted as Betha elbowed him twice in the side, and once he doubled over, she slammed an elbow into his spine. Jari grunted, nothing more. He bit her lower thigh and ripped out a plug of hair, then spat it out.

He smiled, his teeth bloody, and then as quickly as the smile appeared, it was gone. Betha grabbed him by the cheeks, pushed them together, and gave him a headbutt that would have broken a concrete block. Jari stumbled, spun around, and fell flat on his face.

"If dwarf dead, Zog gets eyeballs."

"He ain't dead; he should be, though," Kala said, feeling Jari's pulse.

Satisfied he was alive, Kala rolled him over, wound his own arm back, then backhanded him. Jari groaned and sat up as Kala waved something under his nose. Jari gagged and threw up. He yanked his helmet off and pointed at Betha.

"To hell with you, Betha. You know I'm right. It's the only way we can win this," Jari shouted.

"What does he mean?" Arnak grumbled.

Betha roared and stomped, then kicked dirt at Jari. "He wants to go into Thunderhoof territory. And if I go, I'll be dead before I cross the border."

"Not necessarily," Jari muttered, expelling blood for his nostrils.

"How do you know?" she demanded.

Kala helped Jari to his feet. "If you want to retire, we *need* mercs. Nothing less than the best, and the Thunderhoof tribe is one of the best, right?" Jari asked.

"We can't even pay them, Jari. Have you lost your mind?" Toli asked, joining the conversation.

"Shut it, Toli. Nobody asked you," Gnok said over his shoulder. "I want to hear my cousin out."

Betha threw her arms in the air. "Am I the *only* one with any sense?" she bellowed, turning in a full circle, watching everyone's face. "Well, am I?"

Jari mounted his pony and said, "I've had enough of this bullshit. We need mercs, we need gold, and we need to retire. You guys do what you want. I'm going."

He rode off by himself at first, then one by one, the others followed. Betha stood fuming, the steam rising from her body. Then she sprinted after her friends as they rode to Wolfwalker Valley.

Chapter 8

Jari reined in his pony as the rest of the group caught up. Sprawled out in front of them were the wilds of Wolfwalker Valley, a place where no one but minotaurs roamed, some by themselves, others in bands.

Single minotaurs were nomadic, castoffs of a larger band for many different offenses. If a single minotaur was still alive after a full moon, they were the worst of the worst, foul in every way.

Betha cautiously walked up behind Jari and sniffed the air. She exhaled, her breath misty. He glanced at her. "Your thoughts?"

Betha snorted and scanned the horizon. "They're out there."

Jari shrugged as Zog walked up to them, chugging on a flask of gut-rot. He moved the flask from his lips and then threw an eyeball into his open mouth with relish. "The Mighty Zog is ready."

Sinda and Toli groaned simultaneously behind him. "Well, the crazy orc is ready. Who else?" Jari asked, shaking his head.

Kala, Gnok, Arnak, and Polis stepped forward. "Even the pathetic human stepped forward, Betha," Toli teased.

Polis growled and slapped one hand over his forearm at Toli. "Easy, Pint Size. It was *my* idea."

Betha growled as she stared through him.

Toli ignored the comment and walked up to Betha. "Whaddya say, Beth? Let's go get the mercs we need to get our gold," he said, nudging her side.

Betha snorted and clutched the handle of her battle-ax, her grip so tight it looked like it would snap at any moment.

"Toli, this is a bad idea," she snapped.

"If we can hire them, we'll be out before we find trouble with your band," Toli said.

Jari paused as the information registered. *Toli knows more about her than I do.*

Betha caught Jari's opened eyes. "Never wanted you to know." She paused. "And I never thought Toli would live long enough to talk."

Toli blustered. "Now, wait a hot second, you burly mino—"

Gnok cuffed Toli and moved him back with a sweep of his hand. "Quiet, Little One."

Arnak grumbled his approval, then slid forward and placed a makeshift telescope to his craggy eye. He scanned the horizon like a hawk waiting for its meal. Jari cleared his throat and waved for the instrument.

Arnak handed it over. "Don't go through my bags again, Ha-Nuh-Nah, or I'll kill you," Jari promised.

"Empty threats, Dwarf," Arnak grumbled, handing it back.

Jari moved his hands at a snail's pace as he scouted the country in front of them. *Trees, trees, rocks. Ugh, is there noth—*

He focused on a large body attempting to hide behind a boulder that was far too small for them to hide behind. Jari handed the scope to Betha with a nod. She snatched it from his hands and glanced through it. She saw the minotaur on the other end instantly. Her growl was heard a little farther than intended.

"Thunderhoof," she grunted.

Jari smiled wide. "Looks like we found our escort."

Betha placed her palm on Jari's chest and held him back for a moment. "Jari, I'm friendly compared to those down there. I know you think all of us are honorable. But the fact is, these minotaurs are savages. Nothing nice about them. Nothing..... At..... All. I have one favor to ask," she said.

Jari made eye contact.

"If my band finds us while we're in there, no matter what happens . . . You need to ride away."

"Betha, how could—"

"Promise," she growled.

"I don't unders—"

Betha pushed past him and roared. One, then another, and on it went until ten minotaurs walked out of the shadows. She stomped her hoof several times, roared again, then held her ax high above her head by the shaft.

She swung it into the earth and left it there. "Remember what I said," she hissed and then descended into the valley alone.

The group watched closely as Betha approached, hands out, walking at a leisurely pace, not too fast or too slow. The largest minotaur stepped out in front of her. The two made eye contact.

"You know you're not welcome here, Betha Silentnight of the Iron Skulls," said the minotaur.

"I know, Honor Giver Isafin Toughhide of the Thunderhoof."

Isafin was tall for a minotaur and beautiful among her kind. Both of the male and female minotaurs surrounding her were grizzled, scars crisscrossing their chiseled bodies. But Isafin bore no scars. Her mesmerizing eyes were bright blue with violet irises, the exact opposite of Betha, whose eyes looked like coal in her sockets.

"How have you been, sister?" Betha asked with a stiff bow.

"I'm no longer your sister, Betha," Isafin growled.

Betha clenched her jaw a few times, the sweat on her brow beading on her forehead. She glanced around the semicircle of warriors, some she recognized, others she didn't. Her eyes settled back on Isafin.

Isafin sniffed, her septum ring vibrating. "You bring dwarves." She sniffed again, then yanked her hatchet from her waistband. "And . . . and... an *orc*? You desecrate our lands, sister?" she roared.

The other minotaurs with her freed their weapons and advanced side by side. Betha groaned and took a sad glance behind her.

"I knew I shouldn't have come back, but this was the only place we could come. I will accept my punishment as you see fit, but let my companions go. They only wanted to hire mercenaries."

Isafin lowered her weapon as did her warriors. "Betha Silentnight, you were given a second chance and told to never come back for dishonoring your band. Instead, you bring a mercenary company to our foothills to find warriors thirsty for coin and battle." She sighed. "Either you have gone mad or are desperate. Neither, of which, I find appealing."

Betha glared at her. "I'm neither mad nor desperate. I want to retire from bounty hunting, and I need my kind to kill *my* enemy."

Isafin chuckled. "You always were a dreamer, Betha. And because we are blood, I will not turn you over to the Iron Skulls . . . just yet. Should word reach them that you are with the Thunderhoof, though, you will be turned over. Blood or no blood, you will not endanger my band with a tribal war. Now, bring your companions, and we will discuss this with my kinsmen."

"And the orc?" Betha asked.

"Don't push your luck, Betha." Isafin glanced at the group fifty meters away. "No orcs or that grotesque Hah-Nu-Nah I smell."

Betha trudged up the hill to her companions. They stared at her in complete silence. She exhaled loudly and yanked her ax out of the dirt.

"What happened down there?" Jari asked as Betha walked away.

"Everyone can go except Arnak and Zog. The Thunderhoof will never let them cross the border and enter the camp."

"I'm not going without Arnak," Sinda said.

Jari whistled, and Betha turned around. "We're a band, Betha. Either we all go, or none of us go."

Betha roared so loud, Jari thought his eardrums would split. "No! I gave my word, Jari. Zog and Arnak stay here."

"I won't warn you again, Betha," Jari said, adjusting his helmet, then freeing his ax.

"You've lost your mind again, Jari," Betha said.

"Nope, I believe in honoring my companions. So . . ." Jari spun his ax in his hand and then thumped it on his shield. "Let's see who wins and who loses."

Betha threw her hands in the air. "Damn stubborn dwarves." She dropped her ax and rushed Jari head-on. Jari threw down his ax and shield and dove out of her way. Betha pounced on him before he could move outside her grasp. She picked him up, squeezed him tight, and then shook him like a rag doll. Jari rocked back and forth, and as Betha tired, he slammed his head into her muzzle, once, twice, then three more times, bringing her to her knees.

As her grip released, he slammed his helmet into her one more time, then gave her an uppercut. Betha stumbled back and snarled as she made it to her knees. She speared Jari, nearly snapping her other horn off in the process. Jari gasped, hugged his dented chest piece, and fell. He managed to loosen the leather straps and drop the front of it as Betha tackled him again. She reined blows down on him but couldn't quite hit her mark, the tears in her eyes too hard to see through.

In the moment it took to clear her vision, Jari's giant hands wrapped around her throat. With a loud groan, he kneed her in the stomach and then slammed his head into her septum again.

Betha roared and slammed him into the ground. Jari choked on the dust, the spittle, the nastiness of it all. And in one instant, Betha lay beside him unconscious.

Jari lashed out. *What in the hell???*

He sat up and shouted, "Whoever intervened, I'm killing them."

The sun overhead was blocked out as a shadow stood over him. He squinted up. "That you, Zog?"

"'fraid not, Little Dwarf. I'm Honor Giver Isafin Toughhide, Spirit leader of the Thunderhoof, and blood linked with the minotaur you're fighting."

"What?" Jari asked as Gnok helped him to his feet.

"My sister was told only dwarves could enter our valley." She glanced at Polis in distaste. "Didn't smell you before, *Human*. You're worth less than a drunk three-legged dwarf—and not welcome here."

Toli laughed so loud, he snorted. "Three-legged dwa—"

A quick glance from Isafin stilled his laughter. She turned back to Jari. "We watched with interest as you fought her for your band's honor. We will allow everyone to enter our camp." She glanced at Polis. "Even the filthy human, but he stays with the pigs until we reach an agreement."

Jari spat and nodded his thanks. Gnok handed him a canteen, and he took a long pull. "Why break it up and knock your sister out, then?"

Isafin snorted and pawed the earth. "Because I like her much less than you."

Chapter 9

Jari brushed a low-hanging branch out of his way as their ponies followed the minotaurs leading them up a winding road. Over valleys, through mountain passes, the hours rolled on. Betha had woken up and was sulking at the back of the wagon train, unwilling to speak to anyone.

Jari reined his pony to the side of the path and threw a head nod for the others to continue. As the rest of his company passed him, Betha trudged by. He pulled up alongside her without a word. After a few minutes of awkward silence, he spoke.

"Sorry about earl—"

Betha held up her hand. "You were right. Like it or not, we are a band."

Jari, surprised at her admission, tried to think of something to say.

"There's no need for words, Jari. Sometimes, the best answer lies in silence. Now, leave me to my thoughts."

Jari tapped his pony on the flanks and urged it ahead. He pulled alongside Toli.

"How are you, Jari?" Toli asked, chewing on an apple skewered by his hook.

Jari felt the lump on the side of his head, courtesy of Betha, and winced. "Feel a little better than I did a few hours ago."

Toli chuckled and scratched his chin with his hook, the apple juices running down his chin.

"Do you know what happened to Betha?" Jari asked.

Toli gave a slow nod. "I do, but it ain't my place to say. Ask her if you want to know."

Jari went to protest but was interrupted by a cacophony of horn blasts. Toli held his good hand over his brow. "Can't see nothing from here."

Betha moved beside Toli's mount. "That's because we have been announced to the elders of the village. If we're allowed to enter we will, if not . . ."

"What?" Toli asked.

Betha shrugged. "Then here you will rest in the Pit of Sorrow."

"Pit of Sorrow?" Toli mouthed with wide eyes to Jari as the column began moving again.

The column moved ahead, and then Toli saw it. "*Oh,* a real pit?" he muttered as they passed by. "A really *large* pit."

The pit was twenty-five feet down and fifteen feet across at the top. Skeletons of minotaurs lay piled on top of one another, the ones below them pulverized to dust.

Jari's pony trotted by it. *Dwarven Lords, help us.*

Even the Mighty Zog was intrigued as he stood by the edge. "Zog needs to make pee-pee," he said.

"If that comes out of your britches, they'll throw you in," Betha hissed, pushing the brute forward.

One of the minotaurs strode to the back where the column was. He picked Polis up by the throat and threw him to the pigs. He roared at Betha and walked away.

"What did he say?" Jari asked.

"The human stays with the pigs as agreed."

Jari walked over to Polis and helped brush him off. "Lucky he didn't kill you."

Polis growled. "I hate minotaurs."

"Careful, Lord Polis. A minotaur just saved your life. We'll be back." He glanced at Polis's feet. "Don't step in the pig shit. Boro's troops will smell it for miles."

Jari rejoined the group. Isafin could be heard talking to the elders, but he couldn't see her. Betha took deep breaths and kept her head lowered.

"I would move, Toli," Betha hissed as she shoved his pony to the side.

They heard a minotaur's voice in front of them. "You bring danger to my band, Betha Silentnight of the Iron Skulls. Approach to be judged for this action."

The minotaurs in front kneeled as one and parted down the middle. At the back, in the center, stood Betha, alone, but in control.

Jari stepped out in front of Betha, ax and shield at the ready. The minotaurs that were kneeling stood and fanned out beside the elders, enveloping the group.

Jari spat on the ground. "Oi, Kala Silverbeard. Good day for a fight, isn't it?"

Kala stepped forward with a smile. "Indeed, it is, Brother Jari." He unslung the massive warhammer. "Which of you bellowers is first, then, eh?"

Betha nodded her thanks to them, a slight smirk on her lips. She pointed for both of them to stand aside. She stepped up next to Jari and said, "Remember, whatever happens to me, you get to riding."

"But, Beth—"

Betha ignored him, threw her ax over her shoulder with a roar, and stepped forward. Her hoofbeats felt like they were reverberating through the black soil. She showed no outward signs of fear, but Jari saw the slightest twitch of her fingers. As she reached the center of the circle, she dropped her ax and then knelt.

The oldest minotaur had a chalky body with a silver mane. To his right stood Isafin Toughhide.

"Are your little friends looking for a fight?" asked the old minotaur.

"No, Great Giver Minarrak Orcslayer. They are of my band. We have a bounty to collect on Boro Spiderbinder to the southwest."

Minarrak laughed. "Band? What band? All I see is some puny dwarves." He spotted Zog and roared. He unslung his double-edged great ax. "You bring an *orc* to my camp?" he roared, spittle dripping from his bottom lip.

Isafin placed a hand over Manarrak's chest. "I allowed it. They are here under a banner of truce. The only one who can be voted into the pit is Betha Silentnight."

Minarrak fumed, his misty breath seeping out of his nostrils. He turned his attention back to Betha. "You are no longer an Iron Skull. No doubt, Isafin told you what you risk coming here?"

"She has, Great Giver."

"Fine. So, Betha . . . What is your band's name so that I may address you properly?" Minarrak said.

Betha gazed over her shoulder at her companions, scanning each face. "We are known as the Loners."

"And why do you come here?" Minarrak asked.

"We need mercenaries, Great Giver. My band would only come to our people for help," Betha said.

"Is that a fact?"

"It is, Great Giver. We cannot win without your band. Will you allow us to purchase your warriors' services?" Betha asked.

Minarrak pondered what he heard for a few moments, then whispered to Isafin, who left. "You have created a problem for the Thunderhooves." He wrinkled his nose. "And you have brought an orc and a *human* into our midst. Both carry a sentence of death amongst our kind."

"I understand, Great Giver."

Minarrak sighed, then straightened, and bellowed. "Betha, of the Loners, you have committed unspeakable atrocities against the Iron Skulls, your former band. A runner has been sent to their camp to inform them of your return. You will be shackled and chained where you kneel. The Loners will be able to stay with the pigs until the Iron Skulls arrive, then a decision will be made whether you live or die."

Chapter 10

"It smells like shit," Toli complained, slapping a snorting pig away from him.

Zog sniffed the air. "Zog likes smell."

Arnak rolled his craggy eyes and looked out between the loose boards in the hovel they were in. Betha lay bruised and bloody, shackled to the earth. Arnak snatched the flask out of Toli's hands and walked over to the fence.

Sinda snatched him by the arm. "You can't go out there."

Arnak smiled and touched her cheek. "Worry not."

He leaped over the fence and strode toward Betha. In one movement, he had her head tilted back and the gut-rot down her throat. She drank greedily, even choking it down until her guard smacked Arnak across the face with the butt of his ax.

The guard roared, striking him repeatedly. As he hammered him, Arnak turned on his stomach, using his shell as a shield. Crawling hand over fist back to the group, he allowed the minotaur to land his blows until the last moment, then leaped up, disarmed him, and broke his weapon over his knee as he leaped back over the fence.

The minotaur stood stunned. Arnak roared like a minotaur and kicked the ground around him. Then he shuffled forward and slammed his fists on his hips. The minotaur shook with fury, then stalked off.

Arnak's companions stared at him, eyes wide. Sinda was the first to speak. "You speak their language?"

Arnak nodded and took a sip from the flask Zog handed him, who, then, patted Arnak on the shell. "Brave. Very brave." Zog pulled his choker off and placed it in Arnak's hand and walked off. "Good fight."

Arnak turned the choker over in the firelight. "Thank you," he grumbled.

Zog waved at him over his shoulder and walked into the darkness.

Sinda pressed her question. "How do you speak their language?"

"I was a gladiator for a long time, Sinda. I never thought I would be free. You freed me, but there were things about my past you didn't need to know. I met an old minotaur in the mines near Pula, years and years ago. I helped him escape, and before he left, he taught me his language and customs."

"That still doesn't explain why you did what you just did." She shoved him. "That guard could have killed you," she shouted.

"No, he couldn't. Rendering aid to one of their kinsman is allowed. They can beat you but never kill you. It is a disgrace to kill anyone who helps their kind."

Gnok slapped him on the shell with a laugh. "You never cease to amaze me, Arnak. What did you say?"

Arnak hesitated. "Well, what did you say?" Gnok asked again.

"I said she was my lover," he muttered, walking away.

Gnok roared with laughter. Toli threw a rock and hit him in the chest. "Oi, some of us are trying to sleep."

The following morning, Jari and the others woke to the sound of horns and roars. A stampede of minotaurs wearing black plate armor trudged past them in rows of two. Jari scrambled to his feet. Arnak and Zog knocked him over as they charged out of the enclosure, standing side by side. The last of the guards passed, followed by a bloodred carriage.

"Who's in the carriage?" Toli asked, yawning as he walked out of the hovel.

"How would I know?" Arnak grumbled, walking toward the gate. He lifted the latch, swung his club over his shoulder, and then walked into the roadway. "You coming, or what?"

A large minotaur pushed Arnak back into the enclosure from behind. "Return to your quarters," he growled.

Arnak turned and stared at his aggressor, trying to control his temper, and then stepped forward. "What did you say, Taur? I must have missed it. Did you push me and tell me to step back?"

"I won't warn you again. Wait here until the judgment is passed. If your mate is found guilty, we'll throw her in the pit. If not, she goes free," the minotaur said, then walked away.

"I don't know about the rest of you, but I'm going up there and damn the consequences. I'm not watching them throw her into the pit," Jari said. "Now, who's with me?"

"Lead on, Cousin," Gnok said, checking his axes.

Everyone followed Jari out and walked side by side with him down the worn dirt path, stopping behind the last row of minotaurs. Jari nodded at Zog and Arnak, who led the way around the outer ring, occasionally bumping into the minotaurs to ruffle feathers. The ones they walked past spat at Zog, Arnak, and Polis, who managed not to piss himself.

Near the pit, Jari pushed a minotaur from behind. "Move, Taur!"

The minotaur spun around and reached for him. Jari ducked and slapped her hands away. "Too slow, Taur. Now, move aside so that we may attend our companion's trial."

The minotaur exhaled, its breath clearly visible. With a deep growl, she roared, and the warriors in front of her parted. The band saw Betha on her knees, head lowered, still shackled by her hands and hooves.

Dwarven Lords, be merciful, Jari thought as he walked up the open path.

Betha brought her eyes up and met his. The glance was awkward, filled with shame. He nodded a greeting at her and then fanned out with the rest of their band. All eyes were on the carriage. A chiseled minotaur strode up to the door, kicked out the attached stairway, and turned the handle. After a few awkward moments, an old minotaur ducked under the door frame and stepped down the stairs.

Betha froze, her breath caught in her throat. She lowered her eyes and touched her forehead to the dirt, the other minotaurs following suit. Jari barely noticed the old minotaur. He was too busy eyeing Betha's condition. The new arrival had snow-white hair with sapphire eyes. One could only guess how old he was. Isafin walked over to him and bowed her head.

"Welcome, Honorable Leader Henefin Kagoslayer of the Iron Skulls. Our band is honored you have answered our call."

Henefin didn't even heed Isafin's words. He nudged her aside and strode up to Betha. He knelt beside her and sniffed. "You smell of fear, daughter. Have you come back to pay for the crimes you committed, you worthless mangy she-wolf?"

Henefin moved faster than the others expected him to. He roared, pounded his chest with one hand, and then slapped her viciously across the mouth, cracking her septum ring.

Jari tensed and hesitated. Then he thought better of it and relaxed. Gnok held his hand across Arnak's midsection as he took a step forward. "Now is not the time, Arnak. She must be judged," he hissed, pushing him back into line.

Henefin stood and walked back to the carriage. One of his

guardsmen held out a red satin pillow with a large ornate ax lying across it. Henefin ripped it off the pillow and spun around. He shrugged the cape off his shoulders and raised his ax over his head. The minotaurs with him cheered him on after he took a practice swing.

Great Giver Minarrak walked over and stood in front of Betha. "Honorable Henefin Kagoslayer, you cannot have revenge until she has been voted on by an elected council. Once the vote is cast, if she loses, she must choose death or a contest of arms."

"She's guilty, Minarrak," Henefin roared, slicing both biceps.

Minarrak's growl was low but noticeable enough for Jari to hear. "That may be so; however, she must be judged. You cannot draw blood on *our* sacred land without permission. We captured her, and it is our right on how we proceed. Do you agree, Honorable Leader?"

The bloodlust dissipated from Henefin's eyes, the pure blue returning from ruby red. Henefin slowly nodded, handed his ax to a guardsman, and returned to his carriage. He slammed the door, and the driver urged the large horses forward.

Minarrak glanced at one of Henefin's remaining guards and said, "Follow your leader and inform him the council meets tonight when the moon is highest in the sky."

Henefin's guards led the way, and the others followed, all of them spitting at Betha before walking away.

Jari and the others surrounded her. Minarrak sighed and wiped his matted forehead. "What do you think you're doing, Master Dwarf?" he said to no one in particular.

"I'm watching my friend," Jari said, handing Toli his flask to give to Betha.

Toli knelt next to her and helped her drink. Arnak brought a grey piece of meat out of his pouch and forced her to eat it.

Betha pulled out her broken septum ring. "Your food tastes like shit."

Arnak laughed and patted her on the shoulder. "Feeling better?"

Betha gave a quick nod. "Could do without these chains."

Minarrak waved his guard over to him. "Remove the restraints. She needs all her strength for tonight."

The guard unlocked her shackles and helped her up. "Betha of the Loners, you will be judged tonight when the moon is at its highest peak. Henefin Kagoslayer wants your blood, but until the council votes, you're safe. Do I have your word you won't run?"

"You have my word, Great Giver Minarrak."

"Fine, you may leave with your band and await our summons. I will not waste my guards keeping you under surveillance."

Minarrak walked away with Isafin. Betha smiled at Jari through bloody teeth. "I told you to run."

"And when have I ever listened?" he replied.

"Stubborn dwarves."

"It's just the way we are," Gnok said with a mighty laugh. "And doomed . . . very much doomed."

The band helped Betha as she stumbled back with them. She tripped through the doorway and lay facedown with a grunt. Arnak moved the others and knelt by her side. He used a small flint and started a low fire.

The others piled out of the room except for Jari, who unbuttoned his surcoat and ax belt. He dropped them to the ground and watched Arnak roll Betha over. Arnak glanced at Jari. "Need something, Dwarf?"

"She's my right hand. Can't leave her. What can I do to help?"

"Bring me a cloth soaked in hot water and plenty of cold water to drink. She's dehydrated."

Jari returned with what Arnak needed and then stepped back.

Arnak rubbed his hands together with a loud hum, then slapped them. He applied the hot cloths over her eyes and body and then inserted a new septum ring from his pocket back into her nose.

"Where did you get that?" Jari asked.

Arnak ignored him and rubbed a foul-smelling goo over Betha's body. She groaned and tried to sit up. Arnak gently pushed one of her shoulders down. "Easy, Betha."

"What is that smell?" she gasped.

"Greenrot," Arnak mumbled.

Betha wrinkled her muzzle. "Whatever it is, it smells like Zog's balls."

"Once you wake up, you won't feel any pain."

"Wake u—"

Arnak punched her in the muzzle, knocking her unconscious. Jari pushed Arnak, who swatted him away like a fly. Jari crashed into the pig food with a grunt. Arnak picked him up and then set him down. "She needs rest, Dwarf. Tonight will be the worst trial she has ever faced—if she lives."

Without another word, he snatched his spiked club off the ground and walked out of the hovel.

Jari glanced at Betha. *Sorry about this, Betha. The coins were too good to pass up.*

He sat down and warmed his hands by the fire. The door creaked, and Toli poked his head in. "Hey, Jari."

"Toli."

"Mind if I come in?" he asked.

Jari gave a nod, and Toli hurried inside. "I wanted to check on Betha," he said, watching her intently.

"Toli, what do you know that I don't?" Jari asked, wiping her forehead.

Toli hesitated.

"I won't ask nicely again. What do you know?" Jari pressed.

"Where do I begin?" Toli muttered, scratching his chin with

his hook. "Betha got real drunk one night a couple of years back when you were out hunting down some damn elf . . . I have long since forgotten the name. Betha had a hell of a lot of gut-rot mixed with cow blood. The funny thing about cow blood, it—"

"Toli."

"Yeah, right, sorry. We went for a walk around Port Agu to find some cows to tip." Jari raised an eyebrow. "What? We were out of options. All the bounties had been collected, so we drank, and we strolled. As the moon reached its peak above us, she watched it. I asked her what was wrong."

"And?"

"She told me—"

Gnok and Sinda burst into the hovel. "Wake her up," Gnok hissed, loading his sling.

"What are you on about now?" Jari asked.

"We heard a commotion in the camp," Gnok said, pointing to where Betha had been tied down.

At first, single horn notes were heard but ended as quickly as they started. There was an explosion, and then he heard roaring and bellowing. They all heard the familiar sound of axes smashing shields and weapons striking plate armor.

The group barreled out into the pen, weapons at the ready. "Who's ready?" Jari shouted.

As one, his companions slammed their weapons against their shields and shouted, "Ready!"

They stood side by side, protecting the door. Then they heard a snort behind them and turned. Betha sniffed the air around her for a second and then tried to push past her comrades.

"What is it, Betha?"

"Iron Skulls are attacking," she roared as the pigs squealed around their ankles.

"Then let's get the hell out of here," Polis said, heading to the back of the pen.

"Go clean your pants, human," Betha sneered. "I'm going to help the Thunderhoof."

Jari grabbed her arm. "This isn't our fight."

"It sure as hell is. They didn't hand me over when they were asked to. The Iron Skulls attacked because the Great Giver wouldn't allow my father to kill me," Betha snapped, accepting her ax from Arnak with a smile.

Zog thumped his chest and shoved Betha out of his way. He charged out of the pen with Arnak and Betha close on his heels, the rest of the group behind them. The minotaurs in front of them were mixed in together, several surrounding Minarrak.

Betha pointed ahead, and without a word, she lowered her head and slammed into an Iron Skull from behind. Jari heard the sickening crunch of its back breaking. The minotaur instinctively turned around, a questioning look in his eyes, then collapsed. Arnak leaped in front of Betha, rolled across the dirt, and found his feet. He systematically destroyed horns and shattered teeth as he swung from right to left, forward and behind.

Jari watched as Toli whistled at Arnak and then ran up his weapon. Arnak flipped him over his shoulder and then continued caving in heads.

Toli landed inside the enclosed circle. "Great Giver Minarrak, follow us."

Minarrak glanced down. "Master Dwarf, are you recommending we retreat?"

"No, I'm suggesting we move away from here and let us hire the warriors left alive."

One of Minarrak's warriors collapsed, his helmet and brains landing on Toli's feet. "If we don't hurry, we will die here," Toli pleaded, kicking the bloody brains off his shoes.

Minarrak flicked his wrist, and a knife flew from his forearm and into the throat of the warrior charging through the hole. Isafin charged in with a contingent of grizzled warriors, accompanied by the Loners.

"Then we die fighting, Master Dwarf," Minarrak said, expelling another blade from his forearm.

The Iron Skulls attacking Minarrak never noticed Betha's group attack. Toli rolled out of the circle, knelt, and castrated the warrior he was under. As fast as he rolled out of the circle, he rolled back in. Betha roared, pounded her chest, and then buried her ax head into one of the Iron Skulls.

Jari and Kala stood side by side, Jari making quick cuts to the lower half of the warriors, and Kala swinging his warhammer toward their skulls. Jari pitched forward, his helmet knocked clear off his head.

Above him stood Henefin Kagoslayer. Sneering at Jari, he picked him up by the throat and pointed at Betha. "Stop fighting, or he dies."

Jari struggled, clutching at Henefin's mane. A few quick horn blasts from both sides ceased the fighting.

"You're weak, daughter. You care for this dwarf, don't you?" Henefin sneered, dangling Jari. He sniffed and pointed. "And your human just shat itself."

Polis reddened, then retreated.

"Put him down," she said, pointing her ax at him.

"You fight me, and I'll consider it," Henefin said.

Betha snorted and wiped her arm across her lips, clearing the blood. "All right, Father, you leave me no choice," she whispered.

"Didn't hear you, daughter."

"I will fight you," she roared. "Now, drop him."

Henefin dropped Jari and kicked him forward. Gnok and Kala pulled him back to their group and formed a circle around him, weapons at the ready.

The minotaurs from both clans made a giant circle as the pair squared off. Betha slowed her breathing and closed her eyes.

"Great Giver, I must ask your permission to draw blood on

your land," Betha said with a stiff bow.

"You have it."

Betha slid her ax across both forearms and let the blood trickle to the ground, pooling near her hooves. She glanced at her companions and gave a quick smile. Before she turned her head, Henefin was on her. He swung his ax, barely missing her midsection. She stepped back, rotated her ankle, and threw him past her.

Toli guffawed. "Gotta stay up, Old Taur. She's a little faster than she looks."

Henefin sprang to his feet and charged. He lowered his horns, attempting to gore her. Betha rolled forward, attempting to trip him, but one horn caught her shoulder, driving her back. She roared and slammed her head into the side of Henefin's ear several times until he withdrew the embedded horn.

She rolled away, grabbed her ax, and swung it down from over her head. Henefin caught the ax shaft midair and yanked it from her grip. He threw it behind him, kicked her in the chest, then slapped her across the face. Betha lay facedown in the dust, her breath shallow. Henefin stalked over, picked her up with both hands around the waist, and squeezed.

Jari heard her whimper, then heard her choking on the blood in her throat. As she gasped for breath, Henefin shook her harder. Arnak flew through the air with a bellow, grabbed Henefin's horns, and yanked them forward, the sinews in his arms rippling. With a pop, both horns came free. Henefin screeched and dropped Betha. Arnak placed both gnarled hands around his neck, headbutted him, and then slashed his throat with a flick of his wrist. His knife returned from the mechanical device tied to his forearm.

Henefin stumbled a few feet, arms outstretched, fell to his knees, and then face-first into the dirt. All present stood in stunned silence as they watched Arnak stomp and grunt like a minotaur.

He moved around Betha, roaring while slamming his fists on his sides. He picked up Henefin's bloody horns and shook them above his head, the blood running down his arms.

He shuffled and pointed at the Iron Skulls, making thrusting movements with his pelvis, then picked up Henefin's dead body and threw it ten feet away. He knelt and slammed the horns into the dirt and bowed his head. One by one, the Iron Skulls grunted at Arnak and walked away. The Thunderhooves nodded their approval, some even so brave as to give Arnak a smirk before walking away.

Jari rushed to Betha's side and checked her wounds. She lay still, blood trickling from her nostrils. Arnak pushed Jari away and then lifted her and slapped her on the back. Zog ran to help, and after another few blows, Betha spat out an enormous torrent of bloody phlegm.

She growled and took a deep breath, her chest shaking as she breathed. Glancing at Jari, she gave him a tired smile. "See, nothing to it."

Chapter 11

Arnak walked over to Betha. "Are you okay?"

She nodded with a grunt, smearing blood across her muzzle. Her eyes briefly inspected Henefin, and then she looked back at Arnak.

"Yeah, I'm good. Thanks for the help," she said before spitting out one of her teeth. "Bastard always did hit hard."

Great Giver Minarrak walked over with Isafin. As they approached, Jari led his group in front of Betha.

"Unless you plan on apologizing, I would stop right there," Jari said, readying his ax.

"Master Dwarf, we fought with you, not against you. Betha was supposed to be judged." He glanced at Henefin's body. "But Henefin had other plans. His attack was a declaration of war against the Thunderhoof. We had no choice but to turn her over. It has always been this way."

"Ah, bull—"

"Jari," Betha hissed, "he protected us."

"Don't think so. He left you chained to the dirt, like some sort of brigand. No one does that to my friends. So, we'll have to remedy that, one way or another. Right, Kala?"

Kala swung his warhammer above his head and stretched. "Oh, right, you are, Brother Jari."

Betha stepped in front of Kala. "No."

"Move aside, Taur. It ain't about you." He pointed his warhammer at Isafin. "I want her horns."

Zog gave a gruff laugh in agreement from behind and unslung his club.

Isafin held her hands up as her warriors advanced. "Do you want a battle, Master Dwarf, or mercenaries to kill your enemies?"

Jari thought for a moment and relaxed. "My anger won't let me negotiate the price. Arnak, bring Betha with us. Polis, you negotiate."

"A human? You must be joking," Minarrak said with a snort.

"He knows where the gold is hidden, and how much of it there is," Jari said.

"We care not. We *don't* negotiate with humans," Isafin snorted.

Jari bristled. "You're testing my patience, Taur."

Isafin growled. "Insult me again, Master Dwarf, and there will be no negotiations."

"Jari, we should go," Kala hissed. "Leave Polis to negotiate."

"Fine."

"I don't give two shits that they protected us, Betha. They tied you to the ground and beat you. That alone is a death sentence," Jari shouted, pointing up at her.

"Calm down, Jari. Great Giver Minarrak could have done a lot worse to me," she said, stretching her shoulders.

"Like what?" he demanded.

"He could have ordered a Brashla," she muttered.

"A what?"

"A Brashla, Jari. It is the Great Giver's right for *all* his warriors to have their way with me if he wanted to dole out severe punishment, so, yes, it could have been a lot worse."

"That's disgusting," Jari hissed. "And if they would have tried that—"

Betha sighed. "You would all be dead."

"We could have taken them," Jari insisted.

Betha chuckled. "A hundred against eight?"

"Zog like those odds. Lots of horns, rings, and ears."

"Shut up, Orc. This doesn't concern us," Arnak grumbled after taking a bite of his grey food.

Zog turned in his direction with a wicked smile. "When Zog wants a fight, anyone will do . . . even you, Brother Arnak."

"That a fact?" Arnak asked, snatching his club off the table.

Gnok stepped between them with a wide smile. "Okay, you two, that's enough."

"No, Brother Gnok. Once Zog draws weapon, it must draw blood. Let turtle come."

Gnok paused. "Did you call me brother, Zog?"

Zog nodded.

"Why?"

"Jari said we were band. Among Zog's people, that makes you brother."

Gnok nodded slowly, not entirely understanding, then huffed and walked away. "Well, don't expect me to call you brother."

Jari and Betha stood in silence, staring at each other. "Something you want to ask me, Jari?"

"Matter of fact, I do," he spat back.

"It's none of your business," Betha said, turning her back to him.

Jari walked around and pushed her. "Heed what I tell you, Betha. Toli knows, and I'll be damned if that little bastard knows more than I."

"That a threat, Jari?" Betha asked with a raised eyebrow.

"Take it however you wish," he spat.

Toli moved over to them. "Leave it, Jari."

Jari tossed his head back and slammed his forehead against Toli's nose. Toli stumbled back and landed with a thud. Betha roared and picked Jari up by the throat and hurled him against the wall. He bounced off and rolled forward with a groan. Betha lunged but stopped short of him as the rest of the band moved in front of him, weapons raised.

Betha pawed the dirt and roared, "Move."

"Not likely," Sinda said, settling into a defensive stance in front of the others.

"This doesn't concern you, Sinda. Stand aside or feel the wrath of a minotaur."

"I've had worse wrath to deal with." Before Betha could move, Sinda had her blades to the inside of Betha's thighs.

"I can end you now, and you'll bleed out, but it'll take a while."

Betha dropped her ax.

"Now, pick up Jari and Toli and explain why all this has been happening," Sinda said, sheathing her knives.

Betha snorted for a moment, then sighed. She picked Jari up by the belt and tossed him to Arnak. Toli stood up as Betha reached over. He smacked her hand away with a curse. "Lot of good that did, Betha," he huffed, pinching his nose closed. "Tell them already."

The others waited for Betha to speak. She shook her mane. Her voice was soft at first as if she were gently pulling on a Band-Aid. "My name is not Betha Silentnight of the Iron Skulls. My real name is Nisafin, High Princess of the Iron Skulls."

Everyone quieted as she went on. "It all started when I was young. I spent my childhood learning about how to be a Wind Whisperer." The others looked at her, puzzled. "A Wind Whisperer is a chosen member of the royal house who communicates with the dead to get their blessings for the tribe. As the youngest of my siblings, I was the chosen one. My father, Great Giver Henefin, wouldn't go to war without the blessings of the dead. As I talked to the dead, they guided me to kill everything. My father did as our ancestors instructed and killed everything around us. Only one tribe was left after the slaughter, but they were protected from harm because of an ancient blood oath. My father sought my council, and I gave him my answer."

"And what answer was that?" Jari asked, wiggling one of his loose teeth.

Betha snorted. "I told him the elders forbade him. They were mostly old warriors, nursing mothers, and little ones. My father did not heed my counsel. So, on the night he planned the raid, I snuck to his hut where my brothers and sisters were getting ready for war."

She shuddered. "I barricaded the exits, threw some pitch on the roof, and lit it." A single tear fell from the corner of her eye. "It was over in less than a minute. All those inside perished. My father and sister, Isafin, were out scouting when the fire broke out. They came back and watched me drop the torch as all my siblings were burned alive."

"And then?" Arnak pressed.

Betha chuckled and touched her horns. "My father and I faced off. He broke one horn off and snapped the other midway. It is known as 'The Mark of the Beast.' He couldn't kill me because I was his daughter. But he disowned me and cast me out with the understanding that if I ever stepped foot on minotaur land again, I would be killed."

Jari nodded slowly, then looked to the others. "Damn."

"What?" Betha asked.

"Never before shared my bed with a princess," Jari said.

Everyone laughed as Betha blushed. "In your dreams, Jari. In your dreams."

"So, Nisafin, is it?" Jari asked through a chuckle.

"Among my kind, yes. Among this band, no. By the way, did one of you act like a minotaur when I was out cold?"

All eyes turned to Arnak, who shrugged. "What?"

Betha leveled her eyes with his. "You killed my father, not an easy task. Why did the others not kill you? You don't speak my language," Betha said, sheathing her ax across her broad shoulders. "Or do you?"

Toli cackled. "Beth, that Hah-Nu-Nah is part minotaur by the way he danced."

Betha raised an eyebrow.

Arnak blushed (well, what might have been a blush). He gave a low groan.

"So, is anyone here going to tell me what happened?" she asked.

"Arnak?" Sinda said.

"It was nothing."

"You told one of them you were her lover," Gnok said with a roar of laughter.

Betha, drinking from a horn of ale, spat the contents on Toli. "Gods damn you, Betha. Now I smell like a minotaur." He sniffed his shirt with a gag and walked away, muttering.

"What did you say, Arnak?" she asked.

Arnak shrugged. "I know your culture, so I—"

"Tell me you didn't claim me," she said more in anger than surprise.

"It wasn't like that, Betha," Gnok said, trying to calm the escalating situation.

Betha snorted. "If you know my culture," she stabbed a finger at Arnak, "then you should know I AM your property now."

It was Jari's turn to redden. "What are you on about, Nisa—" She gave him a harsh stare. "I mean, Betha."

Betha spat some blood from her muzzle. Then she imitated the dance that Arnak had displayed after defeating Henefin.

Everyone watched in wonder as her body moved in an elegant sway for one so robust. She came nose to nose with Arnak and snorted.

When she finished, Zog asked, "What was that?"

"The dance of death," she spat, eyes glued to Arnak.

Toli glanced around. "Uh, what does that mean, exactly?"

"It means that as far as the Thunderhoof and Iron Skulls are concerned, I'm *taken* and therefore must give up my ax or—"

"Or what?" Jari shouted over her, trying to hide the fear in his voice.

"Kill the owner."

A pin could have been heard hitting the dirt floor.

I can hear everyone breathing, Jari thought. *Not good.*

"You missed one of my moves then," Arnak grumbled.

"Yeah, and what was that?" she snapped.

"It is not you who is owned. It is I."

Sinda sucked her breath in, then exploded, her tight french braid bouncing off her back. "I absolutely forbid it," she shouted, pointing up at him.

Arnak smiled and touched her cheek. "My choice." He hefted his spiked club, kissed the head of it, tossed it to Betha, and took a knee. "Your loyal servant, Princess."

Betha sat a few feet away, fuming. Sinda walked up to her, and before she could react, Sinda pushed her off a chair and was poised over her throat.

"That's enough, Sinda," Gnok shouted, holding Arnak back with his other hand.

Sinda flicked her wrist and cut Betha just below her eye. "This ain't over, Taur. Far from over," she hissed before storming out.

Zog helped Betha to her feet with a wide smile. "So, Princess, are your royal holes open for the Mighty Zog?"

Betha slammed her head into Zog's chest and gave him an uppercut that would have broken the jaw of any dwarf.

"No. They're. Not."

Chapter 12

Polis ducked under the small doorway. He glanced at Zog, and then at all the blood. "What the hell happened here?"

"Minor dispute," Gnok grunted as he and Kala dragged Zog to an open area, nearest the smoldering fire.

Jari sat next to Betha in silence, wiping his nose with a cloth. They had been so close to each other, yet so far apart. Their eyes caught for a brief instant, and a slight smile crossed Jari's lips. "I think you loosened one of my teeth again."

"You're lucky that's all I loosened, you ass. You tore out a chunk of my leg." She glanced at her wound. "Bastard."

Jari stuck his hand out. "Brothers?"

It was Betha's turn to smile. "Brothers."

"When you two are done kissing and making up, we have minotaurs to recruit, or do you not want to get paid?" Toli asked, packing his bag.

"We need to find Sinda," Kala said, heading out the door with Gnok on his heels. Zog groaned when he came to. He peered around the room, trying his best to see through his blackened eyes. "Damn you, Betha," he roared, springing to his feet. "You pay for that."

Betha rolled her eyes, standing on shaky legs. "Try to make me pay, Orc."

Jari chuckled as he collected his pack. "I'll let you two lovebirds sort this out," he said before joining the others.

As he cleared the door, Zog flew through the air behind him. His pack landed at his feet as Betha followed him out.

"So, Polis, what was negotiated?" Jari asked, glancing at Zog while shaking his head.

Polis spat and saddled his horse. "Fifty minotaurs for half the gold."

Jari eyed Polis for a moment. "How many coins did Boro get off the wagon train?"

"All told, at least one hundred thousand coins and precious gems."

Betha whistled. "So, we get half of that?"

Polis nodded.

"Is that the only stipulation?" Jari asked, lifting an eyebrow.

Polis shook his head. "No. I agreed that Betha would now travel under the Thunderhoof banner."

Betha never slowed as she lifted Polis off his feet and dangled him in the air. "I never agreed to those terms."

Polis gasped, clawing her biceps. "It was the only way they would agree."

Betha dropped him. She spun around and stared at Jari. "You gave him permission to negotiate?"

Jari smiled with a nod. "Doesn't really matter who's banner you march under as long as you're there." He turned to Polis. "How long is her contract?"

"The Great Giver and I agreed on this battle, and after that, a vote will be cast as to who she will fight with from then on," Polis said.

Sinda pushed her way through some brush with Gnok and Kala on her tail. She yanked her daggers from her belt and moved into a defensive position. "Come now, Taur. Die like a warrior, not some lame-ass worthless princess."

Betha roared, slung her ax from over her shoulder, and charged. Arnak tripped her as she stepped forward and picked up her ax. Then he helped to her feet. "You know the rules, Princess."

Betha fumed, her septum ring jingling. She thrust Arnak's club into his hands and moved aside. He stood in front of Sinda and rested his club on his foot. Gnok watched the situation unfolding and stepped up beside Sinda.

"Not sure what you're thinking here, Arnak. But if I were you, I would back down," Gnok said.

Kala moved next to Gnok and slid his warhammer into both palms, his knuckles white. "I'm with you, Gnok."

Jari stepped beside Arnak. "Is this the way it's going to be? We're going to kill each other?"

"He moves toward Sinda, then, yea, I will kill him," Gnok said, tapping his worn ax handle.

Arnak took a step forward. "Now is not the time, Arnak," Betha hissed, placing a hand on his shoulder.

Arnak bowed and stepped behind her. Betha turned to Sinda. "It was his choice to preserve my honor, Sinda." She cracked a smile. "Remember, only around minotaurs must he act like a slave. As soon as we win this fight and part ways with the Thunderhoof, then we will all be equal again."

"And if we lose?" Sinda asked.

Zog snorted from behind her. "Then we all dead."

The rest of the group nodded.

Jari turned his head as the horns from the Thunderhoof camp blasted. Isafin led her warriors down the road, the dust swirling around their ankles. Betha pushed to the front and bowed. "Sister."

Isafin gave a halfhearted nod. "Where are we going?"

"We must go west," Jari said, joining the conversation.

"*The human* has negotiated half the treasure for our clan and Betha of the Loners under our standard. Since you number only eight, and we number fifty, we will draw up the battle plan once we arrive. You can join us if you like." She watched her warriors fidget, then picked her teeth with a sharpened bone. "Or not. It matters not. Once we have the gold, Nisafin will be voted on as to whether she continues service with the Thunderhoof as a merc or goes back with the Loners. These are our clauses. Do you agree?"

"Yea," Jari said.

"It's a group decision, Master Dwarf," Isafin muttered.

The others all nodded individually.

Isafin's eyes hardened as she ran her paw down the edge of her blade. "Let's go kill this Spiderbinder."

Chapter 13

Jari held his fist up as the column walked over a tall peak and into the valley below. Isafin walked over to him, her head at his elbow as he sat on his pony.

"What is it?" she asked.

"Something doesn't feel right."

Kala's mount nickered as the ponies stood side by side. Jari glanced over with a head nod.

"I know that look, Jari. What do you sense?" Kala asked.

"They're out there," Jari muttered.

"Ambush?" Kala asked.

Before Jari could answer, Isafin said, "My warriors want to kill this brigand and go home. Damn an ambush," she said, waving her warriors to follow her.

The rest of the Loners rode up to the ridgeline as Isafin and her group descended into the valley. Betha and Arnak passed, but only Betha acknowledged them. Arnak kept his eyes downcast. Jari could hear Sinda muttering several dwarven curses, which made him chuckle.

Toli cleared his throat and pointed with his hook. "Jari, what's that on the next ridge?"

Jari pulled his small scope out, unfolded it, and placed it over his eye. Scanning the opposite ridgeline, he couldn't see what Toli saw. He held his breath, slowed his breathing, and then saw it.

The slightest glint from a piece of armor caught the sun just right for him to focus his attention. "Damn fools."

Without any warning, Boro's men rolled large fiery haystacks down on Isafin and her warriors. Jari and the others heard the war cries from the attacking force before they actually saw the warriors themselves.

The ground rumbled as the first fourteen-foot Kago stepped onto the ridge.

"What in all the Dwarven Lords' name?" Kala exclaimed. "I've never seen a Kago up close."

Two more joined their comrade on the top. They rained huge, sharpened tree branches into the valley below. Isafin's warriors closed around one another, shields up.

A few dead minotaurs lay impaled on the ground on the perimeter. The Loners watched in horror as hundreds of Red Widows and bands of Frost Elves sprinted down the charred landscape after the burning haystacks.

Kala and Gnok made eye contact and smiled. Both slammed their visors down, touched their weapons, and charged.

"Wait," Jari roared.

It was of no use. The remainder of the group followed suit with their own war cry.

Should have never agreed to this bounty, he thought.

He yanked the reins of his pony back, rearing it up on his hind legs. The pony needed no prompting when its hooves touched the ground. It could smell the battle raging below.

His pony galloped down the hill in the wake of the others. Each hoofbeat slammed into the grass, sending a jolt through Jari's tailbone. With a flick of his wrist, Jari freed his bolas from his belt loop. He stared at the Kago on the ridge and watched more branches impale his mercenaries.

Few hundred more feet.

The pony's mane tickled his nose as he galloped behind the others. A Frost Elf crossed his path. He never slowed as the bolas struck the elf in the head, caving in its cheekbone. Jari's mount dropped its head and bowled the defender under its hooves.

One.

Yanking a knife from his belt, he launched it end over end and caught a Red Widow in the throat that had Toli pinned under five of its limbs. Jari stood up in the stirrups and flung his bolas in every direction.

Two, three, fou—

His pony screeched as its legs were chopped out from under it. Jari flew through the air and landed on his shoulder.

Shit.

He rolled to his side as a large red and black pincher lay poised above his head. As the pincher darted at him, it was chopped off. Black blood and bits of carapace sprayed into his eyes.

"Godsdamn it," he shouted, furiously rubbing his eyes.

He felt a hand on the top of his breastplate. "Let me clear my eyes before we fight, you worthless bag of pony spunk."

Someone lifted him and put him on his feet. After the blood cleared, he saw his group rallying around him. He smelled Betha before his eyes opened. Her musky scent flooded his nostrils.

Ah, good to have her.

Only it wasn't Betha. It was Isafin. She growled at him with a sneer and pushed his ax into his palms.

"There's too many of them. We will fight a rearguard action, leapfrogging until we reach the high ground behind us."

Jari tugged at his bloody beard. "Fine. How many warriors do you have?"

"Twenty that can fight. The rest are dead or dying," she muttered as one of her teeth fell out.

Jari scanned the battle in front of him. The minotaurs had managed to form a ring defense, protecting their flanks, but they were buckling. Jari found his horn and blew three quick blasts to sound retreat. Betha and Arnak fought their way to him.

"We're here," Betha roared, disemboweling two elves.

Gnok and Kala ran up, their ponies dead behind them. Sinda and Toli held each other up and regrouped. Toli had a long gash running across his forehead, and Sinda's braid had been severed, leaving her hair running in different directions.

"Where are Zog and Polis?" Jari asked the others.

"Zog here." He stumbled into the group holding his side. "Hurt, but here."

"Anyone seen Polis?" Gnok shouted.

Betha pointed to the opposite hill. "There."

Atop the opposite embankment was Polis, sitting alongside Boro Spiderbinder.

I'll kill you and boil you in oil, Jari thought.

Zog limped up to Jari. "Too many insects. We go." Jari nodded as he backpedaled, fending off a large Red Widow. Isafin ran over to him and caved in the insect's head. "My warriors will hold the line. We must—"

Her head exploded into multiple pieces, spraying Jari with blood and gore. Behind her stood a Kago, his blue beard dripping with blood, smiling wide.

The Kago swung his club down again, and Jari rolled forward. It roared and reached down to its ankles. Betha ducked as she cut the giant's ankle tendons with broad fluid strokes. He roared and reached down, but she slid past his grasp.

With a final hack, the Kago fell forward onto a group of Red Widows.

"Follow me," Betha roared, leading the others into the woods as Spiderbinder's troops surrounded the remaining minotaurs.

Betha led them through the branches and briar patches, past the overgrown trees and wild berry bushes. They ran single file down a path, tripping and falling along the way. After running for a time, they finally stopped hearing the sounds of battle. Betha slowed as she took deep breaths, scanning the forest around them.

Jari walked up to her and hugged her. "You okay, Brother?"

She gave a sharp nod.

"How 'bout you, Arnak?" he asked.

Arnak felt the wide dent in his carapace. "I'll live," he grumbled, throwing a piece of the outer shell away.

Jari said each person's name individually.

"Gnok?"

Gnok smiled, wrapping a cloth around his wound on his forearm. "Aye, I'm good."

"Kala?"

Kala groaned and dropped a large bag off his shoulder. "A piece of my right ear is chopped off, but got a shit ton of trophies from the battle." He held up his bandaged hand. "And half an index finger chopped off. I really *hate* Red Widows."

"Sinda?"

"I'm okay, just lost my braid and a dagger," she said.

"Toli?"

Blood dripped from his head wound. Sinda unrolled a bandage and wrapped his head. "I ain't dead yet," he muttered.

"Zog?"

"Zog here."

"Good, everyone's breathing," Jari said, sitting on a log with a groan.

"What now, Jari?" Betha asked, sitting beside him.

"Sorry about your—"

Betha waved him off. "Never mind that. They knew the score going in. Comes with the territory." Her septum ring rattled. "Now, what do we do? It's obvious Polis sold us out. He has the blood of fifty minotaurs on his hands. At the very least, I must take him back to Great Giver Minarrak for trial."

"I want that rat bastard as much as everyone here. But he has an army behind him now with Spiderbinder. We can't get him," Jari mumbled.

"Why would he sell us out?" Toli asked.

"More importantly, how did he get time to sell us out?" Gnok said.

"Wish I knew the answer to both questions, but when I do catch him again, I'll shatter every bone in his body to find out."

"Back to what I was saying, I think there's a way," Betha insisted.

"We just lost fifty mercs. How do you propose we do that?" Jari asked. "We'd need a thousand more."

"Not necessarily," she said.

Jari stared through her. *What is she on about now?*

"You might think this is crazy, but I say we ride for Anak'anor and recruit a merc army," she said, cleaning some blood and brains from her ax.

Everyone chuckled. "You can't be serious," Jari hissed. "It's in the far north for a reason."

"I am. I never wanted to go to the Thunderhoof. That was your choice to follow Polis's advice, but I do think we can recruit more mercs if we go further. I want revenge for my sister, even though she hated me," Betha said.

"With what coin?" Toli asked with a smirk.

"We borrow from the dwarves in the mountains," she said, scanning the faces.

Gnok rolled his eyes. "Betha, the other dwarves will never help us. Every dwarf here has a bounty on their head in one way or another."

Kala grunted his agreement. "I'm with Gnok."

"So, who's gonna go, and who's gonna stay?" Jari asked after spitting a wad of phlegm at his boots.

Toli and Betha stood on one side and Gnok and Kala on the other. Sinda stood up, ran her hands through her hair, jostling it in different directions, then walked over with Toli.

"I'm game," she said.

Arnak followed her, relieved to no longer be a fake slave. Zog slid next to Betha. "Zog need coin too."

"All right, that's the vote. Kala and Gnok, you may join us or leave. No one will say another word."

"Shit," Kala muttered, then picked up his warhammer.

He cut his eyes at Gnok. "I may have a bounty on my head among the lords, but I still swore an oath, same as you, Gnok the Rock, and I'll be damned if I'm going to die branded a coward."

Sinda stared at them, her eyes never betraying her thoughts. She finally spoke up. "I'll be damned, Gnok and Kala are Yellow Dwarves."

They both threw her an evil expression. Kala gripped his warhammer tighter. "And what of it, Sinda Rockgut? I've lost as you have. Only difference is I lost my daughters as well as my wife." He yanked his sleeve up to his elbow.

A brand ran from his inner forearm to his elbow. It was the shape of an anvil with a large X over it.

"I killed the dwarves responsible for their murders. And in doing so, they banished me to a nomadic *Yellow* Dwarf's existence. So, the next time you care to call me *yellow*, watch your tongue and your tone. I'll thank you to remember I am *the* Kala Silverbeard of the *Grey* Dwarves, Third Anvalist of Fog Peak."

"The Gray Dwarves are no longer," Toli said.

"One still draws breath on this god's forsaken planet," Kala said over his shoulder.

"And you, Gnok?" Jari asked, his eyebrow arching. "You have a bounty on your head now?"

"Long story," Gnok muttered.

"I haven't seen or heard from you in ten years. What have you been doing?"

Gnok ignored him.

Jari pushed him. "I said—"

The ground shook around them. Zog pointed behind them. "Kago."

Arnak pointed to a cave one hundred yards off the ground path. "We talk later. Follow me." He crashed through more vegetation as he led the group. Nearing the cave, everyone spread out. They moved as one, turning themselves into a shield wall with Betha and Jari on point.

"Torch," Jari hissed as they stepped into the darkened opening. Sinda made a torch quickly and shoved it into his outstretched hand.

He swung it at his feet. Nothing moved.

A cobweb stuck to Toli's face. As he pulled it free, he tripped and knocked a large piece of wood into a pile of metal. The sound was similar to a clap of thunder. Toli pushed himself up.

Jari stared straight ahead and hissed, "Dammit, Toli."

Jari motioned for the others to take a knee, shields together. The dirt swirled around them as a cold gust of wind blew from the back of the cave.

Jari strengthened his grip on his worn ax handle. "Whatever comes our way, show no mercy, take no prisoners."

It started as a low bleat; then it was joined by others.

"What the hell is that sound?" Arnak grumbled, rotating his club in his palm.

Betha sniffed the air, her tongue wagging from side to side. She paused. "Wedge formation—now."

The others followed without question, their shields clinking together. "Who are we?" Jari shouted as he slammed his ax head against his shield.

"Loners."

"Advance," he bellowed, then lowered his visor.

Pure white goats with massive black corkscrew horns and their goblin riders thundered out of the back of the cave. The goblins burst through the darkness and crashed against the shield wall.

Betha swung her ax overhand and split a goblin in half, knocking it out of the saddle. She threw her shoulder into the goat's side and knocked it off its feet.

Jari's bolas and Zog's throwing spears found their marks, taking several riders from their saddles.

"Kill the riders, protect the mounts," Kala shouted, leaving the others to mount one of the riderless goats.

He spurred it forward and raised his warhammer. "For the Grey Dwarves."

Using his knees to guide it, he placed his warhammer in the crook of his arm like a lance and lowered the goat's horns.

The goat bleated and charged. Its horns gored the goblin in front of it, shaking it like a rag doll, spraying its flank with black blood. Kala's warhammer speared two riders riding in a single file as he rode on. He yanked a long ax from his belt and decapitated a goblin running underneath him.

Sinda, Toli, and Gnok mounted and charged behind Kala as the other Loners broke ranks. Built to charge, the goats reorganized with their new riders lined up in a diamond formation and swarmed the remaining goblins as they squeaked in retreat.

With one final push, Kala rode the rest down. With a torch in one hand and his warhammer in the other, he spun his kicking and butting goat with his knees until all that was left were mangled corpses. He dismounted with a groan, his breathing heavy and deep, but he smiled wide and hugged the goat around the neck.

He patted its head. "Good goat."

Jari walked up beside him, his mouth agape. "What was that all about?"

Kala shrugged. "Before the Grey Dwarves banished me, I was a war mount trainer. This is a special breed called a Bohal."

"Bohal, huh?" Jari asked, petting its flank.

"Yea, hardest war beast in the Dwarven Kingdoms. But why would they be out here?" Kala asked, peering into the darkness.

"Someone hand me a torch," Jari said.

Sinda passed him one and lit some more for the others.

"Spread out and keep your guard up. Kala, collect the mounts and wait for us at the mouth of the cave," Jari said.

Kala nodded and started rounding up the war goats as the others crept farther into the cave. The farther the group traveled, the larger the cave became. Jari and the others searched the walls. Mounds of old armor, discarded weapons, and coins lay scattered around them.

Jari and Sinda wandered over to an unlit area. Jari swept his torch by his feet and gasped. Chained to the wall were ten dwarves, broken and bloody. He growled and ran over to them, checking pulses.

"Over here," Jari shouted.

The others sprinted to him and helped check the bodies. "They're all dead," Gnok grumbled.

They had been tortured before death—horribly tortured. Arnak knelt by one and pressed his hand against the dwarf's chest.

"I got one still breathing," he shouted.

Zog ran to the wall and ripped the chain off. Arnak scooped up the body and ran to the front of the cave and out into the sun. The dwarf's chest rose in haggard breaths. Arnak laid him down and pressed both palms on his temples and began to hum. Betha ran to a nearby brook and filled her flask. She returned to Arnak and placed it beside him.

Arnak hummed, oblivious to the world around him. Few, if any, on Labrys could heal someone like a Ha-Nuh-Na. Jari listened to him humming what sounded like a prayer.

A light blue glow enveloped both Arnak and the injured dwarf in a bubble. Arnak shook, his muscles tensing. A few seconds later, the light shattered into a thousand pieces. The dwarf groaned and moved his head from side to side.

Arnak removed his hands and fell back. Sinda rushed to his side, pulled the cork from the flask, and forced him to drink.

"Is he alive?" Arnak muttered.

"Yea," Jari said, feeling his pulse.

"Good, I think I'll take a nap," he mumbled, then immediately fell asleep.

Chapter 14

"How long till he's awake?" Jari asked.

Arnak shrugged. "Hard to say. I put him into a trance so I could operate if I needed to." He checked the dwarf over thoroughly once more with a grunt. "And I won't have to, so I say another twelve hours, and he should be awake."

Jari was only half-listening. His eyes scanned the cave. He gave Arnak a quick nod and walked away. He walked along the walls, running his fingers along the porous surface.

Nothing seemed out of the ordinary. The others in the company had lain down in a circle in the center of the cave, weapons close at hand. Jari gave a quick glance over his shoulder, then to the back of the cave.

Satisfied no one was awake, he pulled his ax from his belt, lifted his torch a little higher, and walked further back. The dirt turned into white sand as he neared the back.

He knelt in the sand. *What the hells?*

In front of him were mounds of arms and armor. Plate, chainmail, and leather lined the wall. Halberds, lances, warhammers, axes, swords, and daggers lay in separate piles, all in different states of disrepair.

Lightweight silver chainmail lay on a table in front of him. He ran his calloused hairy fingers across it, the rings catching his fingernails. He shoved his ax into his belt, lifted the chainmail up, and held it to his shoulders.

Perfect fit. I'll be damned.

A helmet with a thick silver nose guard with two gold-plated cheek guards sat on the corner of the table. Jari picked the helmet up, slid it over his head, and twisted his neck.

Not a bad fit.

Making sure nothing else could harm them while they rested, he returned to his group. Gnok sat by himself, sharpening his ax and throwing knives with a small whetstone.

Jari walked up to him. "Mind if I join you?"

Gnok pointed to the log beside him.

Jari set his newfound treasures down. Gnok eyed the chainmail. "Nice chainmail. Where did you get it?"

"Back of the cave. Bound to be stuff that fits all of us dwarves," Jari said.

Gnok put his weapons and whetstone aside and readied to stand. "Why didn't you say that before?"

Jari placed a hand on Gnok's knee. "Give me a few minutes, please."

Gnok sighed and sat back down. "I was hoping you would let this drop," he said, again picking up his weapons and whetstone.

"Not likely. When were you banished from the Blue Dwarves?"

"Really wasn't banished, per se," Gnok said, sliding his ax head down the whetstone.

"Really?"

Gnok shrugged. "Okay, that was a lie."

Jari smiled. "I know."

"Promise you won't judge me?" Gnok asked.

Jari made eye contact. "Aye, no judgments."

He gave a long sigh and lit his pipe lying nearby. "I fucked Queen Vofida Anvilbender," he muttered.

Jari's jaw dropped. "For hell's sake! She's four hundred years old if she's a day, Gnok. Did you please her while she was using her cane or having her tea?"

Gnok stared through him. "Don't do it, Jari."

Jari pursed his lips, tapped his feet, wrung his hands—all to no avail. He burst out laughing. It was so loud, Betha woke up and roared. "Shut it."

Gnok readied to leave.

"Gnok, Gnok, don't leave. I'm sorry."

Gnok glared at him for a few moments, then sat back down. "I told you not to laugh, Jari," he hissed.

Jari collected himself. "I'm sorry, Cousin. There must be a reason."

Gnok nodded grimly. "Oh, aye, there's a reason."

Jari leaned forward. "So, what's the reason, Gnok the Rock?"

Gnok spat, picked his front teeth, and then took a long pull from his pipe. "She held out on paying the palace guards for months. The boys weren't eating. Our little ones were starving, so I had to do something."

"Why did she hold out on you?"

Gnok shrugged. "How should I know? She's crazy as a Kago's ass."

Jari smiled.

"Anyway, the boys concocted a plan. If I could detain her, they would sneak in and steal our pay."

"So, what happened?" Jari asked, leaning forward.

"I walked into her naked as the day I was born. I went straight to her bed and put it in her hand."

Jari placed his hands over his mouth to keep from laughing. Gnok cracked a smile listening to how ridiculous it all sounded.

He leaned in to finish the tale. "While I'm pumping away to that evil croon's screams of ecstasy, the boys stole the money and ran like hells," Gnok giggled. "When I finished, she yelled out the dead king's name."

Jari couldn't hold it. He fell off the log and rolled on the ground. His laughter echoed through the cave, waking the others.

"What's so funny over there?" Toli shouted before throwing a rock at Jari. "Quiet down, dammit. I smell like minotaur blood, and some damn Red Widow gave me a gash across the head. Now, go to sleep."

Chapter 15

Jari's eyelid popped open when the first ray of light hit it. When he heard the moans from the front of the cave, he scrambled to his feet and rushed over to the dwarf. Encased in a blue glow, the dwarf muttered, then blinked. Jari held his breath as the young dwarf turned to look at him.

"Do you have any water?" he asked, his voice like footsteps on gravel.

Jari snatched his flask, lifted the dwarf's head slightly, and dribbled the water over his cracked lips as the blue hue faded.

"Where are the others?" he asked.

Jari shook his head.

The young dwarf nodded with an extended sigh. "Thought so. Help me up, will ya?"

"Not sure I should," Jari said after a long pause.

"I'm fine, Old Dwarf. Just got the wind knocked out of me is all," he said.

Jari smiled. "It's a little worse than that but all right. Have it your way." He slid his arm under the young dwarf's armpit and pulled him up slowly.

"Aye, thanks, friend."

Jari nodded. "Jari Rockjaw's my name," he said, extending his hand.

The other dwarf shook it. "Bric Firehand," he said in return.

Jari glanced at the hideous burns on top of his hand and fingers. Bric took notice. "Oh, aye, those are from smithing Tok ore."

Jari cleared his throat. "There's none of that metal left on the planet."

Bric raised a bushy eyebrow. "That a fact?" He spat, then licked his lips. "Well, you keep thinking that." He patted Jari on the shoulder, then rubbed his hands. "Now, who's got some gut-rot?"

Jari flipped him a flask. Bric lifted it in his direction and took a loud gulp, then sighed with a smile. "That's the good stuff."

Bric was slender of the waist with brawny arms the size of tree trunks. His blue beard was cropped close to his chin, unusually short for a dwarf. His Tok plate mail and helm were a perfect fit with runes carved throughout.

Jari glanced over Bric's shoulder and watched the others rise. Arnak came out of the trees and walked over. He lifted Bric's chin.

"No worse for wear, I see," he grumbled.

"You worked on me, Ha-Nuh-Na?" Bric asked, after taking another sip.

Arnak shrugged. "I work on any and everyone if they need it."

"Thanks."

Betha yawned with a long growl. She approached them. "Hell of a night, last night." She handed Jari her ax. "Brighten that ax head, will ya?"

Jari accepted it with a grunt of disapproval. "I hope to save *your* ass soon. I'm tired of cleaning your gory blade."

Bric chuckled and looked around. "Lively group. A minotaur, a Ha-Nu-Nah, and an orc among dwarves? Interesting."

Jari nodded. "We're called the Loners."

"I like the ring of that," Bric said. "'And where are you headed?"

"North to Anak'anor," Gnok said, joining the conversation. "By the way, why are you in a cave full of goblins?"

Bric winced and glanced at the cave mouth. "Long story."

"Join us for breakfast and tell us. Let me introduce you to everyone," Jari said, making the introductions.

"The orc over there is the Mighty Zog. Our brethren are Toli, Kala, Sinda, and Gnok the Rock. The Ha-Nu-Nah is Arnak, and Betha's standing by the small fire," Jari said.

Betha tossed some dried beef to Bric. He took a large chunk and devoured it. "So, what's the deal?" Betha asked.

Bric took another bite and chewed. "We were heading to Port Agu to sell weapons and armor. The goblins you fought were what was left of a horde of two hundred that attacked while we camped. They fell on us, slaughtering most." He spat. "And the ones in the cave and myself were captured and tortured."

"How many of you were there?" Jari asked.

"Fifty. Fifty of the finest Black Rock dwarven smiths and miners in the Restless Highlands."

"You're a Black Rock?" Toli asked, looking up from rummaging through his pack. "Your lasses have beards." He shook his head. "Yick."

Bric bristled. "Only married ones. What would you know of it, Little Stump?"

Toli loosened his bolas from his belt. "I'll give you a little stump, Black Rock."

"Enough, Toli." Jari threw him three flasks. "Fill these up. We have a lot of ground to cover today," he said.

Toli muttered something under his breath and walked to the river. Kala led the goats out of the cave and over to Bric. "These belong to you."

Bric smiled. "That's okay. The owners will no longer be needing them. My gift for saving my life."

"We're grateful, Bric. Would you like to journey with us on

our way to Anak'anor?"

Bric hesitated. "Guess I haven't a choice, do I?"

"Good. It's settled. Are the weapons and armor in the back yours?" Jari asked.

"Yes, along with the Tok chainmail and helmet you're wearing," Bric said, eyeing Jari up and down.

"Forgive me. I didn't know," Jari said, attempting to hand it back.

Bric waved him off. "Agh, it fits you well enough. I'll take half price for it with the helm."

Jari glanced at his friends. "We're a little short on coin right now. We were traveling to the Blue Dwarves to ask for a loan. But our situation has changed. If you travel with us and help with a few bounties, we'll have what you need."

"You're bounty hunters?" Bric asked.

"Yea, it's all we know," Gnok said from behind Jari.

"Who are you going after?" Bric asked.

"Boro Spiderbinder and his rogue army," Jari said.

Bric smiled.

"Something amusing?" Jari asked.

"Boro owes me thirty thousand coins for weapons and armor for his army. If you're going after him, I'm in," Bric said.

"We still need money for an army ourselves," Kala hissed from behind Jari.

"I heard Boro has a horde of treasure. I'll give you the weapons and armor we were carrying to sell in Port Agu. You can sell them in Anak'anor to recruit mercs. Sound like a deal?" Bric asked.

Jari stuck out his hand. "Deal. Now, let's go and pack that wagon I saw in the back and ride for Anak'anor."

"Move out," Jari shouted from the saddle of his mount the next morning.

He picked the meanest of the goats to ride. Its horns were sharpened, making it capable of goring any enemy that crossed its path. The horns were four feet long with multiple forks throughout, forming a shield to protect the rider.

I'll name you, Grumps.

Jari leaned over the goat's neck and hand-fed him an apple, then rubbed its horns. He tapped his ankles, and Grumps led the way.

They rode in silence for a good portion of the day, only stopping to water the goats and feed them. Betha and Zog flanked Jari, forming a spear point, the others the shaft.

As they crossed The River of Sorrow that ran the full length of Labrys from north to south, they went over a large wooden bridge made of the finest oak.

Jari reined in Grumps after they crossed the bridge. "Ahead of us lies The Expanse. I need a volunteer to scout ahead and report back any activity so that we can get off this road. Who's in?"

Everyone glanced at one another. Being a merc was one thing. Attempting a suicide mission was another. Jari felt their hesitation.

Come on . . .

Kala nudged his goat forward. "I'll go."

Shit. Why couldn't Zog volunteer?

"All right, Kala. Be careful out there. Ride five miles out along the road, then report back. We'll camp in the woods every time you report back. Take it nice and easy, lest we fall prey to whatever's out there," Jari said.

Bric moved alongside Kala. "If you don't mind, I know the tracks ahead, and where we were ambushed. I would like to ride with him."

Gnok leaned over to Jari. "You sure you can trust him?"

Kala nodded in agreement. "Could use some company."

Jari whispered, "Well, it seems so."

Chapter 16

"They've been gone most of the day," Gnok said, reining in beside Jari at the head of the column.

"Tell me something I don't know, Cousin," Jari muttered.

"Kala should never have taken Bric with him. For all we know, Kala could be lying in a ditch somewhere, and if we do manage to find him, there probably won't be anything left to recognize."

Jari's look silenced him. "We will see."

The group rode for another mile. Jari scanned the sky, trying to find any carrion birds. After what seemed like an eternity, Kala and Bric rode hard over a hill, holding onto their goats' necks.

At first, one, two, three, then *fifty* goblins streamed over the hill chasing them. Kala reined in and shouted. "We better find high ground. They'll be here shortly."

Jari glanced at Sinda and Toli, who were driving the goats leading the wagon. "Make for the trees."

Sinda urged the goats off the path, several weapons falling off the top.

Damn, now what?

"Cousin, any ideas?" Gnok asked, yanking his ax from his waist.

"We won't escape with the wagon. Someone has to divert

them. They're stupid creatures. They'll follow whoever is closest. Kala and Bric are spent." Jari paused. "I'll go. You take command, and I'll catch up," Jari said to Gnok.

"Jari—"

"Gnok, a leader leads from the front, *not* behind." He shoved him. "Go. I'll find you."

Ready, Grumps?

Jari dug his heels into Grumps's side and charged toward the green and brown goblins. Their short black arrows thudded into the ground around him. He could feel Grumps surge with excitement, his ears flattening back.

A few larger goblins surged ahead of the pack. Jari loosened his silver balled bolas and swung them over his head. The wind blew his bushy red beard over his shoulder, the stench of the half-naked goblins wafted into his nostrils.

Without prompting, Grumps lowered his horns and gored the two lead goblins, who were ten yards ahead of the others, their squeals of anguish invigorating him.

Adrenaline surged through Jari's fingertips as his bolas loosed downrange. Grumps shook his head with a loud bleat, tossing the corpses to the side, his hooves trampling them. Jari continued to fire his bolas with loud whoops until they were spent.

"For the Loners," he roared, throwing one of his knives end over end, taking another goblin in the throat. As the group closed in, Grumps lowered his horns and broke left at a ninety-degree angle.

Jari risked a glance over his shoulder as most of the goblins followed him. A group of ten split off from the main group and followed the train.

Shit, well, I got most of 'em.

He continued to ride as more arrows thudded into the grass around him. As he cleared the plains, he rode toward the woods in front of him. Dead trees with massive trunks, branches, and stakes sprawled out around him.

Jari heard a wolf howl behind him.

Great! Wolf riders.

Three wolf riders rode away from the rest of the column and were gaining ground. He shifted in the saddle, reached for another set of bolas in his saddlebag, and felt an arrow slam into the top of his hand.

Ah, dammit.

He dropped the bolas, sat upright in the saddle, and felt Grumps leap. As his goat landed, Jari bounced up, his legs lifting from the stirrups. His left hand caught the saddle horn as gravity pulled him to the right. He pulled himself back into the saddle with a strain and continued riding.

Easy, boy, easy.

A wolf rider pulled up alongside him, and Grumps lowered his horns and tore into the wolf's throat. The goblin flipped over the wolf's head and snapped its neck as it screeched and crashed.

Jari yanked the arrow out of his hand and bore down on Grump's neck, gripping his knees tighter to his flanks. The hair from his mane tickled his nose.

"Achoo."

Jari snorted and spat a wad of phlegm. The wolves howled as they followed, darting between the broken branches and upturned tree limbs.

Let's see how smart you bastards are.

He urged Grumps up a tree trunk, trusting his steady hooves. He heard a yelp as a wolf slipped off the trunk, impaling itself and its rider on a limb jutting up from below.

One more.

Spinning in the saddle as Grumps leaped to another trunk, he reached for his knife handle. He patted his waistline.

Shit.

A moment later, a wolf bit into the chainmail covering his

shoulder and knocked him from the saddle. Both rider and mount rolled over him, the wolf's teeth gnawing on the Tok links.

Ahhhhh, you bastard.

Jari searched madly for any weapon nearby, his fingers stretching. He touched a sharp limb, gripped it, and slammed it into the wolf's ear.

Its head draped across his shoulder, the wolf's tongue wet on his ear. He lay on his back, dazed and bloody. His eyes fluttered open, and the goblin stood over him, blood and spit dripping from his lips.

It screeched, "*Yanka dilaka.*"

Raising its sword above its head, it swung down. As the blade descended, Jari heard Grumps bleating and watched as he speared the goblin. It flew off its feet and landed five feet away on its back, its chest cavity smashed.

Grumps lowered his horns and nudged Jari's hand. With a grimace and groan, he rolled on his side and slowly made it to his feet.

He wiped his bloody lip and spat. "*Yanka blanca* to you too, ya worthless bastard."

"He's out there. I know he is," Betha said, scalping the last goblin at her hoof.

The remainder of the mob had followed after Jari to the opposite side of the field. Once they disappeared from view, the Loners turned around, mustered into formation, and rode over the ten goblins sprinting after them.

One of the goat's flanks had been slashed, and Kala was in the process of sewing it shut while Arnak put it under a trance.

After the cleanup, Gnok checked everyone. "Jari said to keep moving. So, let's move out. We keep close to the woods. Bric, you up for another scouting mission?"

Bric wiped the gore off his blades and gave a quick nod. He swung into the saddle and rode out.

"While he's gone, I want everyone to police up what they can. Strip the goblins of any and all weapons. They will count when we get to Anak'anor," Gnok said.

Toli picked up a crude goblin sword with two fingers. "Gnok, you must be joking. These pieces won't even trade for a mug of gut-rot."

"You let me worry about that, Toli. You just gather it with the others," Gnok said, scalping the goblin in front of him. "Betha, you and Zog loot and scalp the corpses on the plains, then drag their bodies back here, away from the carrion birds."

"I'm no grave digger, Gnok. Ask someone else," Betha snapped, keeping her hand over her brow.

"Betha, Jari left me in charge. Please do as I ask. Just think of all the ears you can sell. I'll give you my loot out there on the battlefield."

Betha cut her eyes at him. "Your loot? What do you think, Zog?"

Gnok smiled and pointed behind her. "Looks like he's on his way already."

Gnok turned around and walked over to Kala. "What happened out there on the mission?"

Kala shrugged as he sewed. "We were riding along the path, about to turn around and report. Then those dirty bastards streamed down a hill beside us like they were waiting for something."

Gnok stared at the open plain. "Ambushed?" he muttered.

Toli walked over to Gnok. "When are you going to look for Jari? He should have been back by now."

"He'll be back. Have patience," Gnok said. He glanced at Sinda. "Sinda, can you get a fire going?"

Sinda shrugged. "Do it yourself. I'm busy scalping," she said, tossing a scalp into a pouch by her feet.

Gnok sighed and rubbed his brow. "I'll do it," Toli said.

Betha and Zog dumped the bodies they carried from the field into the pit where they had thrown the other goblins. Without saying a word to Gnok, they walked over to the fire to count their spoils.

As night settled in and still no word from Jari, Betha finally grew weary of it. "I'm crossing that plain and heading into the woods. I won't leave him out there by himself."

A twig snapped behind her as Jari and Bric walked into the firelight, leading their goats. "Don't worry about me, Betha. Would have been back hours ago, but I saw Bric ride out and went to join him," Jari said, lifting a tree branch out of Grumps's path.

Betha snorted her reply and handed him her ax shaft first. "I just wanted to make sure my blade was clean by morning. Chop-chop."

"What did you see?" Gnok asked, poking the fire.

"Goblins and a handful of orcs are camped on the road about a mile ahead," Bric said.

Zog's ears perked up. "What orcs you see?"

Bric stood by the fire warming his hands. "The orcs wore blue face paint across their eyes."

Zog snatched his blade off the ground and headed for the road. Jari stepped in front of him. "I'd like to know where you're going," he said.

"Not business."

He stormed past him and disappeared into the crisp black night. Jari watched the stars for a few minutes.

"Well, it seems our orc has better things to do," Toli said with a chuckle.

"Form up," Jari said, tightening his leather helmet strap.

He snatched Grumps's reins and mounted. Betha walked over

and calmly took the bridle.

"No need, Jari. Zog will either come back from his run, or we kill him along with his brethren."

Jari gazed into her eyes for a moment, then nodded. He dismounted and walked back to the fire.

"If you're wrong, Betha, The Loner's blood is on your hands."

Chapter 17

As dawn broke, there was still no sign of Zog. The group ate breakfast, packed their kits, and waited for Jari's orders.

Why did you have to do this, Zog?

"Loners, mount up," Jari said.

Kala reined in beside Jari. "And what of Zog?"

"You care?" Jari asked with a raised eyebrow.

Kala huffed. "No, Jari, but he's a Loner, whether or not I like it." He clucked, then tapped his ankles to the goat's flank. "Giddyap."

"I want the wagon on the road with me, Betha, and Arnak. The rest of you will stay in the woods. We'll hit the enemies flank if attacked. Understood?" Jari asked.

Everyone nodded as they packed.

Toli and Sinda urged the goats onto the rocky road.

"We're fish in a barrel up here," Toli muttered as they broke through the tree line.

"We may be, but we have to keep this wagon moving, or we'll never catch up to Boro." Toli watched as her eyes hardened. "And I want my revenge," she hissed.

"I'm sorry about your husband," Toli said, looking straight ahead.

Sinda smiled. "Thank you, Toli. And to answer your comment

from the bar when we first met, I am single."

"I . . . ugh, did I ask that?"

"No, you said it while you stared at my ass. You're lucky Arnak didn't hear you, or he would have killed you for that," she said with a chuckle.

"I still might if your cock jumps out of your pants, Little One. I'll use your skull as a drinking horn," Arnak muttered, walking past them to take point with Betha.

Sinda chuckled and elbowed Toli. "See what I mean?"

Toli swallowed the lump in his throat.

"All right, enough talking up there," Jari said, tossing a few sets of bolas up to Sinda. "Keep an eye out for Zog."

Jari rode alongside Betha. "So, where the hell is Zog?"

Betha shrugged. "That orc does what he wants."

"Okay. But would he betray us?" Jari asked.

Betha shook her head. "No."

"How can you be so sure?"

"He's a member of a company. He wouldn't turn on us. He's not Polis," Betha said.

Jari bristled. "Fine, you were right about him. But I'm still wondering how he got word to Boro."

Betha's snort rattled her septum ring. "I discovered that he used one of the Thunderhoof's homing pigeons under the guise of contacting his *son* when he hid in the back of the pen. The only thing the warrior knew was that he was with us, so he never questioned it."

"So, he set us up?" Jari asked.

"Yeah. He probably offered to lead Boro into Wolfwalker Valley to kill my tribe and sell our horns and other pieces. And in the process, get his son and the princess back. And temporarily put him off from attacking Port Agu."

"And he needed us for what?" Jari asked.

"A diversion. Remember, he planned to go to Wolfwalker

Valley." Betha growled. "But it was your greed that got us into this, Jari."

"*My* greed? What about *your* greed?" Jari demanded.

"I followed your lead—like always. *You're* the one that took this job over an easy twenty Dark Elven scalps," Betha shot back.

"Sorry if I wanted to retire. Oh, that's right. You wanted to as well, right?" Jari barked.

"Break it up, you two. Orcs ahead," Toli said, pointing with his hook.

Zog was riding a Cobry, a rare creature with a large horn at the tip of its nose. Orcs used them for hunting and raiding. Large enough to seat an orc, they had an armored head with enough power to batter down a thick, wooden castle gate. Several paces behind Zog rode four smaller orcs with blue handprints across their eyes. The group neared them. Betha stepped out in front of the wagon.

"You ride with another company, Zog?" she asked with a practice swing.

"No, orcs are merc, like Mighty Zog. Want to join on way to Anak'anor."

Jari cantered up to Betha. "We can't pay them, Zog. You know that."

One of the orcs behind Zog spoke to him in orcish. Zog listened, nodding every few words. He spoke to the other orc as he thumped his chest, then the other one lowered his head.

"What was that about, Zog?" Betha asked.

"Zog remind him, Zog King of Orcs. Do what Zog say do. He hate dwarf."

"That a fact?" Kala asked, riding with Gnok and Bric out of the woods, weapons at the ready.

"Easy, Brothers. Let Zog explain," Jari said.

"Cousin, we made an exception for Zog. If the others hate us as much as we hate them, then let them through, and Kala, Bric, and I will show them some manners," Gnok said.

"Gnok, this is no time for a fight. We're low on numbers and still have a three-day ride to Anak'anor. We need them," Jari said.

"And what of it? I trust Zog. The others will stick a knife in our back as soon as it is turned. Orcs can't be trusted," Kala insisted.

Zog rode over to them. "Zog keeper of orcs. No bother you. I am Loner," he said, placing his fist over his heart.

Bric scoffed and cantered over to Jari, leaving Gnok and Kala with Zog. Gnok stared at the brutish orcs, all four with battle wounds still bleeding from a recent skirmish.

"Why are they bleeding?" Kala asked.

Zog glanced over his shoulder. "They kill goblins to clear road."

Gnok smiled. "All right, Mighty Zog, I trust you. What about you, Jari?"

"I'm all for it. Now, can we please move on and make camp far from here?"

The Loners moved out and stopped when they saw the carrion birds gnawing on goblin flesh. Betha roared and scared the birds away.

"Try not to let all of Labrys know we're out here, will you?" Jari muttered. "Strip the dead and scalp them."

Sinda leaned over to Jari's ear. "Technically, it's the orcs' loot, right?"

Jari bristled at the suggestion. "Zog, are these the goblins your orcs killed?"

"Yes."

Jari sighed. "They have first dibs on loot then. Betha, step back."

Zog translated what Jari had said, and the orcs froze. A slight smile crossed the oldest of the four who rode over to Jari and eyed him up and down.

"Good you," the orc struggled to say, then went with the others to loot the corpses.

"What the hell, Jari? These savages don't even trade. They just equip themselves with the dead enemies' weapons," Toli hissed.

"What the hell does 'good you' mean?" Jari asked the wind.

"It mean, 'thank you,'" Zog said, riding out with them.

The Loners waited while the orcs scalped and looted their dead. After finishing, the group set off. They passed through the rest of the plains, always skirting the edge of the forest. After several more miles, they reached the mouth of the mountains hiding the dwarven kingdoms.

Jari reined Grumps in and raised his fist. "Make camp."

Kala glanced at Gnok. "Never thought I would be back here."

"Me neither," Gnok said, glancing in the direction of his old home. "But here we are."

Sinda urged the goats off the road and into an outcropping of boulders. As she drove around the last boulder, the axle broke. As the wagon capsized, Toli flew off and hit a boulder. Sinda cut the goats free as the wagon tipped over, the arms and armor scattering everywhere.

"Sinda," Arnak roared, pushing everyone out of his way. "Sinda, can you hear me?"

"Push the wagon over," Jari shouted.

The orcs with Zog moved to one side of the wagon and lifted it. With a push from Betha and Arnak, they managed to right it with a crash. Weapons and armor lay everywhere. Arnak kicked and threw them out of his way as he madly searched for Sinda.

"Arnak, over here," Sinda shouted, cradling Toli's head.

Arnak rushed over and knelt next to him.

"Is he dead?" Jari asked, kneeling beside him.

Arnak was silent for several moments as he felt along the base of Toli's neck. Toli groaned and blinked. His eyes fluttered open, and he looked at Arnak. "Did I finally bed Sinda?"

Kala, Gnok, and Jari laughed. Sinda smiled, her cheeks a little red. "Not yet. And if you keep hitting boulders dead-on, you never will."

Toli winked. "So, there is a chance."

Arnak dropped Toli's head onto the dirt and walked away, muttering. Sinda knelt next to him and offered him a flask. "You know, for a stump, you have a really hard head."

Toli grabbed his crotch. "I may be short, but this is *not* stumpy, and it's harder than my head."

Sinda smiled and walked away.

"If you're done flirting, can you get up and help us collect the arms and armor?" Jari asked, yanking him to his feet. "Head on a swivel."

Toli nodded, spat, then started collecting the equipment with the others.

Jari and Betha stood in front of the broken axle. "Any ideas?" he asked.

Betha shrugged. "I'm no carpenter."

The four orcs walked over. Three lifted the wagon, their sinewy arms rippling with exertion. The last one rolled a large boulder under the middle of the wagon, stabilizing it. The others lowered it as a second boulder was rolled under the tail end.

They spoke to Zog, who nodded. "Be back."

The orcs walked into the woods nearby, and after a few minutes, Jari heard the sound of axes cutting wood. They reemerged with wood to fix the wheel.

"We fix," Zog said, walking past the others.

"Pack the arms and armor. Gnok, find some axes for our new mercs," Jari said.

"Like hell dwarven axes will go to orcs," Bric said.

"Remember our deal, Black Rock," Jari said, staring straight ahead. "We get this wagon, and you get half of Boro's treasure."

Gnok picked up four battle-axes and walked over to the orcs. He handed them to Zog and pointed at Jari. Zog held them up and then gave them to the others. Jari watched them smile, their tusks jutting out, and then they returned to their work.

Betha stood next to Jari with Arnak by her side. "That wasn't voted on, Jari."

"No time."

Betha snorted. "Don't forget you can be replaced as a leader if the Loners so deem it."

Jari turned to look at her. "That a threat, Betha?"

"No, it's the rules. I'm just saying what you're thinking," Betha said before walking away with Arnak.

Jari clenched his fist. *Damn you, Betha.* He exhaled and ran his hands through his hair. "Everyone gather 'round."

The Loners formed a semicircle in front of him. "Zog, get over here."

Jari made eye contact with each individual member. "It's been brought to my attention that I gave away loot without a vote. Since we don't have any formal rules, I say we make some now. I propose if a group decision needs to be made, we vote on it immediately. Hands up if you vote yes."

All hands went up.

"I would like to lead this company. But I know several of you would like another leader. Let's go around the group and say who we want to lead," Jari said. "Let's start with Zog."

Zog pointed at Betha. Sinda pointed at Jari. Bric paused for a long moment and finally pointed at Betha.

Kala and Gnok pointed at Jari. Arnak pointed at Betha. The tie-breaking vote went to Toli, who lowered his head.

"Had to end with me for a tie," he muttered. "Now, *that's* what I call dumb luck."

Toli cleared his throat and clenched his hand, then tapped his hook along his pant leg.

Before he could speak, Betha interrupted him. "I didn't vote, and I cast my vote for Jari."

Jari stared at her for a long moment. "What?"

"I've followed you this far; might as well keep on going," she said with a wink.

Toli blinked and wiped the sweat from his brow. "Haven't felt that nervous since the first time I laid three dwarven lasses at the same time."

The tension among the group eased.

Why do I feel like shit?

"So, the group has spoken. Jari is the official leader of our company. What's our next order of business?" Kala asked.

"Loot," Bric said.

"Whoever kills the enemy keeps the loot. If two of us claim the same kill, they will settle it between themselves, and no other member can intercede," Jari said. "Does everyone agree?"

All the hands went up.

"I make a motion that when we vote, the side with the most votes will decide our course of action. But there can only be two options. We don't want a third option, or we'll get nowhere. Any other suggestions?" Sinda asked.

No one raised their hand.

"Then that's settled. Now, I know most of us hate orcs. However, an additional four bodies will help deter any courageous brigands. If I saw orcs and dwarves riding together, I would think twice about attacking," Jari said. "For now, let's get the wagon fixed, and then we'll break camp in the morning."

Jari had somehow managed to keep the group together. After everyone dispersed, he mounted Grumps and rode out toward the plain.

Kala stepped in front of his goat. "I would like to know where you think you're going."

"Riding," he said, clucking for Grumps to continue past him.

Grumps shook his head and leaped out of the trees. The wind blew Jari's hair and beard back. A few cool raindrops fell from the sky as Grumps found his legs. The goat picked up speed in a few moments, and as he sped up, Jari swung his arms wide and tilted his head back.

The soft rain fell heavier. It ran down his cheeks and through his thick, bushy beard, making it run like a faucet.

A wide smile crossed his face. *I love the rain.*

For the first time in a long time, he felt something he hadn't in a long while.

Free.

Chapter 18

Jari spurred Grumps forward, testing his endurance and speed over different terrain. He rode him over hills, down through ditches, over fallen logs, and through briar patches.

Returning to camp, he watched as Kala, Gnok, Sinda, Bric, and Toli rode in a horizontal line toward him. Kala and Bric side by side in the center, their burly shoulders barely swaying in the saddle. The others were looking like pigs on roller skates.

They reined in next to him. "Since this is our first reprieve on our ill-fated adventure, and the wagon is still broken, we should learn formations. Some of you have never ridden in a formal battle, or not at all," Kala said, looking at Toli, who was holding his thighs with a grimace.

"What do you want from me? I'm three feet tall, you jackass."

Kala ignored him. "The first formation I will teach you is similar to our spear formation in hand-to-hand combat. The best rider will hold the tip of the spear, the next two will flank his goat, and the rest of us will ride on the flanks forming the angle of the spear. I think Bric should be the centerpiece and take over drills because the goats have trained to work together with him, and he can control the ebb and flow."

Bric rode forward. "I want Kala on my left with his warhammer and Gnok on my right. Frost Elves keep a distance with bows and are the most dangerous. Keep low on your mount until you're close to them. The Black, White, and Red Widows come in close for the kill. Their carapace and limbs are no match for dwarven steel, but they're still deadly. I want each of you to train with a heavy wooden branch as practice lances we will be using in battle. If we keep a spear formation, the orcs with us can keep stride, and after we crash through the enemy, they can explode out of the flanks, hitting the remainder who haven't been trampled."

He made sure everyone understood. "Next, I want Sinda behind Gnok and Jari behind Kala."

"And what about me?" Toli asked.

"You will ride directly behind me. If and when we break through, you'll give the signal to the infantry to break formation," Bric said. "Form up."

"Ready," he shouted, then urged his goat forward.

The group attempted to form, but Jari and Gnok became entangled, Sinda's goat veered off course, breaking formation, and Toli's goat threw him in its eagerness to keep up with the others.

When Bric realized what had happened, only Kala and he were still in formation. They looked at each other, and Kala rubbed his forehead with a deep groan.

"You must be joking," Kala roared. "Are you mercs or milkmaids? Reform and prepare to charge again—and this time, do it right!" he barked.

They reassembled. Bric at the center, Kala and Gnok flanking him. Jari and Sinda behind them, and Toli right in the middle.

"Charge!"

The group stayed closer this time. Toli managed to stay in the saddle (for a few more yards). Kala's goat butted the back of Bric's goat, sending it careening into Gnok's mount, knocking him from the saddle.

Jari and Sinda were able to ride clear of the mess. Kala and Bric collided as they tried to correct their goats' miscalculation, but ended up clotheslining each other as they righted themselves in the saddle before crashing to the ground.

Toli groaned as he sat up. He rubbed his hook on his temple. "Is it just me, or should I learn to ride first, *then* get a formation lesson?"

"I'm with Toli. I've only been on a pony. These bastards are faster, smaller, and more aggressive," Gnok said, handing Bric his helm.

Bric gave a reluctant nod. "Who here has never sat a goat?"

Everyone except Kala raised their hand. Bric walked over to his goat, picked up the reins, and brought him over.

"I'll give you a quick lesson in what your mount is capable of." He handed the reins to Sinda. "Goats are fickle. They're like us dwarves . . . hardheaded, strong, and eager for battle."

The comment received grins and nods. Bric explained the intricacies of guiding and riding a goat. How to turn, when to spur, and how to fall, if needed. After he explained the concept of riding, he told of the animals' magnificence.

"The Bohal is the most elite goat in the Black Rock. Few live in the wild, and they're almost all bred from our stock. They will charge into a mass of well disciplined Frost Elves, widows, or giant Kagos without a thought. They are bred to be fearless."

Bric ran his fingers along the intricate chainmail around his goat's muzzle and neck. "They are adorned with the finest Tok mail ever made. The only way to kill one is to strike at their flank, but any rider worth his salt would die before their goat was impaled."

A sad smile crossed his face. "The mounts you have are what remains of the deadliest dwarven cavalry in the history of Black Rock, The Hammer and Anvil Brigade."

Jari spit up the gut-rot from his flask. "They're a myth."

Bric corrected him. "Myth?" he laughed. "No, we're real. We never left our borders with the army. Our sole job was to protect our king."

"I heard King Irngud Back-breaker was dead," Kala said as he mounted. "There are no kings of the Black Rock anymore."

Bric nodded. "That is a true statement. Enough of the Black Rocks' history. Let's practice again."

The weary group of dwarves walked in, leading their mounts five hours later. Everyone was either cut, bruised, or both. They walked to the fire and plopped down. Toli was the first to doze, having been flung from his mount eleven times before finally learning to control it.

It had been a strenuous training day that even the most battle-hardened riders would have complained. The goats were hesitant of new riders, especially nonskilled ones.

Toli's goat was the most ruthless of the group. When Toli wasn't looking, the goat would nip at his pant leg and then bite his ankle. Toli finally had enough and dug his knees into its flanks. For that indiscretion, he was bucked off with the extra pleasure of being urinated on afterward.

Kala had ridden his goat masterfully, and when he dismounted, his goat followed him everywhere he went. Bric said it was good luck to have such a faithful mount.

Sinda stayed in the saddle more than Toli, but less than the others. Whenever she was bucked off, she got to her feet, adjusted her knives, and climbed back up to go again. After a few hours, her goat performed how she wanted.

Gnok had a hard go of it. The last time he hit the ground, a rock struck him above his right eye. The gash ran down to his ear, and the wound a quarter-inch wide. Arnak sat by him, sewing him up as Gnok stared at his goat in disgust.

Jari and Grumps rode as if they were destined to work as a team. It was if the goat could read his mind before he gave an order, the animal feeling like an extension of his legs.

When everyone had settled in for the evening, Jari was the only one around the campfire still awake. His beard was caked with mud and twigs. He sniffed his armpits, stood up, and walked to a pond nearby.

Grumps bleat as he walked by. "I'll be right back." He fed him an apple. "See, all better."

He walked to the shoreline, stripped, and waded into the cold pond. The water rippled around his waist as he waded further in. He took a deep breath and submerged himself. The water temperature nearly took his breath away as he scrubbed himself clean. With a loud splash, he resurfaced with a groan and flipped his long hair back. The water dripped from his arms, causing tiny ripples on the surface.

Jari winced as he rubbed his raw shoulders. *The first thing I'm getting in Anak'anor is a padded leather gambeson for that chainmail.*

The moon hung high above him, shimmering on the water below. Few dwarves bathed in the open, most preferring the hot springs deep in the mountain cities. But Jari had been a merc for over one hundred years and had long forgotten he was a Blue Dwarf like Gnok.

He had spent most of his life traveling from one end of Labrys to another, always looking for the next bounty. But he had never actually been to Anak'anor (and considered himself lucky).

It was a large city with towering, spiked walls, a ten-foot moat that ran the city's entire circumference, and large auction blocks for their markets.

Jari trailed his stubby bloodstained finger across the water. He cupped his hands and splashed more water across his face to scrub his beard. As he scrubbed, a branch snapped behind him.

He spun around and stared at two of the largest and most imposing blue-toned orcs he had ever seen. As they stepped out of the shadows, Jari took a step back, the mud in his toes making it hard to maneuver.

The Blue Orcs wore goblin heads as helms. Their armor was piecemeal like most of their kind, their large stone clubs resting on their broad shoulders.

They spoke in Orcish to each other.

Where's my ax? His eyes scanned the shore ten feet in front of him. *Where the hell is it?*

The two orcs stepped into the water and pointed at Jari; then one slid his thumb across his own throat. "You die."

"Like to see you try," Jari said, motioning them forward.

"No weapon," one of them said with what seemed like a frown.

"Don't worry, beautiful. I got all you'll need right here. Come and get some of it."

Jari charged up the middle, neither orc expecting an attack. As he churned the mud, his thighs started to burn. They both swung their clubs. One missed, and the other caught his shoulder, spinning him in the opposite direction. He landed with a shout on his hands and knees in the water along the rocks at the bottom.

Stones?

Coming out of the water, he gripped the large stone he had and whipped it at the orc on the left. The stone hit with such force, his eye exploded.

The other orc, not concerned with a silent attack anymore, roared and charged. Jari ducked and sank under the water in an attempt to make the shoreline. He felt the hands of his enemy tighten around his throat from behind, pushing his face further into the mud and rocks. The air bubbles from his struggle started to lessen, his struggle weak.

"Spear formation, charge."

The orc glanced up and brought his hands up, attempting to protect himself.

"For the Loners," Toli bellowed, riding Grumps at the point of the spear. He lowered his horns and gored the orc in the pelvis, shaking it so violently, a piece of his rack embedded at its waistline.

Toli vaulted off Grumps's back. "The dwarven lasses' asses—"

He landed on the orc's head and stuck his hook in its neck. "Zog, you get the eyeballs, and I get the coins."

Zog roared his approval as he churned through the water to assist.

Toli slid down the orc's back with a grunt and dug his hook further into its neck like a fishing lure, shredding its vocal cords.

The dying orc reached back and yanked him forward by the ankle, snapping it in two. Toli screamed but yanked harder on the neck, his face a mask of determination. "Die, you . . . rotten . . . worthless . . . piece . . . of . . . shit," he said, accentuating each word.

As the orc collapsed forward, it snatched the hook, ripping it out with a torrent of blood. He swung Toli out by the arm and crushed his lower arm with its jaws.

Toli screeched as the orc released, then clamped down on his neck as he recovered from the shock of his arm being crushed. Both of them plunged into the red, frothy water.

"Toli!" Betha roared.

Zog lifted the dead orc and threw him ten feet onto the opposite shoreline. The others brought the last orc down, hacking it to pieces.

Jari gasped as he burst to the surface, his face covered in mud. "What on Labrys was that?" he shouted, swiping at his eyes.

"Zog, get Jari to shore," Betha shouted as she searched madly for Toli in the water. After a few seconds, she found him and pulled him out of it.

"Arnak, help me," she roared, clutching Toli to her chest.

Arnak splashed toward them and helped her to shore. She fell to her knees and laid Toli's broken and mangled body on the grass, the others anxiously crowding around them. Arnak touched Toli's shoulder.

Toli gasped and gurgled, frothy blood leaking out the sides of his mouth, "Jari . . . is Jari . . . okay?" he managed to gasp, his eyes flickering side to side in his eye sockets.

Betha made eye contact with Arnak, who shook his head, then lowered it.

She nodded slowly and leaned down to his ear. "He's fine, Toli. You saved him."

For a moment, his eyes were clear, and he gave a sad smile. "Good," he mouthed, then his head rolled back.

He was gone.

Chapter 19

"I'm all right," Jari said, wiping his face with a rag.

Blinking the rest of the mud away from his eyes, he smiled at Zog. "Thank you."

Zog nodded.

"Where is everyone?" Jari asked.

Zog pointed to where the group was standing, then walked away. Jari followed behind him. He saw the blood-soaked sand first, then the small body of his friend. He stepped around Kala, who had his head bowed.

Toli lay on the ground, his arms folded across his chest. His broken hook lay under his other hand, dented and cracked. Betha had cleaned the blood away from his mouth, but he saw the section of his neck that had been ripped out.

Without looking up from his body, she hissed, "Enjoy your swim?"

Jari stood silent, his dwarf hood blowing in the cool breeze. "Betha, I . . ." He stopped speaking as a tear fell from his eye. "I'm sorry."

She kissed Toli's forehead, closed his eyes, and stood up. Taking a deep haggard breath, she lowered her head and took three bounding steps with a roar. She speared Jari's naked body. Her half horn pierced his left side as she lifted her head. She put both arms on his shoulders and hurled him back into the pond.

The others restrained her as she drove her legs forward to finish the job. It took every last member of the group, including four orcs, to take her to the ground. Only Bric remained by the side, watching and waiting. He waded into the water and lifted the unconscious Jari and slung him over his shoulder.

He walked past the group as Betha reached for his ankle. She tightened her grip. "Give me Jari," she hissed, gripping his ankle.

"He didn't intend for this to happen, and Toli would not want you to kill him in revenge. It wasn't his fault." He shook her hand loose and continued.

"Let her up," Kala said, backing up.

Betha slowly regained her feet and walked over to Toli. She picked him up, his body small against her arms.

"I will prepare the body and burn him when the sun rises. Keep Jari out of my sight, or I'll kill him."

The first ray of light broke through the velvet night sky, its orange beam warming the crabgrass. It had been a starless night . . . a perfect night for an ambush. The Loners watched from a distance as Betha stacked the logs she cut from the nearby trees. Toli's body lay under a sheet close by.

"I'm going to help her," Jari said, stepping forward. "If she kills me, vote for a new leader."

Kala and Gnok both stepped in front of him. "I wouldn't suggest that just now. Give her time," Kala said.

"Time we don't have. It was my screwup, and it's my job to patch it up."

He pushed by them, dropped his ax at his feet, and stepped forward. He cinched the bandage around his wound and gasped.

Please, don't kill me, Betha.

Blood pounded in his ears as he took each step toward her. When he was about fifty feet away, Betha lifted her head and sniffed.

"I smell your piss-stained pants from here, Jari Rockjaw. You're not welcome here."

"I understand that. I just came to apologize."

Betha spun with a roar. "I said, leave."

"Toli wouldn't want this," Jari pleaded.

"Toli's dead," she roared.

Jari let the salty tears fall from his eyes. "I know, Betha. When I left camp to wash, I should have brought backup. I thought it was safe."

Betha snorted, her body shaking, then her shoulders sagged. "So did I," she whispered.

Jari took a tentative step forward, his wound screaming at him to stop. He lowered his head, then stared at the bloody white sheet atop Toli.

"And I'm sorrier than you'll ever know. I wish you didn't come to my rescue and just let me die. It would have been better that way."

Betha dropped her ax and snatched Jari in a bear hug. He winced when she embraced him but didn't say a word. Her grip was worth the pain. They held each other for a time, neither wanting to break away.

"I'm sorry," Betha said.

"Me too."

The others walked over and started helping Betha and Jari cut and place the wood by Toli's body. They built a wooden pyre exactly three feet off the ground.

Betha and Jari held Toli's body between them and then placed it atop the wood. The others gathered around while Arnak and Zog poured oil onto the body and the wood.

Zog brought Toli's hook over to Betha and took a knee. "The

little one," he said.

Betha held the hook, then handed it to Jari. Jari held it one last time, then kissed it. He placed it at Toli's feet and stepped back. Then he turned to face the others.

He cleared his throat. "Toli Hookhand was my friend. He wasn't the best merc or the toughest. But ask any merc who served with him what he was, they would tell you, a comedian. Some would think to be remembered the comedian instead of a devout warrior would be a dishonor. But the truth is, there is comedy in tragedy and tragedy in comedy. Face it. Toli liked big dwarven lasses' asses."

A few of the others chuckled and raised their flasks.

Jari continued. "I never got to tell him what a great friend he was or how much I was going to enjoy retirement with him and Betha." He gave a slight smile, a tear glistening in the corner of his eye. "He was one of the best mercs I ever served with. So, raise your flasks to Toli Hookhand, the horniest merc we ever knew."

The Loners gave a cheer, then Arnak and Zog set fire to the funeral pyre.

The wood popped and cracked as the blaze sent smoke billowing into the air. Arnak's humming was low at first, then gradually louder. The others joined in after listening, and soon, the Loners were all humming together. They continued to hum for another few minutes, then dispersed.

Betha and Jari stood at the ashes of the funeral pyre, not saying a word. Jari reached into his pouch and pulled out several gold coins. "Here's for some gut-rot when you get there, till you find a new crew and get your own coins," he said, flipping them into the smoldering ash.

Betha clapped him on the shoulder. "Ashes to ashes, dust to dust. May he ride with the Dwarven Lords until the end of days. Now, let's find out who those orcs were."

Jari gave a sharp nod, then gripped his ax handle, his knuckles white. They walked over to the others and sat by the fire. Gnok was busy cooking bacon in the skillet, while Sinda kept an eye on the forest around them, sharpening her blades.

Sinda hadn't spoken since Toli's death. Jari caught her eye. "You okay?"

She smiled. "I enjoyed our conversations. May he rest with the Dwarven Lords."

Jari swallowed the lump in his throat. He raised his flask and took a swig. Then he moved closer to Zog with Betha. Zog and the other orcs were cleaning and sharpening their axes. They had smeared ash from the pyre across their eyes and lips.

"You want to tell me something?" Betha asked Zog.

"Orc kill Toli. We go kill orcs."

"What do you mean?" Jari asked.

"Orcs sent by Ur'gak, Queen of Blues."

Jari choked on his gut-rot. He hurried to his saddlebag, fished a parchment out, and walked back over.

"I have a bounty for her. Just could never track her down. You know where she is?" Jari asked.

Zog nodded and thumped his chest. "Zog mate."

Jari and Betha glanced at each other. "*Mate?*"

Zog shrugged.

"You mean your orc-bearer?"

Zog nodded. "She try kill Zog. I kill her now."

"Does she have little ones, Betha?" Jari muttered.

"We're mercs, not lovers, Jari. How in the hell should I know?"

One of the orcs spoke to Zog.

"What did he say?" Betha asked.

"He say he hate Blue Queen more than dwarf. He go kill her for little dwarf."

"Not a bad idea, Jari. I could go with some revenge before we go to Anak'anor," Betha said with a coy smile.

"Zog go alone."

"Our friend, our fight, Zog. Show us where she lives, and we'll kill them all," Betha hissed.

Zog hesitated for a long moment. "Very dangerous. Many not live."

"Name of the game, Zog." Jari glanced over his shoulder. "Loners, votes needed."

The Loners assembled around Jari. "I've found out that the orcs who killed Toli are minions of Queen Ur'gak of the Blue tribe. I have her bounty here. I vote we go and avenge Toli. Who votes aye?"

"How much is the bounty?" Gnok asked after he spat on the ground.

"Two hundred gold coins," Jari said.

"I *liked* Toli, but risking it over two hundred gold coins seems crazy to me," Gnok sighed.

Arnak yanked Gnok's hand up, nearly pulling it out of its socket. "We are in," he grumbled.

Every other hand went up without hesitation. "Killing a Loner will always be avenged, no matter the cost to the others," Kala said, stretching with his warhammer behind his back.

"This will be extremely dangerous. There is a solid chance some of us won't make it back," Betha said, cutting in. "Just so everyone knows."

"Zog lead way."

"And what of them?" Gnok asked with a head nod at the other orcs. "Can we trust them?"

Zog gave a nod. "Toli give Zog eyes from kill. They like and will help sneak in."

"Oh, goody," Gnok muttered, walking to his mount.

Chapter 20

The morning sun blazed brightly overhead. The further north they rode, the hotter it became. The Blue tribe wasn't far, hidden in a local area with dead trees and large boulders.

"It figures that shrew would hide in the far reaches across the continent," Jari muttered, navigating Grumps over another rotten, termite-infested log.

The landscape was barren around them, offering nowhere to sneak in. Zog held his arm up and motioned to a group of large boulders a hundred yards away on their left. Smoke rose on the horizon in front of them. Jari pulled his scope to his eye and scanned the area. He watched the large Blue Orcs milling about between little huts.

He pocketed his scope and urged Grumps forward after the others. Zog knelt in the rock formation, talking to the other orcs. He thumped his chest several times and pointed at the huts.

"Any idea what's being said?" Gnok asked from nearby.

"Nah, I'll wait for Zog to tell me," Jari said.

The orcs finished talking, and then three of them slipped away from the group. Zog walked over to them. "Two scout tribe, one go get more orc."

"Getting more orcs?" Betha asked.

Zog nodded.

"We can't pay them," Jari said with a sigh.

"They fight with Zog. No coins."

"I'll be damned," Gnok and Kala said at the same time.

Arnak walked over. "I'm not sure I trust a legion of orcs to fight on our behalf."

"I'm with Arnak," Sinda said.

"We don't have a choice. Either we trust Zog, or we forget it. There's no way in without the idea he came up with," Jari said.

"What happened to voting?" Sinda asked.

"Are you kidding? Four of those orcs aren't part of our group, and Bric isn't either. Toli's vote is no longer. We have to trust Zog. He's a Loner," Jari said, clenching his jaw.

Zog smiled at the group. "I am Mighty Zog. Follow me."

The group made camp without a fire. Zog and Betha drew the first two-hour watch, then Gnok and Kala, and finally, Sinda and Arnak. Jari and Bric worked together as a roving patrol, checking their defensive position and riding forward to ensure no orcs infiltrated their lines.

After an uneventful night, the sun rose, and the two scouts returned and reported to Zog. They spoke for a few minutes, Zog nodding along intermittently.

Several hours later, the last scout sprinted in and pointed to the forest. Zog ran over to the other Loners.

"Good orcs wait in forest, ready for attack," he said.

"Sounds good," Jari replied. "What's next?"

"We kill," Zog said.

Jari walked over to Grumps and rubbed his new stump, the former horn embedded in the orc that killed Toli.

"Thanks for coming to get me," Jari whispered and patted his head. "And for being the last mount Toli rode."

He mounted Grumps and pulled a set of bolas out of his saddlebag.

Here we go again.

Betha walked over with a smile. "Ready, old friend?"

Jari adjusted himself. "Hell yeah. Now, where has Zog run off to?"

Betha pointed over her shoulder. Zog was riding up the hill on his Cobry with the other four orcs.

"What's the signal?" Kala asked, riding up with the others.

"Where's Arnak?" Betha asked, glancing around.

"Preparing the healing tents for those wounded," Sinda said, checking her blades.

"He's going to help orcs?"

"He's a healer. That's what healers do," Betha said with a shrug.

"So, again, what's the signal?" Kala insisted.

"Orcs don't have to use a signal. They just charge," Betha said with a snort.

There was no noise at first, then the rumbling and crashing of trees hit like a clap of thunder. Zog led the charge atop his Cobry, galloping down the hill with such intensity that he was nearly ten feet in front of the others.

A band of thirty bloodthirsty orcs burst from the tree line behind him, some mounted on Cobrys as well, but most not. Horns and drums sounded the alarm in the Blue Orc camp. An orc with a large ornate headdress inside the camp lifted her bow and fired. The long arrow impaled an orc riding beside Zog.

Jari pointed at the Loners. "Betha, take the middle where Toli was positioned. Where's Gnok?"

Gnok stumbled out from behind a rock, whistling. He mounted his goat and took another long swig.

"You good?" Jari asked.

Gnok nodded with a wide smile.

Jari sighed. "Spear formation."

The goats moved into position with Bric at the center. He held his arm up for everyone to see. "Ready when you are, Jari."

Jari smiled, reared Grumps on his hind legs, and bellowed, "For Toli Hookhand!"

"For Toli," the others cheered, then spurred their mounts forward.

For once, the Loners formed in a spearhead and rode forward. With Bric in the lead, they charged out of the outcropping of rock they were positioned behind, flanking the camp.

The orcs with Zog crashed through the mud huts, flooding the center of the camp. The screeches, growls, and groans of dying orcs filled the air around them. The Loners rode over the last bit of open ground as spears and boulders landed around them, Bric at the tip of the spear.

He lowered his goat's horns and gored a Blue Orc through the side, the goat trampling it under its hooves as it moved on.

"Break formation. Only kill the Blue Orcs, none of ours," Jari bellowed above the din of battle.

Just as they had practiced, the spear separated with Bric riding straight up the middle, the others peeling out like a banana while Betha cleaved limbs from the orcs caught unprepared by the onslaught.

She roared and bellowed as she went into a bloodlust craze, her eyes wide, pupils dilated as the adrenaline, grief, and violence overtook her. Jari watched in horror as she slew orc after orc.

Cutting, slicing, disemboweling, again and again and again, until eleven bodies in different pieces and chunks were left.

A large Blue Orc raced toward her from behind. Jari pointed and screamed Betha's name. As the Blue Orc approached, Betha dropped to her knee, swung her ax overhand as she whirled around it, and then buried her blade in the center of its back as it lumbered past. The orc gave a puzzled look and collapsed.

Betha turned and clotheslined another orc as it tried to retreat with a roar that reverberated through the camp. She put her knee in its back, snapped its neck, and then stood and wiped the blood from her muzzle.

Queen Ur'gak was surrounded by her last few orcs. Zog dismounted and spoke to them, thumping his chest. The orcs threw down their weapons and stepped back.

The queen snarled and pointed at Zog. She spat on the ground and screamed at him. If Zog was insulted, he didn't show it. The Loners walked over to where the former lovers stood face-to-face, snarling at each other, their tusks jutting out farther than usual.

Ur'gak spoke first, and Zog listened. He pointed at Jari and Betha, then spoke. The two continued to argue until Zog nodded.

He walked over to Jari. "Ur'gak say she die fighting."

"So, she won't go quietly to Port Agu." He spat. "Good. Betha, you want this?"

Betha saw Zog's head lower. "Zog, you want this kill?"

Zog's head shot up. "Yes. Must revenge little one."

"Make her suffer," Betha said, stepping back.

Jari gave her a side glance. "Thought you wanted that kill."

"I did. But Toli would find the humor in those two fighting. I'd kill her before she got a practice swing in." She looked over her shoulder. "Besides, I've got more than my share of kills, and that's all I wanted. My revenge is quenched."

Jari muttered. "I've been holding onto that bounty for two years." With a sigh, he handed the parchment to Zog. "You have the bounty. Now, kill her."

Zog nodded in agreement and roared. He thumped his chest, and the orcs made a circle. Jari and the others walked away to scalp and loot their dead as Zog and his former mate began to fight.

Chapter 21

Zog dropped Ur'gak's head in the grass. He sat down next to Gnok on a log a little small for him, but it would do. Gnok handed him a rag with a chuckle.

"An orcish lovers' quarrel. Best one-on-one fight I've seen in a long while. She almost made you a eunuch." He roared with laughter, trying not to spill his gut-rot. *"Three times."*

Zog growled and wiped his gore-stained face. The blue ash he had spread across his eyes melted away during the battle, leaving the corners of his eyes tinged blue.

The surviving orcs sat behind him, eating and talking amongst themselves. They fought hard, losing half their numbers in the ambush, but for those who had survived, they now had a better village.

One of the orcs traveling with the Loners walked over to Betha and thumped his chest. "Me, Muk. You kill good."

Betha gave a curt nod and tapped her chest. "Betha, and thanks."

"Befma?"

"Beth-a."

Muk shrugged and took a knee. He handed her Queen Ur'gak's recurve bow, then walked away.

The bow was extraordinary in both sight and feel. Betha slid her fingers along the lower limb, over the worn bone grip, and along the upper limb. She stood up, raised the bow, and pulled the bowstring to her armpit.

She slung it over her neck and walked over to the wagon that Bric had brought up after the battle. One of the pieces she looted recently was an orc helm. Dirty as it may have been, and once probably built by a Frost Elf, she removed it and walked over to where Muk was eating. He stood to greet her.

She held the helm up and placed it in his waiting hands. Muk roared his approval and pulled it on. "Friend," he said, patting her on the shoulder.

Betha smiled. "Friend."

Making her way back over to the fire, Gnok said, "Making friends with all the orcs?"

Betha snorted at him. "Mind your tongue, Gnok. Keep drinking cow blood and gut-rot and talking nonsense, and I'll rip your face off."

Gnok chuckled. "Like to . . ." he hiccupped, "see you try."

Betha lunged forward and knocked him to the ground. Jari stepped over a dazed Gnok. "Easy, old friend. We need all the Loners we can get."

"Then sober him up, Jari. He's been drinking a lot more lately," Betha said before storming off.

Jari helped Gnok up and brushed him off. "Why are you drinking so much?"

Gnok shrugged. "I want to stop killing everything and retire. We lost one Loner already, and the longer we take to arrive at Anak'anor, the more we're sitting ducks. So, I'm enjoying myself 'cause we don't know *if* we'll even make it there."

Sinda walked by them, leading her mount. "If you're drunk in the next battle, I'll vote to strip you of your position." She kept walking, not bothering to look at his expression.

Arnak strolled behind her, a blade of grass in between his

teeth. "Me too, Gnok. Tighten up."

"Let's continue our trip to Anak'anor, shall we?" Jari said, mounting Grumps.

"And what of *them?*" Kala asked, nodding at the orcs.

Jari glanced at Zog. "What now?"

"Orcs stay here. Zog only."

"So much for an escort. We stick to the woods and do the best we can to make it to Anak'anor," Jari said, rubbing his eyes.

"We can't make Anak'anor," Bric said from behind. "Our only chance is to make for the Black Rock."

Betha grunted and glanced at Jari. "He's right. We'll never make it with enemy patrols tracking us with a wagon of goods being towed behind us. And hiring Black Rock Dwarves will guarantee our safe passage through the mountains."

Shit, we'll never make it anyway.

Jari groaned. "Fine, who votes to ride to the Black Rock?" He scanned each face as everyone raised their hand. His eyes rested on Gnok for the last vote. The pair made eye contact, and after what felt like an eternity, Gnok raised his hand.

"The vote is settled. We ride for Black Rock. I want Sinda and Zog on the wagon. Make sure we have enough javelins and bolas to keep the goblin patrols at bay. Toli, I . . ." Jari shook his head. "Sorry, I meant Kala and Bric, take the point, and I will bring up the rear with Grumps."

"No use arguing," Kala said, mounting and heading to the front.

They started down the dirt path, eyes searching every fluttering leaf, every shaking branch, every squawk from a crow overhead.

The first day brought them closer to the Black Rock but not far enough. They made camp just outside the borders and set up defensive positions.

After setting up his tent, Jari walked over to Bric, who was staring in the direction of the Black Rock.

"You all right, Bric?"

Bric gave a curt nod. "I'm the last of The Hammer and Anvil Brigade. A lot of mothers, wives, fathers, and children will know their kin are dead tomorrow when we arrive at the gates."

"But at least they'll know what happened," Jari said.

Bric chuckled. "That they will."

The Black Rock was the most reclusive of all the dwarven tribes. Unfortunately, the last king had died, and with no heir, the Black Rock became autonomous.

In years past, the Red, Blue, and Gray Dwarven Lords arranged to travel to one city to discuss trade and defensive alliances. The city chosen rotated between all three, but the last time any of them met was a quarter century before.

When the whims of men, traveling bands of murderers, and the encroachment of different races invading their lands occurred, the once-mighty dwarves locked themselves away. Dwarves unhappy with the decision, like Jari, became mercenaries rather than live the life of a miner with a dwindling population.

Bric spat and pulled his flask from his hip. "Have you ever been there?"

Jari shook his head. "No need." He stared at the peak ahead of them. "Minor thought. What do we do about Zog?"

Bric smiled. "Let me worry about that." He walked over to the fire and lay down, leaving Jari with his thoughts.

"Jari, you ready to go?" Betha shouted.

The night had passed peacefully. Jari groaned and rolled over, a piece of his beard in his mouth.

He spit the hair out. *Yuck.*

He pushed himself up and rubbed his eyes. "Give me a minute, Betha."

Betha snorted her impatience. "Let's go."

Jari muttered under his breath, then mounted Grumps. Once everyone was assembled, Bric led them down the dusty road. The Expanse was a no-man's-land filled with wild animals, lionfolk, bear kin, cyclopes, and banished Kagos, among other dangerous creatures.

The group stopped as they exited the forest and looked at the desert landscape. The sun beamed down on them, and within minutes, all were sweating.

"I hate this damn place," Gnok muttered to Kala, who was removing his breastplate with a sigh.

"Gonna be a long day," Kala said, attaching it to the saddle.

"Keep alert out here," Bric said. "The scorpions are larger than our fists with enough poison to kill you and your mount."

"That's just great," Betha murmured.

"Zog eat bugs."

Everyone turned in his direction. "Why doesn't that surprise me?" Arnak grumbled.

Bric led the group in a single-file line. The Expanse never offered any shade to any that crossed it. Usually, the other dwarven tribes could skirt the edges of it and make it to their own mountain ranges. But the Black Rock and any traveling to Anak'anor had to cross it.

"Conserve your water. It will take half a day to clear this, then it's up one of the most dangerous mountains on Labrys," Bric said with a chuckle.

Hour by hour, the dunes rose and fell around them. For the past hour, vultures circled above them, waiting for their opportunity. Jari held his hand above his brow.

"Good thing I only have one eye," he muttered, wiping sweat from his brow.

"Surprise you can still see after Betha kicked your ass the last three times," Gnok said.

"Luck, pure luck," Jari muttered.

"Really?" Betha asked, glancing up.

"Okay, maybe not."

The group laughed.

Hours later, the entrance to the Black Rock opened. Ragged and exhausted, the Loners stumbled into a grove of trees with a small pond in the center. Gnok and Kala were the first to drink from the icy water.

"Why is it so cold?" Kala shouted as he poured more on his head.

"It's filled with the souls of the dead," Bric said, walking past them.

Kala and Gnok gagged and spat, scratching water off their tongues. "Was he serious?" Kala asked Jari.

Jari shrugged. "Probably. Let's just listen to what Bric says we need to do."

"Leave the goats and the wagon. Follow me," Bric said, sliding his Tok chainmail over his chest, his demeanor changing.

"Are you preparing for battle?" Arnak asked.

"Nope."

The others followed him up the mountainous terrain. The path was barely wide enough at some points for any of them to walk shoulder-width apart. Zog, Betha, and Arnak had to place their backs to the mountain for most of the trip, their feet slightly hanging over the ledge of sharp black rock.

"Zog no like heights."

Arnak slipped, and Zog caught him. "You're not the only one," Arnak grumbled.

"You good?" Sinda asked up ahead.

"Fine."

The farther up they climbed, the colder the weather became. Bric moved with surety as he climbed higher and higher.

"Is it just me, or should we be burrowing into the mountain, not up it?" Betha grumbled to Jari as she followed behind him.

"I'm not sure. The Blue Dwarves dig into the earth. This is something else. I've never been here," Jari said.

Betha snorted. "Hope it ends soon. My hooves are killing me."

Jari chuckled. "Toli would have loved that one."

Betha smiled. "Yes, yes, he would have."

Finally, they came around the last bend, and there in front of them stood the Black Rock in all its glory, the castle's spires so high, they seemed to reach the heavens.

The walls were sanded down from rough-hewn rock, giving it a slick, glasslike finish. Angled down at them from the battlements were bolt shooters called Vesps. They shot long quills that took two dwarves to load and were mainly used for larger enemies like trolls and Kagos. Every few feet along the wall were gargoyles with open mouths that spewed liquid mercury onto unsuspecting enemies below.

Bric raised his hand and stopped their party. "Welcome to the Black Rock."

They stood in wonder at the sight of the fortress as it overwhelmed their senses.

Jari stood next to Bric. "I've never seen anything so, so . . ."

"Magnificent is the word you're looking for," Bric said with a laugh.

Jari could only nod.

The portcullis creaked as it raised. Dwarven riders mounted on Bohals rode out to meet them. They pulled up short of them.

One rider rode forward, his Bohal's corkscrew horns shiny. It sniffed the air around them and bleated.

"You dare tread upon the Black Rock?" the dwarf asked after raising his face shield. He frowned and freed his ax. "And you brought an *orc*?" he roared.

The guard's Bohal bleated and lowered its horns. Bric stepped in front of Zog, who was licking his lips.

"Easy, Thron Irongrip," Bric said.

As Thron charged, his Bohal came to a halt, throwing him over its horns. He rolled to Bric's feet.

"Blast that damn Bohal!" he shouted, flicking sand out of his beard.

Bric extended his arm. "Need some help?"

Sputtering and spitting, Thron blinked and scampered to his feet. He dropped to a knee. "Prince Bricon, my apologies."

All at the same time, the Loners said, "*Prince?*"

Bric faced them. "Please let me reintroduce myself. I am Prince Bricon Firehand, regent of the Black Rock dwarves, defender of the realm." He gave a mock bow. "And this fine dwarf is the captain of the guard, Thron Irongrip."

Thron remained in a kneeling position as did the other dwarves behind him. Betha pointed over his shoulder. Bric sighed with a nod.

"Rise, my fellows," Bric said.

The dwarves stood and surrounded their leader. Thron was the first to embrace Bric, followed by the others. After a few moments, Bric pointed in the Loners' direction.

"May I introduce our guests." He made the introductions. "Now, see to it that they're taken care of."

The dwarves with Thron mounted, saluted Bric, and rode off. Thron shook Bric by the shoulders, then slammed their foreheads together.

"It's good to see you, lad," Thron said, never taking his eyes off Zog. "And you travel in the company I would love to kill."

Zog waved him on. "Zog ready, Dwarf."

Bric held Thron back. "Easy, Thron, he's with me."

"As you say, my Prince, so shall it be," Thron muttered. "Where are the others?"

Bric smiled, ignoring the question. "Loners, please follow me inside, and we will ready your quarters."

Chapter 22

"He's a prince. How'd we miss that?" Betha asked, gazing out the window.

Jari shrugged. "Looks like we'll be without our best rider moving forward. Hope he honors our deal with the weapons and goats." He glanced at Zog, who kept his war club in his hand, his knuckles taut. "They won't attack you, Zog."

Zog stared out the window. "You worry Dwarf, Zog worry Zog."

Kala walked over to the window and put his hand on Zog's elbow. "As the Dwarven Lords are my witness, I will fight and die beside you, should they attack."

Zog nodded.

"Sinda, me, and Arnak are with you as well," Gnok said from his corner.

Jari tossed Zog an apple he was holding. "As are Betha and I. We're Loners"

The guards had brought them to a lavish room with wide bay windows and plush beds. Food and drink were brought in after they settled. And they were told that when Prince Bricon was ready, he would see them.

Soon, there was a loud knock on the door. Betha opened it, and Thron walked in. He eyed the group wearily. He walked around as more of his guards poured in the room behind him.

"Prince Bricon has informed me of what happened south of here with The Hammer and Anvil Brigade. Which of you is the healer who saved our prince?"

Arnak stood, keeping his shell to Zog. "I'm the healer."

Thron smiled. "We of The Black Rock Guard are in your debt. Whenever you or your companions need shelter, you are welcome here."

"Thank you," Arnak said woodenly.

"Now, to the business at hand. Prince Bricon has told us about your problem, and we would like to help." He made eye contact with Zog. "We will help you reach Anak'anor, but it will not be dwarves who will go with you."

Jari looked at his companions. "Okay, then who will?"

"Our prisoners." He walked back to the door and opened it. "Follow me."

Thron led them through the hallways and down several flights of stairs. Once they reached the bottom, they stepped into a cellar with a dirt floor.

"I've got a bad feeling about this," Betha hissed to Jari.

"Calm, Betha, calm," Jari whispered.

This is not looking good.

Thron went to an oaken door and unlocked it. The guards with him pulled on the heavy chains, which emanated a loud groan. Large cages sat stacked on one another. Inside the cages were orcs. More orcs than Jari could count.

Zog roared and lifted his club, then took a step toward the guards. Betha and Kala grabbed his arm and pulled it down. "Not now, Zog. Free your people, and we'll return here, I promise. But not today," Betha said, pressing her nose to his.

"Is there a problem, *Orc*?" Thron taunted, raising his ax.

Zog threw down his club, stormed past his mates, and knelt by an orcess with a little one to her breast. "Loners must free them."

With brute strength, Zog ripped the padlock off the cage and swung the rusted gate open. He helped the orcess up and held the little orc who was teething.

"We will take your prisoners, one and all, even the dead and dying. Is Prince Bricon aware of this?"

Thron roared with laughter. "Who do you think helped capture them? We're Black Rock's. Opportunists, we are. Whatever sells, we sell. Now take this trash outside, keep the goats and the wagon. It is our payment for the prince."

Jari bristled. Kala leaned into his ear. "Easy, Jari, we're outnumbered. Let's help Zog and make for Anak'anor," Kala said.

Jari growled. "Thron, we will take them."

Thron waved to his guards, who walked into the room and began unlocking cages. Most of the prisoners were orcs, but there were a few other races mixed in with them.

"Our business is concluded, brethren," Thron said, making his way to a side door.

"And Bric?" Jari asked.

"Busy. He wishes you a good day. And if you have any prisoners in your travels, we will purchase them at a quarter of the price. If we do meet again, I'll kill that orc, so come *orc-less*," Thron said with a roar, pointing at Zog, then closed the door behind him.

"Let's leave, Jari," Betha said, pushing her way to the front.

The Loners led the prisoners out of the mountains and down into The Expanse. Helping them down the mountain was no easy task, but all of them made it safely to the bottom. Arnak set up a walking triage as they descended. He went to work on the orcesses and their little ones, known as orks.

After everyone made it back to flat ground, Jari and the others quickly separated the walking wounded from the dying. Sinda, Gnok, Zog, and Betha split up with Zog translating the best he could.

The prisoners had been held awhile; no one was quite sure how long. A few ragged dwarves were sitting by themselves, trying to light a fire.

Jari and Kala approached them. "You lads all right?" Kala asked, handing one of them a flask of gut-rot.

"Aye, been locked away for a long time."

"What's your name?" Jari asked.

"Mori Greygrog."

Mori was slim for a dwarf. He was bald, with a thinning salt-and-pepper beard that ran down to his knees, his skin dusty.

"Jari Rockjaw is my name, and my brethren is Kala Silverbeard. What mountains are you from?" Jari asked.

Mori sighed. "From a place that is no longer," he muttered.

Kala made eye contact with him. "What?"

Mori smiled, revealing several missing teeth. "We're Grey Dwarves."

Without thought, Kala leaned forward and wrapped him in a bear hug. He roared with laughter. "I thought *I* was the last one."

He laughed at Kala's embrace. "The Grey Mountains have been empty for years. How long have you been a captive?"

Mori exhaled. "The better part of seventy cycles. We are all that remains of the once-proud, Death Hammers." He chuckled. "All three of us."

Kala sat next to his new allies. "The Death Hammers . . . They were in the final defense of the Iron Highlands," Kala exclaimed, both eyebrows raised.

Mori rolled his sleeves up. On both sides of his forearms was a hammer crossing a skull with a burn mark straight across it.

"Dwarven Lords," Kala hissed.

Mori chuckled. "I wish they were there. Sadly, that *battle* was the end of us Grey Dwarves. King Thrakrul Ironmaster was killed, along with fifty-seven of the best damn dwarves I ever served with. The rest of our kin tried to protect themselves but were put to the sword."

Mori's eyes clouded. "There were too many enemies. They flooded into the mountain, killing everything that moved. Attempting to save the king, we formed a protective box and pushed our way outside, losing most of our company in transit. In the mêlée, a Kago killed the king, and the rest of our brothers perished. Me, Vognok, and Dodtrot are all that remain." He paused. "Well, besides you, Kala Silverbeard of the Grey Dwarves."

"Actually, I'm Kala Silverbeard of the Loners now," he said with a wide smile.

Jari smiled and listened to the conversation for another minute, and then left the long lost dwarves to talk. He wandered through their makeshift camp. Little orks played with sticks and rocks, hitting each other as frequently as possible, roaring at the top of their little lungs every second they could.

Zog sat by a fire with a handful of mercs, talking about his many exploits, captivating those around him. As Jari walked further on, he saw the area Arnak had set up for an infirmary.

He watched Betha, Sinda, Arnak, and Gnok help each other with different orcs. Some struggled to breathe, and some lay dead outside the tent where a large orc was dragging the bodies into a deep pit dug in the earth.

Little blue hues covering sick orks could be seen by the firelight as black as the night was without a star in the sky. Jari turned the corner and sucked his breath in. Here lay the bodies of the dead orcesses and little orks. He watched as a small ork sat crying over his mother's corpse.

Jari knelt next to him and smiled. No language needed to be

used as the ork put his head in the crook of Jari's arm. Jari stayed there for a time while the ork slept.

Finally, a familiar voice sounded behind him just as he was dozing off. "Zog take ork."

He knelt, cradled the little one to his chest, and smiled at Jari. "Proud Loner." Then he walked into the darkness.

I wonder who he meant . . . me or him?

Standing up, he walked into the tent. All the Loners were busy. He pitched in where he could, applying bandages, picking up amputated limbs, dragging dead bodies to the pit.

When one prisoner would die, Arnak would roll them off the makeshift tables for a new case. Jari, covered in green blood and gore, kept pulling the never-ending supply of limbs and dead to the pit.

How many lived?

After rolling the last body in, he couldn't count the bodies in front of him. He'd killed many orcs in his time as a bounty hunter. Hell, it was a natural instinct, like breathing for the bitter enemies. But this . . . This was different. Killing mercs was one thing. Torturing a little one was against everything he stood for, no matter what race of being it was.

The big orc looked down at him, his tree-trunk arms drenched in sweat and gore. "Good you."

Jari smiled wearily. "Good you too."

Chapter 23

"Jari, we're not here to save the world. We're here to *retire*. I vote no," Betha snapped at him across the fire.

"Betha's right, Jari. Your plan is insane," Sinda said.

"What? To go in there and kill those responsible? I see no other way." He opened the tent flap. "I just burned more little ones than I care to count," he shouted.

"Not fight," Zog said.

Jari looked at him incredulously. "What was that, Zog?"

"Vote no."

Jari turned away, red in the face.

"I'm with Jari. Too many little things were killed," Kala said.

"If we leave, more will live. Let the dead rest here. We can come back," Arnak grumbled.

Jari glanced across from him. "Gnok, I know you're with me."

"Much as I would love a fight, it won't be with fellow dwarves, no matter who they kill," Gnok said.

Sinda made eye contact with Jari. "I'll avenge Loners, like Toli, but not some orcs. I signed on to kill Boro."

"Well, five against two. The group has spoken," Jari sighed. "Mark my words, we'll be back here—one way or another."

"Where to then?" Betha asked, changing the conversation.

"Orc need safe," Zog said.

"That they do, Zog. Go find out how many will join us as mercs and who will need shelter," Jari said, buckling on his ax.

Zog left the tent.

Mori and his crew walked into the tent. "Hope we're not interrupting."

"Not at all. Business just finished," Jari said.

"My dwarves need arms and armor. You need bodies for scalp hunting. We'd like to join up," Mori said.

"We got dwarves," Betha sneered. "What do you bring to the table?"

As one, all three dwarves pulled knives from their belts and flung them at her. One knife skimmed her knuckles, causing her to drop her ax. Another one sank to the hilt in her septum ring. And the last knife sliced the rope cord around her pants. She roared as she snatched them while they fell.

Mori smiled wide and gave a mock bow. "We bring experience."

The other dwarves howled with laughter. They wiped the tears from their eyes as Betha stalked from the tent, shouldering Mori aside.

"Kala, fix up our new recruits with arms and armor," Jari said.

Mori paused. "Who are you hunting, by the way?"

"We're heading to Anak'anor to raise an army. Then we move to kill Boro Spiderbinder. Probably never heard of him."

"Nah. But then again, I've been locked up for seventy cycles. How much is he worth?" Mori asked, replacing the knife he threw.

"About sixty thousand coins from the Ekapian Empire, plus all the loot you can tote back on your Bohal. Do any of you ride?" Jari asked when he saw their expressions.

All three shook their heads at the same time. "I hate those goats. Had to clean their stalls for years," Mori spat. "And I'll never clean up after another one again. You want a rider, give me a pony."

"Okay, that answers that question," Jari said with a chuckle. "So, you guys are going to hunt Boro?"

Mori and the others laughed. "For sixty thousand coins, I'll fuck that old crone who runs the Blue Dwarves."

Jari burst out laughing. Gnok gave him an uneasy glance and mouthed, "Shut it."

The Grey Dwarves left with Kala to get weapons and armor. Jari excused himself and walked outside. The camp was silent, not a cricket chirping.

Where do we go from here? What if we don't make it to Anak'anor?

Question after question ran through Jari's mind while he sat on a large rock, surveying the scene in front of him. At best, there were fifty orcs in prime condition to fight. Most huddled around their families, if they had any, and those without stayed together by another fire.

Orcs on Labrys were split along a caste system. Mercs like Zog were of a different caliber, more interested in coin and scalps than their place in orc society.

The ones resting in front of Jari were of a lesser class known as Jabirs, not destined for anything but a life of hard labor. Zog had been one until he became a merc. The ones with them had lived a simple existence until their capture, not bothering a soul.

Betha walked into the cool night air, her breath misty in front of her. She stretched and twisted her torso. Jari could hear her bones popping from a few feet away.

"Getting old, Betha," he said from the darkness.

Betha spun and had her bowstring to her shoulder before Jari could blink. She fired an arrow and hissed, "That you, Jari?"

He walked into the firelight holding an arrow as tall as himself. He tossed it at her feet. "Your aim is shit, but, yea, it's me. Who else would challenge a minotaur in the dead of night without an armed escort?"

Betha grunted and lowered her bow. "Lucky I didn't kill you."

"Lucky you're a shit shot."

They both chuckled. Jari glanced at the sky. "I miss Toli."

Betha nodded. "Me too." She turned to face him. "Sorry about my vote earlier."

Jari waved her off. "No, you were right. We're not in the revenge business. Don't know why I even cared. They're just orcs."

Betha touched his shoulder. "Because we're Loners, not flesh hunters. And they may just be orcs, but they, like Zog, are good. Contrary to popular opinion, not all orcs are bad. They're not all mindless minions hell-bent on destruction. They have families and little ones too."

Jari scanned the faces around them. "It just doesn't seem right. Dwarves mixed in with orcs. We have hated each other since the beginning."

Betha cleared her throat. "Your best friend is a disgraced minotaur; your healer is a Ha-Nu-Nah. And your other comrades are disgraced in their own ways. And the rest of your army is orcs." She burst out laughing. "Jari, if anyone should be grateful that these orcs are with us, not against us, it should be you."

Jari shrugged and spat. "We really are doomed, aren't we?"

Betha clapped his shoulder. "Only one way to find out."

The decision was made to escort the orcesses and their orks to the former Blue tribe village miles back down the road. The train stretched one hundred yards behind Jari as they moved along. Halfway through the day, they reached the edge of The Expanse.

Jari reined Grumps in and glanced at Kala. "This is going to take a while. I need to ride ahead and mark the path. We should cross tonight to help alleviate the hardship on the little ones."

Kala shifted his weight in the saddle. "Agh." He spat. "They're orcs."

Jari chuckled. "Aye, they are, but weren't you helping them recover?"

"Piss off, Jari," Kala said, nudging his mount and turning it around. "Make camp," he bellowed. "See you when you get back, Jari."

Jari urged Grumps forward and took a sip of water. He rode out into The Expanse and its hot dunes. Grumps bleated and leaped forward.

Keep your energy, old friend.

They rode along the sand dunes, searching for ambushes or creatures. Several hundred yards in, he saw buzzards circling above him. Riding a little further, he saw several horses standing around a few bodies.

Jari dismounted, pulled his ax from his belt, and approached. He raised his bandanna over his nose to block the swirling sand and walked over.

The horses neighed and edged away from him. The men lay facedown, several black arrows sticking out of their backs. Jari knelt and yanked one out. He sniffed the tip and pushed it away.

Goblin poison.

He scanned the dunes and waited. Not seeing any trouble, he searched the men's pockets and found little to nothing. He was about to turn away when an object in one man's boot caught his eye.

The glint from the silver object seemed to keep his attention. Without a thought, he removed it from the victim's sock and examined it closer.

I'll be damned—a compass.

Jari held it up and spun on his heel, checking for true north. He stared at it for a few minutes, drinking from his flask. Grumps bleated. He stood up and tipped the flask into Grump's mouth, who drank it greedily. As he spun in a circle, the compass didn't point north.

Why the hell won't this show true north. It only points south.

As he pondered the compass, the winds blew the sand in his direction. He shielded his eye, tied the horses together, and attached them to Grumps's saddle.

Time to get out of here.

He mounted Grumps, freed his bolas, and tapped his mount's flanks. The pair wound their way back through the dunes, his eyes continually searching for unseen enemies.

Once they were clear of the dunes, he rode Grumps to the camp. Betha met him at the entrance. "You all right?"

Jari dismounted. "Yeah, I'm good. Found some dead humans. Brought their horses back. Hook them up with the premade litters and use them to cross that terrain. How's everything here?"

"Our team went in search of food with the Grey Dwarves," she said, untying the horses. "I'll go water these animals."

Jari walked over to his tent and found a bowl of water waiting for him. He dipped his cupped palms in the cold water and splashed it over his face.

The water sent a shiver down his spine.

Damn, that's cold.

He peeled his armor off and poured the rest of the water over his barrel chest. Then he scrubbed weeks of dirt from his skin, knowing full well that he would be covered in dirt by the morning.

That sand gets in every crack of your body.

After washing, he hung his Tok chainmail to dry and walked shirtless back into the camp, which was now a beehive of activity. His team had returned with several birds and a mountain lion.

"Not enough meat," muttered an orcess, walking by with her small orks.

Jari waved Betha over. "Slaughter a horse," he mumbled, ashamed he gave the order.

"Really, Jari?"

Jari didn't blink. "They're starving, Betha. Better to have full bellies than die of hunger in that mess we'll cross tonight."

"Fine," Betha said, freeing her ax.

"Collect the blood. I hear it's a delicacy for them."

"Ugh, that's disgusting, Jari."

He laughed. "Might as well have some happiness," he said before opening his tent flap to get some rest. "Wake me when the moon is highest in the sky."

Chapter 24

The moon shone down as Jari exited his tent. The order had been given to break camp several hours after they had eaten, and his was the last tent standing. After exiting, several orcs made quick work of packing it.

Jari mounted Grumps and surveyed the line behind him. "Keep moving if you want to live. It will take half the night to cross. If we are attacked, protect the orcesses and orks. Preserve your water. You're gonna need it," Jari bellowed. "Forward."

The column wound through the dunes, the Loners splitting their group with Jari, Betha, and Zog on point. Sinda, Arnak, Gnok, and Kala rode at the back of the party, protecting the rear. As they proceeded, birds of prey could be heard squawking above them . . . waiting . . .

The stars overhead did not provide enough light for the journey. Every twenty feet, a torch would light the way. Creatures of the night slipped beneath their feet, causing some of the orks to cry out.

Jari and Zog rode ahead several times, checking for any ambushes. Zog's Cobry nipped at Grumps, who bleated and tried to gore it several times. Each time, Jari would chuckle and pull his head away from the giant Cobry. The pair headed back after checking the surrounding area.

After the group traveled for several hours, the sun peeked over the horizon. As the group reached the edge of The Expanse, the sun was beaming down hotly. Wiping sweat from his brow, Jari reined in and stopped the column. He nodded to Zog, who rode forward.

"Ride into the village and let Muk know we're coming and to see if he will help us get everyone inside," Jari said as Betha approached.

"Where's he going?" Betha asked, walking to the front.

"Going to talk to his friends."

Zog rode back over the dunes, a few orcs in tow. "Orcs help us."

Jari motioned the column forward and followed Zog. He led them to the village, which had been renovated since they left. The destroyed huts had been rebuilt, and in the center of the camp, a large well had been dug.

A large orc stood in front of Grumps and thumped his chest. "Muk."

Jari smirked. "Yes, I remember. How are you?"

"Now, *Chief* Muk."

"Good." He glanced over his shoulder. "We need you to protect the orcesses and orks."

Muk leaned around Grumps to look and then back at his camp. "Muk help."

"Thank you, Chief Muk."

Zog and the others helped the orcs traveling with them into camp. Kala, Gnok, and Sinda started a large fire on the outskirts of the camp to cook the leftover horse meat.

Muk and Zog talked with the other orcs, deciding who would go and who would stay. Jari walked around the camp, helping where he could. Most in Labrys would never help an orc due to their propensity to kill any race. But the longer Jari spent around them, the more he saw the care they showed one another, especially the orks.

Zog and Muk walked over. "Orc fight with us to Anak'anor. Then return to camp," Zog said, mounting his Cobry.

"How many orcs will join us?" Jari asked.

Zog waved the orcs over, and Jari counted twenty. "This many."

Betha snorted behind Jari. "That's quite a few. What do we pay them with?"

"They fight for freedom," Zog said. "Orcs loyal."

Jari and the others mounted and rode out of the village and headed back toward Anak'anor.

The newly formed group rode across The Expanse, never once stopping. The orcs were bred for the terrain and the pain. Once over the treacherous ground, they quickly cut across to the Blue Mountain ranges.

Jari rode at the point with the others, Betha always at his elbow. As they crested a hill just before the mountains, a swarm of goblins and a cyclops lumbered down behind them.

"Form spear," Jari bellowed.

The Loners moved into formation. Jari sat at the point with Grumps bleating and pawing the wet earth.

The orcs followed Zog, Betha, and Arnak into the center. Jari reared Grumps onto his hind legs. Betha pulled her bow and sent an arrow downrange, hitting the cyclops.

Jari laughed. "Loners, we have the cyclops. Orcs take the goblins, then reinforce."

Zog nodded and shouted to his brethren in orcish.

"Charge!" Jari shouted, lowering his visor.

The group rode in formation, Sinda's mount lagging behind the others. She lowered herself onto its neck and urged it to catch up. The goat responded and caught up on the wing.

Jari and Kala burst through the goblins, trampling them under hoof, and headed for the cyclops. They heard the orcs and goblins screeching at each other as the Loners split like a banana.

"Form a circle," Kala shouted before firing his bolas in the cyclops' direction. The beast swung its arm wide, missed Kala, and knocked Gnok from the saddle, his goat tumbling after him.

Betha charged up the middle, battle-ax raised, with Arnak by her side. As the cyclops faced them, it swung and hit Sinda, who was flanking Arnak, throwing her from the saddle.

Arnak roared and launched a vicious attack, swinging his club like a miner with a pickax. For every blow the cyclops landed, Arnak smashed its kneecaps in response. After a few blows from the cyclops, Arnak was bloodied and dazed, and as he staggered back, he covered Sinda when he fell.

Betha advanced and swung her ax, hacking off one of its hands. The blood sprayed across her body as she spun past the next hurried attack. She pulled a knife from her waist and slammed it inside the creature's groin before rolling through its legs.

Mori and his kin charged into the fray with Zog behind them. Mori yanked a blade from his forearm and waited for the cyclops to attack. As its hand reached for him, Mori's kinsmen hacked off several fingers.

The cyclops recoiled and brought its hand back to its face with Mori along for the ride. Nearing its eye, Mori launched his dagger into the center of it, then lumbered up its sinewy arm and on to its head.

Betha freed her bow and fired an arrow into the back of its skull, sending it to its knees. Mori gripped its ear as it fell.

As it landed on the bloody grass, the knife sank into its brain stem. Mori chopped the ear off and walked off, drinking deeply from his flask.

"Nothing to it," he said with a wink, walking past Jari.

The goblins lay strewn about around them. The orcs stood by as Jari collected his team. "Everyone all right?"

Sinda, Gnok, and Arnak had taken the worst of the beating. Sinda had a cut above her eye that would require stitches. Arnak spat out a few teeth with a smile.

"Damn good fight," he said, sitting Sinda down to stitch her up.

Gnok shook his head and pushed his broken nose back in place with a crunch. "Ooouch."

Mori walked over. "When fighting a cyclops, kill the eye, kill the beast."

Betha nudged Jari. "What of the loot?"

"Scalp and hack off ears what you killed. Let the orcs take most of the goblin loot, though. Not worth an argument for the shitty stuff," Jari said, leading Grumps away.

Zog walked over to the orcs and let them know what Jari said. They immediately began scalping and looting, often pushing and screaming at one another to establish dominance.

Jari moved over to Mori. "You fight well."

Mori smirked. "Hope so. Been at this a long time. Been cooped up and got a lot to catch up on. We're plenty rested, though."

"That you are. Are you going to claim your loot?"

"The cyclops is your minotaur's loot. My kin and I share everything. But when we go after Boro, I'll be working side by side with her for our trophies."

Jari could only smile.

I've got the strangest group of mercs on Labrys.

After Zog and the other orcs collected the eyeballs, they policed up the weapons and armor, then torched the bodies. The group continued through the forest until they reached the base of the mountains.

Jari raised his fist as they reached the edge of the forest. "Make camp. We will make for Anak'anor in the morning."

As the orcs set up camp, the dwarves in the company set a fire and sat with Betha and Arnak. Pipes were lit, and gut-rot passed around.

Kala propped his feet up on a log and tilted his head back. "This be the life."

Gnok chuckled. "Aye, for outcasts like us, it is."

Betha dropped her pouch at Jari's feet. "My pouches are getting full. The scalps from the dead are heavy, but that cyclops head is a pain to carry around," she said, glancing at her prize a few feet away.

"Must you keep that damn head near me?" Sinda asked in disgust.

"Sinda, that head is worth five hundred coins without an eye. With an eye, it's worth eight hundred. You think I'm trusting anyone not a Loner around it, you're very much mistaken," Betha grumbled.

Damn, Betha. You don't ever trust nobody.

Jari rested his back against a gnarled tree trunk, listening to them bicker. He dug in his pouch for his pipe and tobacco. *I haven't even had time to smoke my pipe. I really need to retire.*

He lit his pipe and slowly blew the smoke out his nostrils. The sky was dark. Only the true star beamed in the night. For once, he heard the chirp of the crickets, the squirrels jumping from branch to branch, and a boar rooting around in foliage behind him.

The night is beautiful. I wish it would stay like this forever.

Chapter 25

Betha stood over Jari. "Wake up."

Jari groaned and blinked his eye. "How long was I out?"

Betha turned around and watched the others sleeping. "You're the leader of this rabble. You have to get up first."

"Aye." He sprang to his feet and stretched. "You ready to go?"

"This head lowers in price the longer we delay," she growled. "And I want my money."

"How far you think we are from Anak'anor?" Jari asked.

"A day, maybe more. Depends if we get ambushed again."

"Let's try not to let that happen," Jari said, pulling his chainmail over his head. "First thing I'm buying in Anak'anor is a cotton gambeson. This chainmail is chafing my nipples."

Betha rolled her eyes. "We still have some pickled horse meat and gut-rot. Let's get these orcs moving. You start with the cooking. I'm going to excuse myself to the forest."

Jari dug in his pack for his cooking pans and then set a fire. The food supplies were lower than they should have been. He was missing a loaf of bread and a bag of pickled horse meat.

Damn thievin' orcs.

Kala walked up, chewing on a piece of pickled meat. He caught Jari's eye and shrugged.. "What?" he asked with his mouth full.

Jari shook his head and started cooking the meat. He and Kala chitchatted while the meat cooked, and the orcs woke up. Little by little, the two groups began sitting nearer to each other; not too close, though.

Zog smiled as he approached the fire.

"Orcs ready."

"We will be too as soon as this finishes. We have one more day, and we're safe. Thank them for coming with us."

"Okay." Zog snuck a piece of meat out of the pan, walked back to the others, and sat back down.

After everyone ate, they packed their gear and gathered around Jari. "We are a day's ride from Anak'anor. Once we get there, the orcs are free to return to the village with Chief Muk, or they can join us as mercs."

Zog translated. Jari watched a few heads nodding. He swung into the saddle and turned Grumps in the direction of Anak'anor. The others followed suit.

They rode for most of the day, Betha always within arm's reach of Jari. Regular goats don't usually have endurance, but a Bohal was a completely different animal.

Grumps led the way, jumping over downed trees, briar patches, long reed grass on the open plains, through muck-filled water holes, and dirt that looked more akin to mud. Whenever they rode across any bad terrain, he'd hear Betha curse under her breath.

They rode until they reached a pond that lay near the entrance of the Red Mountains. The orcs with Zog were on edge. If a Red Dwarf, or their cousins, the Silver Dwarves, rode in a war party, they would be attacked and given no quarter.

"Dwarves on the outside. Make a diamond, so the Red Dwarves up there know we're mercs," Jari said to those standing around him. "It's a half-day ride to the city. Let' push it."

The group continued down the path for another quarter mile

and found the road through the mountains blocked.

What the hell?

Jari scanned the area with his spyglass. *Nothing. Now what?*

Betha pointed into the mass of boulders ahead. "I think they know we're here."

A Frost Elf walked out of the hiding spot, lit an arrow, and fired it into the sky. It landed with a thud near Gnok's mount. Gnok dismounted and snatched the arrow from the ground and ripped off the parchment attached to the stem. He brought it to Jari, who opened and glanced at it. "Anyone speak their language?"

Arnak stepped forward and took the document. "It says we must pay for entrance. One hundred coins a head."

Betha laughed. "That's rich."

A large group of Frost Elves flooded out of the woodlands in front of them like termites in a tree. In all, there were close to forty elves protecting the only path leading to Anak'anor.

Jari turned to his comrades. "Either we pay about a thousand coin, and the orcs leave, or we ride over them and collect the loot. Who's voting?"

Zog's hand went up first. "Lots of eyes." He licked his lips.

One . . .

Gnok, Sinda, and Arnak voted yes. Kala gave a wide grin and patted his mount with a raised hand.

All eyes turned to Betha. "What?"

"Your vote?" Jari hissed.

"I can't vote. My hands are on my bow, dumb ass. Let's get that loot."

The orcs with Zog thumped their chests and roared.

"Right! Orcs out front, shields up. Loners attack in spear formation behind them," Jari said.

Zog translated.

The orcs strode out in front of them, set in two rows, ten

across. Arrows started raining down, pinging off their shields. The Loners trotted forward, forming behind them with Mori and his brethren.

"Loners, get in close, else those arrows will find their marks," Jari said, then took a deep breath. "Charge."

The orcs sprinted across the open plain, tearing through the dry mud. One fell, then another, and another as they charged. Betha slipped past the others, her bloodlust taking over.

All was silent around Jari for a moment, and then he realized why. A score of arrows fired in unison rained down on them as they closed the gap.

He spurred Grumps forward and rode hard to Betha, Kala following suit. He lagged behind her as they closed in. Then the Frost Elves appeared to flee.

Ten yards . . .

Five yards . . .

Thre—

The shock of a blow rolled him out of the saddle and into the mud as the orcs and Loners smashed into the elven line.

The sounds of battle raged around him. He gasped for breath, yanking his muddy helm off. He glanced down and saw the arrow embedded in his Tok mail.

I'm hit. For the sake of the Dwarven Lords, I'm hit. He felt his chest. *Where's the blood?*

He struggled to his feet. Something pushed him back into the mud, the arrow shaft snapping off in the process. He rolled out from under the weight in time to see one of the Grey Dwarves, Dodtrot, hacked to death by three elves. With his last ounce of strength, Dodtrot threw his ax overhand and hit the Frost Elf poised over Jari, then collapsed.

Grumps bleated and pushed on Jari with his horns. Jari was still on the ground. He groaned and gripped one of them. The sounds of battle raged around him. Grumps pulled him out of the mud, then swung around to gore an elf. Then he shook him loose and stood protectively next to Jari.

Jari's vision blurred. He heard someone yell far off in the distance. "Jari . . . Hey, Jari, you okay?"

Gnok?

Gnok was yelling and banging him on the shoulders.

Jari shook his head and spat. "Yeah, I'm good."

"Let's go, Cousin."

Jari followed him into the fray that was soaking the ground with green and red blood. He could see Betha, Arnak, Sinda, and Zog fighting side by side. Kala was still mounted. He rode like a pendulum, swinging his warhammer as he crossed the battlefield, picking off lone elves. His Bohal was bleeding from numerous places.

A Frost Elf pointed at Jari and charged. The elf slipped in the mud. Jari conked him on the head, rendering him unconscious. An orc pushed him forward and slashed the defenseless elf's throat.

"My kill."

Jari turned around and followed Gnok. Only a handful of elves were still fighting. They were quickly put to the sword, their cries of anguish soon silent. A young elf lay against a boulder, a deep gash in his side. An orc raised the elf's chin and readied his weapon.

The elf stared back, his dark blue eyes cold, unforgiving. Jari gripped the orc by the elbow and pushed him aside. The orc leaned in and screeched at Jari, nose to nose.

"He say, his kill," Zog translated.

"My prisoner."

Zog translated.

Jari unhooked a large bola from his belt and tossed it to the orc. "Trade."

The orc sniffed the air and snatched the weapon, then stalked back with the others, looting.

"Zog, get Arnak. I want this one alive."

Chapter 26

"Why the hell do we need a prisoner?" Betha shouted while she scalped another elf.

"We don't, but we'll need a guide to Boro, and I bet he knows just where to go," Jari said, leaving the wounded elf with Arnak.

The battle had been costly. Three-quarters of the orcs had been killed, leaving only five.

Jari surveyed the carnage. Mori stood in the center of the killing field, his armor dented and gory.

"You all right, Mori Greygrog?" Jari asked from a few feet away.

Mori shrugged as he stared at the faces of Dodtrot and Vognok, lying side by side around a dozen Frost Elves. "They died free dwarves, with solid dwarven steel in their hands. Can't really ask for more than that, can you?"

"Nah, I guess you can't."

Jari left Mori with his friends and walked over to his group. "Everyone all right?"

Kala and Gnok sat side by side on a boulder, their scalps and trinkets in their bags, both covered in gore.

"How are you doing, Jari Rockjaw?" Gnok asked.

Jari shrugged.

"You have an arrowhead in your Tok mail. You're lucky to

have that armor. These orcs could have used it," Kala said, examining the orc bodies.

Jari fished the arrowhead out, along with a few of the ringlets. He drank from his flask, and then said, "When we're done looting, pull everyone still alive into the trees behind us."

Sinda sat beside Arnak as he put a trance on the young elf. "Can you save him?" Jari asked, approaching.

Arnak nodded.

"Why would you help him?" Sinda spat.

"Need a tour guide to get Boro. And almost all the tribes fight alongside him. Don't want to be wandering around without him when we track that bastard down. Besides, we'll use him as long as we need to, then throw him away," Jari said.

"What makes you think he'll talk?" Sinda pressed.

"Gut feeling."

"You mean a gut-*rot* feeling?" Betha snorted from behind.

Jari spun around. "Geez, Beth, you almost gave me a heart attack."

"Wish I could. Now, what's the next plan?" she asked.

Jari pointed. "We're going up that steep incline. Then we're going to amass an army to kill Boro."

"Doesn't that sound so easy," she snorted.

After everything had been looted, they burned the bodies. Mori buried his comrades near the Blue Mountain, digging almost all night by himself.

Everyone was sound asleep except Jari, who volunteered for the first watch. He sat atop a large grey boulder. The moon hung in the sky above him, twice its normal size.

If only I could retire before I die. At the rate we're going, we'll never make it to Anak'anor.

Deer picked at the grass fifty yards away from him. He watched them through his scope, sipping on his gut-rot, trying his best not to catch a buzz. Grumps bleated beside him. Jari had done his best to wash the blood from his coat, but all he did was succeed in turning Grumps's white fur into a dull orange.

Jari found an apple in his pack and fed it to him. He stroked him behind the ears as he chewed. Grumps pressed his muzzle into Jari's chest with a soft bleat.

"I know. I love you too."

The next morning brought stiffer muscles, Jari's body screaming for sleep. He did manage to catch a few hours, enough to make the city.

He groaned as he mounted Grumps. "We need to ride as fast as we can from Anak'anor. We number only fourteen now."

Kala spat. "And one prisoner along for the *ride*."

Jari gave him a sharp look. "Do you wish a vote on something, Kala?"

Kala ignored him and rode off toward their destination, Gnok on his tail. Mori rode up beside Jari as they set out. "Are we still planning on collecting on Boro?"

Jari chuckled. "Bet your ass, we are."

"Good, I will ride with you until the Dwarven Lords split our path."

"Dodtrot saved my life back there," Jari confessed.

Mori nodded. "I saw. He was repaying our debt. He chose that, instead of saving Vognok."

Jari's eye bulged. "What?"

Mori gave a weary smile. "Our order, The Hammer and Anvil, were bodyguards. Our lives were only for each other and our king. We lived for seventy cycles in the depths of a hell I hope you never see. And when you freed us, you allowed us a second chance. Vognok would have killed him if he hadn't saved you."

"I would save my friend before a stranger," Jari said.

Mori smiled again. "And that's why you're a merc making coins, not a Grey Dwarf who is bound by an oath to repay all debts with his life, should that be the case."

Mori rode off after Kala and Gnok and left Jari with his thoughts and dust.

The last leg of the journey to Anak'anor was uphill. The steep incline made it almost impossible for the orcs to keep up with mounted dwarves.

Betha struggled with the climb as the air thinned around them. The group climbed higher and higher until they finally reached the plateau of Anak'anor.

"How can any mercs live up here?" Betha growled.

"They get used to it, I guess," Jari said.

Anak'anor was massive-- situated on the top of the cliff, the back of it lining the edge of a cliff all the way around. Sentries with hard looks were posted at the crenellations above them. Jari rode forward under the portcullis, the others following him. They rode through the congested thoroughfare, the stalls full of armor, weapons, and relics. Once inside, Anak'anor looked like Port Agu, the sections of the city divided between the different tradespeople.

Kala rode up to Jari. "Where do we go? We should sell the wagon and its contents before too many suspicious eyes are upon us."

"What about him?" Kala asked, pointing at the elf.

"Let's get him to an inn and let Arnak work on him," Jari said, looking around. "Do you know where to go?" Jari asked, scanning the signs above the doors.

A worn sign shaped like a sheep hung above the door that caught his attention. *Little Bo Peep? Is that a brothel?*

"Little Bo Peep—what the hell kinda name is that?" Gnok asked from his perch on the wagon. "A whorehouse?"

"Looks a little sketchy to me," Arnak grumbled.

"Zog think too."

Jari swung his leg over the saddle and dismounted. "Well, my ass hurts, and like Kala said, we need to unload this sharpish."

"Let's get this moving," Mori mumbled, keeping an eye on the mercs walking around him, especially the Red Widows.

"Betha and Kala with me. Everyone else, wait here," Jari said. "And try not to kill anybody."

He heard a few gruff laughs.

He opened the door and stepped into the room. *Why does this seem like a really bad idea?*

The inside of the tavern made the outside beautiful. Few, if any, patrons even glanced up from their drinks. A Red Widow tended bar, chattering away at a large one-eyed orc. The widow pinched the orc on the ass to keep him working.

Two guards sat on stools on either side of the door, their weapons a little too far out of reach. Jari gave them a head nod and searched the room.

Oh good, it is a tavern.

He found the scalp master at the back of the room, counting out coins to a merc. Jari strode over, the others right behind him. The scalp master was an older, grizzled minotaur.

Jari stepped aside. "Well, Betha, you're up."

Betha caught the minotaur's stare. "She looks a little ornery."

Jari nudged her. "Sell the head in your pack and negotiate for the wagon, please."

Her growl was his only answer. She stepped forward and rested both palms on the table.

"I'm looking to sell some things," she said.

The minotaur raised an eyebrow, then continued counting. "And what might that be?" she asked, her voice raspy.

Betha pulled the cyclops head out of the bag, rigor mortis already taking its toll on her prize. She dropped it on the table with a thud.

"How much?"

The scalp master examined it and pulled on its sharp teeth. "Good specimen, this. I'll give you three hundred."

Betha barked a laugh. "Elevation getting to your head, Elder? Thought you said three hundred. I'll take eight. The eye alone will fetch two hundred from a merc."

The minotaur paused. "Six hundred is my final offer. Take it or leave it."

"Done," Betha said, picking up her coins. "Now, I got my comrades out there ready to do some serious trading. Hope you brought enough coin. While I have you sort them out, I need to find someone who will buy a ton of Tok mail."

The scalp master leaned back in her chair and tapped her chin. "Information in the Bo Peep ain't cheap."

Betha slid ten coins back over. "If it's any more than this, I'll fight you for it."

She smiled, her lower jaw minus half her teeth. "There is a bullywug down the road that buys certain metals. Tok mail is in short supply up here. He's in the last house on the left, across from a plum vendor. Tell him Canth sent you. I'll straighten out your friends in the meantime."

"One last question," Betha said. "I need to hire about five hundred mercs. Who here in Anak'anor has the numbers I need?"

Canth sighed, her septum ring rattled. "Horgash, the great mud dweller is who you're going to see. Ask him when you get there."

Back outside, Jari filled the others in. After Canth emptied her purse buying all the scalps, ears, and dried eyes, they led their mounts down the street. Few of the eastern mercs ever traveled this far . . . Port Agu served the same purpose. But Anak'anorian mercs were different in just about every way. Honor and courage meant something to soldiers of fortune in Port Agu—but not here. These mercs killed anything and everything—no rules, no regulations; just coin.

The group reached the last house on the left, the front looking like a large marsh with plants and stagnant brown, soupy water in the front yard.

Jari pinched his nose. *I think this is it.*

Flies buzzed around the fence surrounding the property. "Well, you going in or not?" Betha asked, pushing him forward.

Jari cut her an evil glare. "You going?"

Betha balked. "Nope."

"I'll go," Kala said, gripping his warhammer.

Jari wrinkled his nose. *Damn, this stinks.*

The pair unlatched the gate, which swung open with a loud creak. "Oh, that's not creepy," Kala said, keeping one hand on his knife.

As they crossed the putrid front lawn, the door in front of them opened. A small dog that could fit in their palm barked as they approached. A large bullywug with wide eyes and molting yellow skin came to the door and picked up his dog.

"You lost, Dwarf?" he croaked.

"No, I'm looking for Horg—" Jari glanced at Kala, who mouthed *Horgash.*

"—gash is who I'm trying to find."

Horgash croaked. "Depends on who wants to know."

Kala smiled. "I've got Tok armor for sale."

"That a fact?" cooed Horgash.

Horgash peered over their shoulders at the wagon laden with arms and armor. His eyes lit up, and he gave a low croak. He shouldered between Jari and Kala.

At the wagon, his fingers moved around the different pieces, his fingers tapping constantly. "This is fine Tok mail, so it is." *<ribbet>.* "Let's go inside."

Jari and Kala followed Horgash through the muck and mud. Inside, the building was sparse. Books and trinkets lined the left side, and specimen jars lined the right. Jari stared at the different jars.

Tiger testicles, ogre's brains . . . What the hell is this?

Horgash caught his stare. <*ribbet*> "Those are my treasures. Not for sale."

Thank the Dwarven Lords for that.

Kala picked up a book and blew dust from the cover. He sneezed several times. Jari chuckled. "You all right over there, Kala?"

Kala grumbled and put the book back on the shelf.

Horgash sat behind a table in the center of the room, surrounded by books, melted candles, and half-eaten meat pies. The dog licked at one of the pies.

Eck.

"So, how much do you want for your Tok mail?" Horgash asked.

"Fifty thousand coins," Jari said, sitting in one of the vacant velvet chairs.

Horgash croaked with a grin. "Stop pulling my leg, Dwarf. That lot isn't worth more than ten thousand."

Jari steepled his fingers in front of his chin. "What are you drinking in the flask on your hip, Horgash? Cows' blood?" Jari glanced around the room. "I'll take thirty-five thousand, not a coin less."

The dog gave a sharp bark.

Horgash whispered something in its ear. "Mooky thinks that's fair. Okay, bring the wagon around back, and we'll even up."

Chapter 27

Mooky, the dog, pissed on Betha's hoof. She growled, picked it up by the tail, then handed it to Horgash. "Damn thing pissed on me."

She could hear the others snicker behind her. Sinda barked, and Mooky barked back. They unloaded the wagon and moved everything into Horgash's warehouse next door. Sweating and tired, the others waited impatiently by the door for Jari.

Horgash handed Jari a chest full of coins. "Thirty-five thousand coins."

Jari handed it to Zog, and Horgash showed them the door.

As Jari exited, he paused. "Horgash, you know where I can find five hundred mercs looking for work?"

<*Ribbet*> "Why would you need so many?"

"Just a question," Jari said.

Horgash chuckled, then croaked, "You'll want to find Kippa, the recruiter."

"Human?"

"No," Horgash said.

"Where do I find this Kippa?"

Horgash pointed to the top of the hill. "The compound you're looking for is up there. Tell them I sent you."

And with business concluded, he shut his door.

"We can't all go," Gnok said as everyone closed around the wagon.

"Right. I'll go with Betha," Jari said.

"What about us, Jari?" Sinda asked from atop the wagon.

"Take the elf to the inn we passed back there on the left." He pointed at it. "Go get us rooms for a few nights, and we'll be along shortly."

The groups split up. Jari and Betha trudged up the dirt road and into the courtyard. The building was massive, from its A-frame roof to its ornate woodwork.

Some would venture to say it was a mercs paradise . . . All the weapons, drink, and debauchery every killer craves. Practice dummies stuffed with hay were hacked at by mercs of every race: little ones, big ones, tall ones, short ones. Anak'anor did not discriminate. It was for everyone.

Jari inspected the mercs. *This really is a melting pot.*

Betha watched two minotaurs spar, both equally matched. In another corner, a small human and an orc traded blows with wooden sticks, the human getting the better of the orc. Battling beside them, two gnomes wrestled in the dirt, each clawing for an orange baton just out of reach.

This place is insane.

They walked to the door. "Help you two with something?" asked the guard, sliding his palm to his sword handle.

"Looking for Kippa. Know where I can find him?" Jari asked.

The guard chuckled. "You mean *her*?"

"Her? Of course, her, my good man," Jari said.

Betha rolled her eyes. "You're a constant embarrassment when it comes to males and females. Why does every merc need to be male?" she hissed.

Jari shrugged. "Force of habit, I guess."

The guard pushed open the door. "You'll find Kippa in the back, behind the belly dancers."

The pair entered the dim room. A large bar was crowded on the left with mercs yelling over one another for more drinks. The right had a large octagon with fighters inside. Mercs crowded around the cage, betting on fighters. The smoky haze lingered in the ceiling. A few steps in, the dwarven belly dancers, both male and female, appeared. Betha roared with laughter.

"Oh, if only Toli could be here with us." She smiled wide. "For the dwarven lasses' asses."

Jari smirked.

They weaved through the crowd. At the back, two more guards stopped them. "State your business," one said.

"Looking for Kippa. Horgash, the merchant, sent us," Betha said, stepping in front of Jari.

The guard gazed at Betha's battle-ax, then over his shoulder. "Leave the axes, and you can pass."

"Leave my ax to a merc in a place I don't know? You must be joking," Betha sneered. "I'll lop your head from your shoulders instead."

The guard made a move.

"Stop," came a bellow from the back.

Jari snuck a peek around the guard. Through the haze, he stared at an enormous figure hunched over a table. Betha stood toe to toe with the guard.

"Let them through."

Jari and Betha walked around the guard, Betha mouthing some obscenities. They approached the hooded figure. "I'm looking for Kippa," Jari said.

"You found her."

"Come a long way to find you, we have," Jari said, pulling on the back of a chair.

"Did I say sit?" Kippa bellowed.

Jari froze and stared under the hood. *No way in hell . . . a Loxodon?*

Kippa threw her hood back and leaned into the light. "Your heightened breathing gives you away, Master Dwarf. I take it you've never seen a Loxodon up close."

"I well, I—"

Betha pushed him behind her. "Bellow at my friend again, Kippa, and I'll cut your tusks off."

"That a fact, Taur?"

Betha smirked. "Any time you wish, Old Mother."

Kippa moved her trunk along the table and then pushed the chair back. "Lucky you bring a Taur, Dwarf. She is very beautiful, too beautiful to travel with the likes of you. Sit, please."

Betha sat and pushed Kippa's sniffing trunk out of her way.

"What brings you to my palace?" Kippa asked.

Betha glanced over both shoulders. "A palace? Are you blind, Loxodon?"

Kippa grinned. "A female can dream, can't she?"

"Enough with the flirtations. We came to ask for your help," Betha said after taking a sip from her flask.

"Oh, really? I did hope this would be you trying to be recruited into *our* ranks." Kippa leaned back. "But I'll entertain the idea. What do you require from us?"

"I need five hundred mercs to collect a bounty," Betha said.

Kippa chuckled, grinned, then exploded with raucous laughter. She slammed her fist and trunk on the table, splitting it in half. After regaining her composure, she said, "*Only* five hundred?" The mercs behind her laughed. "Why would you need that many for a bounty?"

Betha's septum ring jingled. "We're going after Boro Spiderbinder."

Everyone around Kippa grew silent. "And what you need with my old pal, Boro?"

"King Zista in Port Agu is offering a massive reward. Half a million coins," Jari said from behind Betha.

"Half a million?" Kippa mused.

Betha cut her eyes at him.

"Of course, we would cut you in on half of that," Jari continued, sliding a chair over. "Mind if I sit?"

Kippa waved her trunk dismissively.

Jari nodded his thanks. "You help us, we help you. Think of how much two hundred and fifty thousand coins could buy."

Kippa rubbed her hand across her chin, lifting her trunk to hide her eyes. (It's always in the eyes.)

"Is what he says true, Taur?"

Betha paused. "Yes, it's true."

Kippa lowered her trunk and tapped her hands together. "Fine. On one condition, though."

"Name it, and it's yours," Jari blurted out . . . too soon.

"I get to *fuck* your taur. And I have a trinket of some value that was stolen from me. Sentimental value, you understand. Not worth much in the hands of others, but to me—priceless. A nasty dwarf by the name of Logrulir Metalbraid stole it from me. My guards tracked him to Barren Bluff."

Jari's head lowered. *Shit*.

"What say you, Master Dwarf?" Kippa pressed.

Betha growled. "I'm not fucking you if *that's* what you're alluding to."

Kippa sighed, her trunk tapping what was left of the table. "Well, the offer stands if you change your mind."

Betha gave her a smirk and a roll of the eyes.

"We're in. Now tell us what you want us to retrieve," Jari sighed.

"Why for the Dwarven Lords' holy assholes would you agree to track down this rogue dwarf in one of the most dangerous places on Labrys, Cousin?" Gnok asked, sitting down. "The Barren Bluff. You have to be kidding me."

"Calm down, Gnok. Let him explain," Kala said. "There must be a reason why he would sign up for a suicide mission."

Jari shrugged, attempting to hide his red cheeks. "About that. I may have made a teeny lie in the process."

"No worries, old friend," Kala said. "It probably matters little. I mean, we made it to Anak'anor, for the Dwarven Lords' sake."

"I told Kippa that the bounty on Boro's army from King Zista was half a million coins."

Kala lunged across the table, his meaty palms gripped tight around Jari's throat. "You lying, no-good sack of Bohal spunk."

The others tore them apart. Jari rubbed his throat.

"So, let me get this right. You signed us up on a suicide mission for the Bluffs, *then* signed our death warrant when Zista doesn't pay them?" Arnak grumbled.

"Yes."

"Has this retirement idea made you crazy?" Kala demanded.

Jari could only shrug.

Mori joined the heated debate. "Supposing we survive the Bluffs, bring back this item to Kippa, who is a crazy Loxodon, right?"

Jari gave a sullen nod.

Mori gave a hint of a smile. "That's what I thought. And then you want us to manage somehow to destroy Boro's army with her loaned-out army?"

"In so many words, yea."

"Understood. And how are we supposed to come up with half a million coins?" Mori asked before lighting his pipe.

"I'll find a way," Jari said.

Mori took a long drag, then exhaled through his nostrils. "I'm not a Loner, but I vote we go."

Oh, thank the Dwarven Lords . . . One.

"I'm with ya until I kill Boro," Sinda, said, then tapped Arnak on the shoulder. "You in?"

He nodded.

Two, three.

"Betha?" Jari asked.

She nodded.

"Zog?" Jari asked.

"Zog want eyes."

Jari blinked and shrugged. "I'll take that as a yes. Gnok and Kala?"

Gnok spat and nodded. "No one will call me a Yellow Dwarf."

Kala's gaze burned into Jari's chest. He tugged his white beard for a long minute.

Silence.

"This is the stupidest idea you've had yet, Jari. If I die like Toli saving your ass, my blood is on your hands."

"I can live with that," Jari said, rubbing his weary eye.

"So, what are we chasing? And how far down the rabbit hole do we need to go?" Kala asked with a sigh.

"We're looking for a trinket that a dwarf took named Logrulir Metalbraid," Betha said.

"Metalbraid? Why do I know that name?" Gnok muttered.

Mori groaned.

"You know *everybody*, Gnok. Who the hell is that?" Jari asked, unpacking his bag.

"The most wanted Grey Dwarf left alive," Mori grumbled, fishing his whetstone out of his pocket.

"There are more?" Kala asked.

"Nope, just him, you, and me."

"Thought you said, you and your kin were the last," Kala said.

"Among *authentic* Grey Dwarves, yes. But Metalbraid and his band of cutthroats sold us out in the final days, opening the passage for the enemy to surround us. Metalbraid was at one time a Death Hammer," he spat. "Agh, traitors."

"I hate traitors," Sinda said.

Mori smiled at her, his eyes catching the candlelight. "Dwarves don't *ever* forsake their honor. But he's different. He's more daemon than dwarf now. The heart that grows inside of him is charred and twisted."

"Zog kill dwarf. Get eyes."

"What of the Frost Elf?" Arnak asked.

"Shit, I almost forgot. Is he still with us?"

"I have him in a trance right now. He shouldn't be moved," Arnak said.

"Will he stay asleep until we return?" Jari asked.

"He should. I'll check his dream patterns and adjust accordingly."

"Then we're off," Jari said with a clap.

Chapter 28

Barren Bluff looked just like it sounded: barren but with no real bluff. The entrance was chiseled into the mountainside, away from the sun. The two wooden doors in front of them didn't appear to have moved in hundreds of cycles. The cobwebs, spiders, crawlers of all sorts slithered back and forth in the damp darkness that encased the doors.

"That's hundreds of cycles old," Gnok said. "Metalbraid didn't go in there."

"Yes, I can see that, Gnok," Jari said, examining the sides of the defilade closest to him.

"What now?" Sinda asked.

"It's obvious he didn't go in the front door," Jari said. He knelt and traced his stubby fingers in the dirt.

Tell me what I want to know.

The dirt ran through his fingers, leaking out in front of him.

Grumps meandered over to the brush with the other goats. Chewing the dry scrub, he bleated and yanked on a particular one. Jari glanced up and walked over. "What have you got there?"

He took the rope from his goat's mouth and followed it. It was tied off to an iron bar, hammered into a trap door.

Hell yea.

"Got something."

The others crowded around him. "Zog, if you wouldn't mind."

Zog gripped the bar, yanked, broke it at the hinges, and then threw it over their heads. "Sorry."

Jari peered down into the pitch-black abyss. He glanced back over his shoulder. "Anyone have a candle?"

Zog handed him a pouch.

"What the hell is this?"

"Fire."

Jari scoffed, then opened it. Inside were little balls of an unknown substance. He pulled one out and rolled it between his thick fingers. The black ball smelled of oil and some other substance he couldn't readily identify.

"Give Zog." He picked it out of Jari's fingertips. "Watch magic."

He crushed it inside his palm and blew into his closed fist. The ball made a whistling sound and started smoking. The others backed up, all eyes on Zog's palm. With a smile, he dropped it into the hole.

Light sprang from the opening. The ball was floating in the air, illuminating everything below it. Down inside, they saw steps cut into the side of the wall. It wound all the way to the bottom, then disappeared.

Betha nudged him. "Go on, hero. Your stupid call. Your stupid ass goes first."

"Fuck off," he mumbled.

He walked to Grumps, dug in his worn leather bag, and removed his compass. He slung his ax over his back and checked his knives and bolas. "My stupid idea. I'll go first." He squatted at the entrance and then swung his leg over the side. "See you at the bottom."

He took his first awkward step, then another, and another until he was a dozen down. The others followed him, single file. The group descended into the darkness, the orb of light following Jari.

They reached the bottom in no time. Jari took his last step and then into the white sand. The orb gave him enough light to see down the corridor. The others gathered around him, waiting on him.

The cave they were in was large, with a single passageway into the darkness. A cold, sharp wind blew, sending a shiver down his spine. He pulled his ax from his back and rotated it in his palm. For the briefest moment, he felt the urge to run and never look back.

I'm starting to lose my nerve. Dwarven Lords, help me.

The others followed him as he navigated down the hall. He glanced at his feet and held his fist up. Kneeling, he traced the outline of well trodden footsteps. "Someone has been here recently."

Gnok grunted and cleared his throat. "Let's go kill this son of a bitch and get the hell out of here. Something doesn't feel right."

"Got that right," Kala said, sliding his palm across the wall. "Let's get to business."

Jari led them farther down until the tunnel branched off in three directions. "Oh, great," Gnok sighed.

"What's the plan, Jari?" Betha hissed.

He knelt at the entrance of each tunnel. The footprints went down all three. He stood up and brushed the sand from his hands.

"Betha, you take Sinda, Gnok, and Arnak down the left. Zog, you and the orcs go right. Me, Mori, and Kala will go down the middle. Kill anything and everything. It breathes—it dies."

"How will we find each other again?" Betha hissed.

"Knowing your smell, Betha, we'll find you no matter what hole you disappear down," Kala said, heading down the center.

Betha threw a fistful of sand at the back of his head.

She and Jari touched blades with a smile, then headed their separate ways. "See you in hell," Betha said.

Jari grinned. "Or at the end of the tunnel."

Jari and his band traveled silently, their feet barely making any imprints. The tunnel was wide enough for all three dwarves to walk shoulder to shoulder. Kala's breastplate kept rubbing Jari's shoulder.

"You should have left that breastplate behind," Jari said, shouldering him aside.

Kala puckered his lips. "You'd have to kiss me first, deary."

The sound of hammers striking anvils traveled down the tunnel. Jari cautiously led the way, searching the ground for footprints. As they closed in on the sound, Mori placed his hand on both their shoulders. "If Metalbraid still lives, he's mine."

"Fair enough," Jari said.

"How many mercs are with him?" Kala asked.

Jari shrugged. "She didn't say."

"Oh, this is really a stupid idea," Kala grumbled as they proceeded.

As they exited, Jari noticed Betha and her group on a tier above them. As the cave opened up, the walls had rows of rings along the edges like a coliseum. They traveled all the way up the side and out of view. Zog and the orcs walked out a few hundred feet to his left.

Sprawled in front of them was a small village. A single plume of smoke rose from the center. Jari motioned to Betha to flank them from the high ground and Zog to follow him.

The orcs and dwarves walked side by side up the narrow road to the outskirts of the village. In the center, dwarves hammered on anvils, sweat pouring off their forearms and faces. Jari waited as Betha moved into position, her bow by her side, ready for action.

The small group walked into the village and formed a semicircle. The dwarves in front of them were covered in blue. Whether it was paint or pigmentation, Jari couldn't tell, but they appeared armed and ready for a fight.

These are no Grey Dwarves.

Kala leaned over and hissed, "What the hell is this?"

Jari focused on them. More stepped from the shadows as the hammering came to a stop.

A large dwarf, nearly five and a half feet tall with arms the size of steel beams moved forward, an ornate hammer in each hand. "Help you with something?"

"You Metalbraid?" Jari asked.

"I am."

Mori slid closer to Jari. "Let's kill him and be done with this."

"Mori Greygrog, that you?" Metalbraid asked.

Mori growled in response.

"Do we have a problem?" Metalbraid asked, tapping the hammers together.

Jari pushed Mori back and hissed, "You have a problem when I say you have a problem. Now, step back." He turned his attention back to Metalbraid. "He has no problem. I'm here to retrieve Kippa's ornament."

Metalbraid smiled and opened his arms wide. "I won it fair and square, I did. If you want to take it back with you, it'll cost you."

"Why don't we just kill you first?" Jari said.

Metalbraid snapped his fingers, and more dwarves appeared out of the tunnels behind them. "You owe me a new gate that the orc broke." He lit his pipe and puffed until the ember glowed orange. "You're outnumbered four to one. If you insist on fighting, I'll order your deaths." His army moved into position. "But I'll tell you what . . . You came for the trinket, right?" Jari nodded. "Fine, I'll give it back, but I want something first."

Betha and the others were escorted down to where Jari was standing. Jari made eye contact with everyone. Each nodded.

All vote yes. No need to lose people for no reason.

"Name your price."

"Got an infestation problem in the lower halls. Don't want to lose any of my dwarves hunting. I'll let your mercs go down and clean it up for me."

Jari clenched his fist, his knuckles white. "What's down there?"

Metalbraid smirked. "A bunch of things. Spiders, goblins, and the like. Nothing a band of mercs such as yourselves can't handle."

What else?

"And what leads them?" Jari asked.

"Not entirely sure myself. But it's stealing my ore, and the mountain doesn't yield what it used to. You find out what it is that is stealing my stuff, and I'll give that sore sport her trinket back. That's the deal."

"Let me discuss it with my band," Jari said.

Metalbraid twirled his fingers, and the dwarves behind them melted back into the tunnels.

"Great. Another fucking roadblock," Kala groaned while stretching.

"Two choices. Either we hunt, or they kill us," Jari said.

"I'll go," Arnak grumbled.

"What about you, Zog, and your orcs?"

The orcs nodded. "In."

"Sinda?"

She shrugged. "Okay."

"Mori?"

"I'm not a Loner. But if you're asking me, I'll stay and kill Metalbraid."

"Gnok?"

"Hell, I'm with Mori. He's a traitor and needs to be dealt with."

"Betha?"

She raised her battle-ax. "I'm with you."

"Kala?"

"I'm with you, Brother."

Jari walked to Metalbraid. "We're in. Show us the entrance we need to go down, and we'll kill this thing."

Metalbraid waved one of his dwarves over. "Show them to the crypt."

The Loners followed the Blue Dwarf down through the village and into a small antechamber at the back of the cave. A double wooden door lay embedded into the floor, its brass rivets catching the firelight. The blue-shaded dwarf left, and the others stared at the door.

"This is a horrible idea," Gnok muttered. "But since this is the group's decision, I'll go first."

"No argument here," Kala said.

"No. My plan, my lead," Jari stated, stepping forward, unslinging his ax from his back.

Arnak and Zog each grabbed a door handle and yanked up on them at the same time. The hinges gave a loud squeal in protest, then swung open. Stone steps led down into the dark. Jari went to the wall, picked up a torch, and then led the group down the steps.

He spat a wad of phlegm from his throat. *This should be fun.*

Chapter 29

Down the stone steps they walked, some solid, others loose. They seemed to go down forever. Jari's torchlight was all that lit the way. Further and further they walked in silence, their boots and hooves making noise as they descended.

"Where the hell are we going?" Kala hissed from behind.

"When I know, you'll know," Jari hissed back.

Jari's foot splashed in a puddle, and he fell forward. He threw the torch behind him and, with a grunt, fell face-first into the oily water. "Son of the Dwarven Lords," he cursed.

There were a few snickers behind him.

Betha pulled him up by his belt, and he could feel her smiling at him in the dark. "Torch," he hissed as the others crowded around him at the base of the steps. "I got a feeling there will be plenty to kill down here. When we find what we're looking for—" A loud shriek suddenly echoed around them. Jari turned his head and then glanced at his comrades. "*That.* Kill it, find the ore, kill some more, and then we're out of here."

The shriek came at them again.

"I guess we should follow that lovely voice," Sinda said, freeing her knives.

Jari led them further down the hall. More torches hung on the walls, and as they passed one, a member would light it and hand it back until most in the group had one. The fives orcs brought up the rear with Zog. Arnak stood watch over Sinda. Kala, Gnok, and Mori held the middle, and Betha and Jari took point.

Something hissed near Arnak, and he slammed his club down instinctively. Then he swung his torch toward the sound. At his feet lay a dead rattlesnake, it's head inches from his feet. He took a step back and wiped his brow.

"Careful where you step. Arnak, I need you in the center of the group with Sinda. One of us gets bit down here, and we don't have you, we'll never make it out. Betha, your bow at the ready."

They followed the shrieking further down the tunnel. Jari held his fist up, knelt, and listened. He heard a sound coming their way. "Form ranks."

The group fell into position, Jari at the point. The voices walked around the bend and into them. The goblins stood no chance. Betha, Arnak, and Zog, with the other orcs, lashed out with their long arms and hacked the five goblins to death before they could utter a sound. What they were carrying fell at their feet.

Jari picked up a loose piece of ore and tossed up and down a few times. "Well, looks like we're on the right track. Scalp 'em and hide them."

"Where do you think they're coming from?" Arnak grumbled, pulling two bodies out of the way.

Betha threw a few scalps and ears to the orcs. "Who cares. We need more scalps. Let's hunt everything in here."

"That could take at least a day, maybe more," Kala hissed.

Betha ripped a scalp off that sounded like Velcro, then pointed it at Kala. "Shut it, Scalp Master. We're hunters, so we hunt. We'll kill Boro in good time, but I, for one, am not passing on free money."

"Zog agree."

"Nobody asked you anything, you hairy beast," Kala spat.

"Zog Loner. Zog count."

"*I'm* the leader, and *I* make the decisions. We kill what we need to and then get the hell out of here. More scalps out in the world than this disgusting shithole," Jari said, leading the way.

They walked a few hundred yards, and then the tunnel opened up. The cave was huge but not as large as the one above them, but large enough. Around a fire sat at least twenty goblins, all chewing on something.

The dirt was red clay, different than the white sand also above them. Goblins destroy everything, even the sand.

I hate these little bastards.

Hundreds of bones were scattered all over, some animal, some humanoid. Jari noticed another tunnel leading out of the back of the cave.

"So, this is a goblin area. There's another tunnel back there. If this is a goblins' nest, then these are simple workers. I hope this isn't what I think it is," Jari said, adjusting his Tok mail.

"What you thinking?" Betha asked, taking a knee.

"Remember years ago when I took that side mission while you ventured north with Toli for a contract?" he asked.

Betha nodded.

"I joined a group of dwarves who chased down a tribe of goblins. A soul crusher, Queen Niz'gaa, led them."

"And?"

Jari pulled up his sleeve. Four lines that looked like whip marks lay across his skin. "The tentacles of a spider queen." He touched his shut eye socket with a wince. "She cut my eye out and killed my company. The healer we were with saved me but perished in the process. If this is her group, I know for a fact that some of us are not going back up top."

Betha sighed and shook her mane. "Jari, I'm not sure if it's Toli's death or your lack of desire to keep being a merc. We're mercs. *We* die. Hell, it's what we do best. You need to find your courage again. Toli wouldn't want to see you like this."

"Like what?" he asked.

"Like someone pissed in your gut-rot."

He gave a curt nod.

Zog chuckled. "I did."

Jari pushed him playfully.

"Now, let's go get this money. Loners, form ranks," Jari said. "Shields high, visors down. March."

Jari moved forward, locked in place with Kala and Betha at his elbows, the others forming a spear with the orcs in the center. A shrill horn sounded, and the goblins sprinted to their weapons. Betha's bow brought several of them down as they scampered toward them. Some of them mounted emaciated mountain wolves, beasts known for their tenacity, with white coats and black bands across the rib cage. The orcs with the Loners threw their javelins and rocks, killing several more before engaging in hand-to-hand combat. Jari, Gnok, Kala, and Sinda all fired their bolas simultaneously, killing a score.

One, then two, then three charged at them. The spear formation split with Jari, Gnok, and Arnak splitting off to the left. Sinda, Kala, and Mori split to the right side. The orcs led by Zog roared as they collided with fifteen goblins. As that group engaged, another twenty goblins sprinted across the muddy red field from somewhere further back.

Jari loosed all of his bolas. He pulled knives from his belt and began throwing them end over end at his attackers.

One, two, three. Dammit, a miss.

He heard a growl of pain and fear from behind. One of the orcs with them had three goblins attempting to hack him to pieces. Jari ran to his aid. He swung his ax, decapitating one goblin from behind. The next one spun and attacked. Jari rolled forward, thrust a knife in its crotch, and rolled by. With a flick of his wrist, he threw another knife and caught the third goblin in the throat. The second one was still screeching until Betha stomped on its head.

The wounded orc smiled. "Good you." He returned to the mêlée.

"You good?" Betha asked, winded.

"Aye."

With no time to talk, Jari charged back into the brawl. He hacked and slashed, dodged and weaved, spun and rolled. More goblins came. More goblins died.

The muddy sand was awash with green goblin blood. The Loners regrouped during a lull in the fighting. "Everyone all right?" Jari asked, his breathing heavy.

"Zog lose one."

Jari nodded. "Form up—shields together. We're almost through this. When we kill it, we will become one of the most famous merc companies out in Labrys."

They did as ordered, their shields interlocking with a clang. Another score of goblins, all mounted, rode over the corpses and slammed into the spear tip. The orcs in the middle hacked and slashed as the riderless wolves careened by them. One of the orcs swung his jagged scimitar so close to Jari's head, he heard a *whoosh* of air pass his ear, the blade hacking a goblin in half a foot away.

A roar in front of them stopped the fighting cold, sending the goblins fleeing.

A Shocker gave a screech while three large, venomous boars walked across the sand and stopped in front of them, their tusks long and curved, deadly saliva dripping. The Shocker was nothing but bones and a large orange glow holding them together. It stood seven feet tall, its eye sockets burning red.

It boomed. "Who dares disturb my rest?"

"I've come to collect a bounty. You've been stealing ore from the dwarves above you," Jari said, stepping in front of his comrades.

The daemon crossed its bony arms. "They do not own the

mountain. I do."

"I'm 'fraid not, daemon. We need to collect, so surrender peacefully, and I'll make sure you get locked up, nice and safe, or fight—and we'll destroy you."

The daemon chuckled.

Jari glanced at his comrades' dirty and bloody faces.

"Who are we?" he roared.

"Loners."

"Let's give 'em a taste of our steel. Zog, you and the orcs take those boars. The rest of you with me."

They advanced, tight, senses heightened. The Shocker spread its long limbs and pointed. The boars galloped toward them. Zog and his orcs broke ranks and fought them head-on. Zog gave orders in orcish, the words guttural and harsh. A boar gored one of the orcs who was engaged, its tusk bursting from his back. The orc grasped the tusks behind him as Zog beheaded it, both hitting the ground.

Two left.

He had no time to watch as his group surrounded the Shocker. It let loose a loud shriek and attacked. Jari was the first to charge, his ax slamming into its bony wrist. The ax lodged, and the daemon tossed it away and punched Jari. He flew back ten feet and landed with a loud groan. Betha engaged next and slammed her ax in its breast bone. It bounced back, flew out of her hand, and she landed with it a few feet away.

Gnok, Mori, and Kala engaged while Sinda and Arnak attacked with projectiles. "Aim for the orange glow," Mori shouted. "Ignore the bones."

Gnok ducked one arm, moved in, and swung his ax underhand into the orange abdomen. It let out a shriek. Gnok shouted in pain and pitched forward between the daemon's thighs. The boar that hit him pawed the ground, ready to finish the job. Jari sprinted over, jumped on its back, plunged a knife through its ear and into its brain. It bucked him off in its death throes. One of its tusks embedded in the orange glow under the daemon's rib cage. The daemon staggered back.

Sinda sent a bola directly into its eye, shattering the ruby-red orb. The daemon shrieked again, flailing wildly. One arm swung at Sinda. She rolled back, came to her feet, and swung her ax at the hand. It made contact and shattered the ax head. She cursed and pulled her backup knives. The arm swatted and sent her sprawling.

"Sinda," Arnak roared, charging past the daemon's grasps.

He masterfully weaved through its well aimed blows. He slipped in front of the orange glow, covered himself with his blue healing cover, and jammed his fingers into its rib cage. His fingers searched frantically for the heat source. After a moment, he yanked down with everything he had. The orange orb popped free of the rib cage with a resounding clap of thunder.

The explosion hurled Arnak in the opposite direction. The blinding light seared through the cave, pulsating, sending energy bouncing off every wall. Jari and the others shielded their eyes.

Then the light faded.

Jari groaned as he sat up. "Anybody alive?"

Betha rolled over on her side, patting herself down. "Yea, I'm here. Some of my hair is singed off, but I'm alive."

Gnok yanked his dented helm off and coughed. "Damn boar speared me. I think I broke a few ribs, but, yea, I'm good."

"I'm here," Kala said.

Jari glanced around. "Zog?"

Zog walked through the smoke with two orcs in tow, bloodied and bruised. "Zog here."

Sinda rolled onto her back and felt her jaw. "Arnak, you okay?"

Silence.

"Arnak?" Sinda repeated.

She scrambled to her feet, saw his crumpled body, and hurried to him, followed by the others.

She cradled his head in her lap. "No... no... no. It can't be."

Jari leaned in and felt for a pulse. "He's not dead. His pulse is weak, but it's there."

"What do we do?" Gnok asked.

"Let's carry him out of here and try to help him when we get back to the surface. Move," Jari said, helping Zog hoist him over his shoulder.

Jari stared at the carnage. *Dwarven Lords, help us.*

Chapter 30

Taking the last step, a haggard and haunted group of adventurers left the underground. Zog set Arnak down and pressed his stubby fingers to his neck and grunted. "Still live."

The blue hue enveloping him still glowed, though now, it was faint. The group sat around him or leaned against the wall, the gore of battle smeared among their sweat. Jari groaned. He knew it would come to this. It was bad enough to lose a few orcs to the dungeon, but losing Arnak was catastrophic. He knelt by Arnak's side and touched his rocklike hand. Sinda wept next to him, trying to wake him. "Arnak, please, wake up."

One eye cracked open.

"I'm here," he whispered.

Sinda hugged him close. "Oh, thank the Dwarven Lords."

Kala, the next closest healer, felt along Arnak's limbs, grunting as he did. He stopped, felt the back of his carapace, and sucked his breath in. "This is not good."

He waved to Jari and eased Arnak forward. Jari sucked his breath in as well. The shell was cracked from top to bottom, exposing his organs. A blue hue pulsated faintly along it.

How is he not dead?

Kala and Jari made eye contact. "Build a litter to carry him. We need to find Metalbraid and get some fresh linen to cover the crack." He knelt in front of Arnak, who was wheezing. "Your shell is badly cracked. We must fix you, but we don't know how. Can you tell us?"

Arnak gave a grim nod. "I'll be dead before you secure the ingredients I need to heal myself. Leave me here and go."

Sinda burst into tears. "Absolutely not."

"'Fraid not, Brother. You're a Loner. Never leave one of ours behind," Jari said.

Arnak groaned. "Very well, but it's a waste of time. Get me back to the inn, and I'll tell you where to find the items."

Mori blocked the exit. "I came here to kill Metalbraid."

"Now is not the time, Brother Mori," Kala said. "We must get ours to safety, or he's dead."

"Not my problem, I'm not a Loner."

"We freed you," Gnok hissed, loosening his ax. "Now stand aside, or Kala really will be the last Grey Dwarf."

"Easy, Gnok," Jari said, restraining his arm. "He's not the enemy."

Gnok growled. "If he keeps my brother from receiving the help he needs, then, yes, he is the enemy."

"Mori, please step aside. You can die down here over the ghosts of the past, or you can keep hunting with us and make coin," Jari said.

Mori's shoulders sagged. "He killed everyone I ever loved. He's a traitor, and should it be my death, then so be it."

Jari walked over to him. "For the love of the Dwarven Lords, I beg you, leave this be. Join us—no reason to die for no reason. You can help train new recruits back in Anak'anor. But right now, we must get our companion out of here."

Mori stepped aside.

"Loners, move," Jari said.

The others left as quickly as possible to help Arnak back to the city. Jari stayed behind to meet with Metalbraid. As he walked into the village, Metalbraid stopped hammering the iron he was working by the raging fire. "What do you have for me?"

Jari dropped the bag of bones that was the Shocker at his feet. "I lost some of my orcs, and my healer was critically injured, destroying that daemonic monstrosity in the depths. I want that trinket, and I want it now."

Metalbraid grinned and clapped his hands. "Of course, of course. Down to business." He tossed him the trinket. "Send my regards to Kippa."

Jari caught it. "Why steal it anyway?"

"I didn't. We were playing cards, and she put it in the pot. I cleaned her clock, and she sends mercs after me. And now she is responsible for your healer. I'm not the enemy . . . she is."

Jari stuck the trinket in his pocket. "Did you really sell the Death Hammers out?"

Metalbraid paused. "An accusation, nothing more."

"Mori Greygrog says differently."

Metalbraid smiled. "I bet my brother does. Always was a liar."

"Brother?"

"Yes." Metalbraid picked up his hammer. "Same father, different mothers. It is true we were both Death Hammers, and it is also true that I helped plan and execute the ambush that killed the king. But he left out the part that he helped me. When our father found out, he banished me and sent him to the Black Rock dungeons as punishment."

Jari's jaw dropped.

Metalbraid chuckled. "Don't look so shocked. Dwarves care about their honor, but to dwarves like us, coin is the *selling* motivator. You rescued a thief, nothing more. If you leave him around your valuables, he will rob you blind."

"Then why does he want to kill you if he's only a thief?"

Metalbraid grabbed a new piece of ore. "Because I killed our father with his help and collected the bounty on his head. He wants his share, but I built this village with it. Be careful, Jari Rockjaw. Trust is a valuable commodity. Don't spend it on a thief."

After several hours of travel, they rode through the portcullis of Anak'anor. Arnak was moaning and talking to himself. He had paled, and his protective blue hue had all but faded. They struggled up the winding stairwell at the inn. Finally, after making it through the door, Jari knelt by his side. "Arnak, you're dying. What do I need to fix you?"

Arnak coughed. "A few of the ingredients will be readily available. Only one will be a journey to get to. And there is no guarantee it will be there."

"I'll take that chance."

"All right, I'll need night bindweed, moon ceed, and life lilac. Those are lying about outside the keep. But the corrupt milfoil will be at the Merrimond Top."

The air was sucked out of the room at the last comment. Kala muttered several curses under his breath and wiped imaginary dust from his shoulder. "So, here it ends. Thought it couldn't get any worse."

"It always gets worse with dwarves," Gnok muttered.

Jari didn't buy into the doom and gloom. "Fine, that should be possible. I'll take Grumps to Merrimond Top, then ride back here. Half a day up, half a day back. I will be back. How long do you have Arnak?"

Arnak gave a weak smile. "Less than the day it will take to get. Let me die in peace."

Jari ignored him. "Sinda, you stay by his side. The rest of you search for the herbs. I'll return."

Jari left the room. He saddled Grumps and turned him around. Betha walked out after him. "I'm going alone, Betha."

"Like hell you are. Already lost Toli; not losing you too." She stretched. "Now, if you don't mind, let's go get the milfoil we need and save Arnak."

I hope like hell we can.

The pair crossed over the Blue Mountains and headed for Merrimond Top. After traveling several hours, they reached the base of it. The climb up the mountain was steep. Only a goat could scale it with a dwarf on its back. Grumps was the goat for the job. Jari held his hand over his brow and scanned the trail in front of him.

"Mighty long way, Betha. You sure about this?"

Betha shouldered him and Grumps aside, who bleated his displeasure. Jari followed behind her, sliding his bolas into the palm of his hand. Betha had her fingers on the bowstring, an arrow nocked. As they traveled, several fist-sized rocks rolled down the mountain and skidded across their path. Betha held her paw up and sniffed.

"You smell something?" Jari hissed.

She sniffed a few more times, then shook her mane.

The further they climbed, the thinner the air. Betha started wheezing halfway up, and Jari tried to help her. She shrugged his hand off her shoulder. "I'm fine, thank you very much."

Who are we fooling? Arnak will be dead before we get back.

"Let's hurry. Don't want Arnak dead. It will be impossible to find such a good sword brother," Betha said, tightening her grip on the bow.

A howl echoed through the mountain passes.

"Coyote?" Jari asked.

"Porkukula."

A porkukula was a mix between a coyote and a lion. Two-headed and meaner than a rattlesnake. Few, if any, ever came down from the Merrimond. As they rounded the corner, two stood snarling on the overhang.

Speak of the daemons.

Betha yanked the bowstring to her shoulder and stared down the sight. Jari calmed a bleating Grumps, who pawed the dirt and leaned his horns forward, ears slicked back. The two porks growled and changed colors from white to half red and blue.

"What now?" Jari hissed.

"Get off Grumps. Give him room to help. Pull your ax. I'll fire, you two do the hand-to-hand combat."

"Grumps isn—"

"Your stupid ass got us into this."

"My stupid ass will get us out of here. I know, I know."

He dismounted, keeping his eye locked on the porks. *You ready, boy?*

Grumps bleated.

Jari unslung his ax, slammed his visor down, and headed up the path. He freed his backup knife and took a defensive stance a few feet from them. Betha's arrow snapped by his ear with such force that he felt the heat.

"For the Dwarven Lords." He charged straight up the middle. He heard several more arrows *whomp* by his head. Grumps galloped by him, lowered his horns, and headbutted the pork on the right. Jari switched his direction and cut left, heading straight for his enemy.

As he neared it, the pork leaped and caught Jari midstride. It knocked him back a few feet, and the two tumbled together down the trail. They rolled off the path and into the brush. The pork bit him with as much force as it could muster. Jari's Tok mail rings groaned as the pork shook both heads back and forth, attempting to rip off his ax hand. Jari cuffed the closest head to him. It howled and released its grip. The knife Jari was carrying had been knocked out of his hands during the fighting, his ax nowhere to be seen.

He punched the pork a few more times, then headbutted both

heads several more times. The more pain he dealt, the more aggressive the pork became. He headbutted it another three times, and one skull crushed. He heard a bleat, then Grumps's horns speared it from the side and brought it down within inches of Jari's chest, killing the last head. Jari pricked the tip of the horn that had burst through with his finger. "Back up, Grumps."

The other animal lay at Betha's feet, several arrows embedded in its chest cavity.

"Not the fight I was looking for," Jari mumbled, stumbling back onto the path with Grumps in tow.

"Not the fight they were looking for either," Betha said, kneeling next to the bodies, her skinning knife gleaming in the sun.

After they skinned the carcasses and harvested the meat, they moved on with their journey. Jari led Grumps as the air thinned even more. Both wheezing, they trudged around another loop and into a large snowdrift. Betha hesitantly touched the snow with her hoof and drew it back. "I'm not walking in that snow. My hooves will crack. You go on up there, brave heart."

Jari grumbled, spat, and handed the reins to her. "Convenient excuse."

He rolled up his sleeves, rubbed Grumps, and headed up the narrow path to the top of Merrimond. The vegetation was all but dead except for some pine trees which were still flush with needles.

It's like finding a needle in a stack of needles. Where the hell am I going to find corrupt milfoil? There's a foot of snow up here.

The black flower with white lines emblazoned throughout the leaves would be easily noticeable if the snowstorm hadn't set in as he reached the pinnacle. Over on the left, he saw a small cave entrance. He trudged through the knee-high snow, his curses heard halfway down the mountain.

I hate caves.

He knelt at the mouth and peered inside. Nothing seemed to be moving. A cold wind roared across the entrance, chilling Jari to the bone. *The Dwarven Lords hate a coward.* He pushed his ax head into the snow and stood. The cave was dark, and with no torch, he searched around for anything he could use. *Wish I had Zog's*—He fumbled in his pocket and found the little magic ball. *Aha!*

He crushed it like Zog had and then rolled it into the cave. Instinctively, he readied his ax and shield and slammed his visor down. His footsteps crunched in the snow as he took short steps. He scanned the darkness ahead. Every time the magic ball stopped, he would kick it a little further. The ball came to a stop when it rolled up against a skull. Jari knelt and lifted his visor, peering into the black.

Nothing moved.

The skull in front of him was bleached white, and the teeth sharpened to a point. As he studied it, a loud wail bounced off the walls around him. Jari sprinted to the ball, picked it up, and then ran to one of the walls with it. His breath came in gasps. He surveyed the five feet in front of him, his shield held just below his chin.

"Who dares bother The Friedd?" the wailing voice asked.

"I'm Jari Rockjaw of the Loners. I'm on a mission to find corrupt milfoil for my wounded comrade."

Silence.

"Why do you think I care about your companion?" the voice asked again after some hesitation.

"I don't. But you asked me—"

"I know what I asked," it snapped.

"I just need the milfoil, and I'll be on my way," Jari said, tightening the grip on his ax.

"Why do you think there's milfoil in here?"

"I don't, but there's at least a foot of snow covering the

flowers out there. Thought I'd try here. Damn cold out there," Jari said.

Silence.

The wail started low, then grew louder. The shrill sound rose until Jari fell to his knees and covered his ears. His eardrums felt like they were caving in. And then all at once, it stopped. Jari slowly slid his palms from his ears. *What in all that's holy—*

An apparition appeared in front of him. "You risk certain death coming in here, Dwarf." Its translucent hand picked up the bleached skull and tossed it to him. "Some have already found this to be true. You were right to guess the milfoil is here."

Oh, thank the Dwarven Lords.

"But you must answer three riddles, and then I'll give you what you seek."

"And if I lose?"

The ghost smiled. "Then you join your brethren."

Jari peeked around the sentient being. In rows stacked upon rows were heads of every shape. Large skulls, small skulls, in between sizes too. He swallowed the large lump in his throat. "Fine, I'll play. What's the first riddle?"

The ghost hissed . . .

You can touch me,

You can break me,

You should win me if you want to be mine.

What am I?

Jari pondered the question. *You break a mug of gut-rot, you can touch it, but I wouldn't win it, I'd buy it. I can touch ore, my pickax can break it, but I wouldn't win it, I'd mine it. What if it's metaphorical? It's freezing in this cave; you have to be strong—*

"You're a heart."

More wailing. "Fine, Dwarf, you got lucky on that one. Now, for the next one," it hissed. "What has cities, but no houses; forests, but no trees; and water, but no fish?"

Jari leaned against the wall. *Cities, forest, water? What would have all three but not what you would expect them to have? Cities, forest, water?*

He grinned. "Easy, that's a map of Labrys."

Jari felt a blast of cold air. The ghost was nose to nose with him, its breath misty with the odor of an old shoe. "You're cheating, aren't you, Little Dwarf?"

Jari raised his hands. "I hold nothing but thoughts."

The ghost wound around him, its face next to his ear. "Final round. If you win, I'll give you some of my precious milfoil. And remember, if you lose . . ." It glanced over its translucent shoulder. "It won't be long till I add your thick skull to my collection."

He clapped his hands. "I'm ready."

"Let's see how smart you *really* are. There's a one-story building in Anak'anor where everything inside is yellow. Yellow walls, yellow doors, yellow furniture. What color are the stairs?"

Jari sucked his teeth and then spat. He shut his eyes and slowed his breathing. He repeated the question over and over. *Stairs, stairs, they should be yellow, right? Nope, too easy. They're brown. Stairs are always brown. Wait . . .* His eyes snapped open. "There aren't any—it's a one-story building."

The ghost hissed. Then a screech, the likes of which Jari had never before heard, knocked him into the wall. With a grunt, he pushed back with all his might. But the noise pinned him physically where he was. His sweaty palms pressed against the freezing rock. He pushed one more time, and the screeching stopped. His momentum landed him facedown at the apparition's feet.

"I should kill you, Little One."

Jari shoved his visor up. "A deal is a deal. I won fair and square. Now, my milfoil, please."

The specter vanished. Jari rose to his feet and drew his ax. "Come back, you lying bastard."

Corrupted milfoil flowers floated from the ceiling. "Begone, Dwarf, before I change my mind."

Not waiting, Jari collected the flowers, turned, and sprinted for the exit. As he cleared the threshold, the entrance transformed into a rock face. *I'll be damned.*

Without wasting a moment, he plodded through the snow, the light white powder filling his boots. One foot in front of the other, he finally made it back to the road. Hunched over at the waist, he gasped from the effort. Jari finally walked back and handed the flowers to Betha.

She sized him up and snorted, "You okay? Looks like you've seen a ghost."

"Nah, piece'a cake. Let's get back to Arnak."

"How is he?" Jari asked, entering the room.

Sinda glanced up, her eyes red-rimmed. "His breathing is barely audible."

"Did he leave any directions?" Betha asked, nearing him.

"With Kala," Gnok said with a shrug and lay the moon ceed stalks on the table, near the mortar and pestle. Moon ceed was a long green blade of grass with a red tip, known to act as a paste when ground with night bindweed.

Night bindweed was a small ball with multiple spikes jutting from all different angles. The plant yielded a strong fruit known to clean your insides out. Zog laid the night bindweed next to the pestle, and Mori draped the purple life lilac over them.

Mori bled from numerous lacerations across his face and along his arms, little red bumps parading up and down his forearms. "I hate red ants," he grumbled.

Mori volunteered to attack the red anthill while the others collected their flowers. He knew the price, but he owed Arnak and repaid his debt. The life lilac lay inside an anthill, by the queen. No one knew how the plant survived underground, but some said red ants dug a water source, and the flower grew from there. It bloomed to a deep indigo within the mound, but only one petal poked through the top of the hill.

Mori sat down at the table with a hiss and a wince. Kala handed him a bowl of white stringy goo. "What's this?"

Kala grinned. "Little something to smear on those cuts and bumps." He moved on to Arnak's side. "He told me before passing out that I would need to make a paste and then apply it. After packing it into his shell, I'm to sear it with a hot poker. He said that should infection set in, he will die."

"That's comforting," Betha groaned.

"Let's get to work," Kala said, ushering everyone except Jari and Sinda from the room.

"Sure you know what you're doing, Kala?" Jari hissed near his ear.

"Shut it or leave, Jari."

He poured several drops from his canteen into the mortar and then picked up the moon ceed stalks and freed his ax, the stalks still rigid. Kala hummed a tune and chopped the stalks into paper-thin slices. He swept the shavings into his palm and dropped them into the bottom. Next, he moved the night bindweeds over and smashed the face of his ax down on the spiked sac. An orange mucus leaked from one, then another, until all ten were leaking. He squeezed the fluid sacs into the pestle with the moon ceed like an egg yolk.

Jari gagged at the smell. "I think I'm gonna b—" He vomited in the corner.

"Dammit, Jari," Kala muttered.

Undisturbed by the projectile vomit, Kala focused. The life lilac went next. The tough shell of the flower had to be cracked like a lobster claw. After smashing his ax on it a few times, it released a black powder with the smell of a Bohal corpse baking in The Expanse. Jari gagged again, and his insides emptied once more. *Didn't even need the bindweed.*

Kala gently moved the cup to the edge of the table, and with an open piece of parchment, he swept the powder into the concoction. "Jari, give me the milfoil."

Jari wiped his mouth with the back of his sleeve. "Huh?"

"The milfoil, you worthless Bohal."

"Oh." Jari fumbled in his pockets and yanked out several of the flowers. The final ingredient, the most precious and rarest flower on Labrys. Kala rubbed his palms together with the petals between them, the heat building. The humming coming from his lips was soft at first, then louder until it reached a crescendo. With a thunderous clap, the flowers exploded into a coarse white powder. He carried the ingredients over to Arnak. Sinda peeled back the sheet covering his shell.

The blue protection force had faded. Now, everything was exposed to the air. Caramel pus ran from the crack, and it smelled like his bowels had evacuated. Jari gagged for a third time. Kala blew the white powder along the crack in his shell. A light enveloped the half-inch crack.

He hurried to the table, ground the ingredients, and made the paste. "Sure hope this works." Returning to Arnak, he smeared the white paste with yellow specks into the fissure. He painted it along the shell for a few minutes. "Jari, get the poker from the fire downstairs."

Jari fetched it, the burning red ember emanating a powerful heat. Kala snatched it and gazed skyward. "Dwarven Lords, be with us," he said.

Then he seared the wound, the smell of burnt flesh wafting through the air.

Jari's face contorted in a grimace and a gag—then he passed out.

Chapter 31

"Does he breathe?" Gnok asked from the doorway with the others in tow.

Kala sighed. "He does, but I'm unsure for how long." He ran his palm over his nose and mouth. "I've prayed to the Dwarven Lords for his survival."

"But we can't wait for him to heal. We must track Boro down. He grows stronger every day," Jari said, rinsing his hands and mouth in the washbowl nearby.

"Leave him? You can't be serious, Jari," Sinda gasped.

"I wish we could wait, Sinda, but we have a bounty to collect. Arnak would tell us to go if he could speak."

"And elf?" Zog asked, pointing to the corner and tightening his grip on his weapon.

"Is he alive?" Jari asked.

Zog nodded.

"Jari's right. If we wait, Boro gets stronger. And if he employs too many, we will never defeat him, no matter how hard we try," Betha said.

Arnak groaned.

The Loners rushed to his bedside. "Give me some gut-rot," he muttered, his tongue swollen.

Zog thrust a flask into his hand. Arnak tried to tip it, but couldn't. Zog nudged the others aside and helped him drink. Arnak took small sips and nodded his thanks.

"How long have I been out?" he asked.

"A day," Gnok said.

He winced. "Where's Sinda?"

She held his hand. "I'm right here." Arnak squeezed hers. "Good to know. I'll be on my feet in no time. I see you found the milfoil." He gave a half smile. "And you won against Mella the Friedd?"

Betha cut her eyes at Jari, who kept his eyes on Arnak. "Yea, piece'a cake."

Arnak winced after a soft chuckle. "Not many alive can say that beside you and me," he grumbled.

"You've faced her?" Jari asked.

"Oh, have I. We were companions before she died." He coughed. "When she did, I fastened her soul to the cave to guard the only ingredient that could offer everlasting life. But it came with a price. Those who steal the milfoil while she rests die forever in the cave. Those who win can leave, but the milfoil dries up."

Jari searched his pockets. When he pulled out the milfoil, it had turned to ash. "How did it work for you?"

"You must have said something about me, or she read your mind," Arnak said, trying to sit up. "She's a mind reader, well, was."

"What happened to her?" Jari pressed. "She seemed very angry."

Arnak chuckled. "Suppose she would be. A hundred years ago, she lost her mind and attacked our group of companions. I'm not entirely sure why she did. I tied her to the cave after we put her down." He attempted to sit up a few more inches.

"Easy, Tortle, rest," Gnok said, gently pushing on his shoulder.

Arnak winced. "I think I'll take your advice," he said as he lay back down.

Jari exhaled and glanced in the corner of the room. The elf sat cross-legged, fingertips touching. "What the Dwarven Lords is he doing?" Jari asked.

"Pray," Zog said.

Everyone looked at him with skepticism until the elf spoke. "The orc is correct. I'm praying to the Frost gods for deliverance."

"Keep praying. Your gods don't live here," Gnok snapped.

Jari held up his hand and silenced Gnok. The Frost Elf had seemed to regenerate on his own. The bindings lay by his feet, and he looked like he had never seen battle, or that he should have been dead.

"How are you not dead?" Jari asked, taking a knee in front of him.

The elf shrugged.

"What's your name?" Jari pressed, offering him a flask of gut-rot.

He waved off the gut-rot. "Never could stand the taste of dwarven brew." He paused and touched his face, which should have been ravaged from the fight. He had taken an ax blow across the nose and down the cheek. "Before I tell you my name, I'll answer the question in your head. Your tortle healer enveloped my body with a healing spell. My will drew on his energy and healed me faster than it would have taken myself." He gave a weary smile. "My name is Sithril Frostsong of the Frost Caves."

"Sithril, huh?" Jari turned and introduced his company. "Now that we're acquainted, tell me where Boro is, and we'll let you walk out of here."

"Deep in the mountains, near the Frost Caves."

"Whoa, that's like a weeklong march from here. I thought he'd be closer," Jari said.

"He was closer, but winter set in, and he escaped to replenish his stock and manpower. Then he will raid in a few weeks," Sithril said, stretching. "The more important question is, what will be done with your healer?"

"Damn, I almost forgot him," Jari said, turning around.

He scanned his companions' faces. "Now what? We can't take Arnak with us. I vote to leave him here in care of Kippa's healers. Let's vote. Who votes along with me?"

No hands went up.

"I'm the only sensible one?" he muttered, stroking his beard.

"No, you're the only one here saying we have to kill Boro. Don't be self-righteous, Jari," Sinda spat.

"Wait. You were all for killing Boro. Now you change your minds?" Jari asked, incredulously.

"My companion's worth more than revenge or coin," she hissed, sliding her hand to her knife handle.

"Easy, Sinda. We're all friends here," Betha said, sliding near Jari. "Let's vote, and then we'll continue our journey."

Sinda's lip twitched. "You know where I stand, just like everyone else." She turned. "Only our illustrious leader doesn't get it."

"C'mon, this isn't my fault," Jari said.

"Actually, Brother, this *was* your call. We have followed you without question. But asking us to leave our friend to collect a bounty is insane. And what's worse, you ask us to leave him in an unknown city with a merc commander whose only interest is in fucking me. I vote to take Arnak with us," Betha said.

"If we take him with us, infection will set in and kill him. I would prefer not to take such a risk," Jari said, widening his arms. "But if all of you vote to move out with him, then we shall. Anyone with me to leave Arnak behind for his own safety?"

Again, no one's hands were raised.

Unbelievable. This is going to be a huge mistake.

"Master Dwarf." Sithril stood. "I will do my best to help keep him alive. He allowed me to survive, so I will help him."

"That's okay, Sithril. You told me where Boro is. That's all I needed," Jari said with a wave of his hand.

Sithril walked over by the bed, his eyes never leaving Sinda's weapons. She tensed and rested her hand on her knife handle. "Watch your step, Elf," Sinda spat.

"Master Dwarf, you killed my merc company, and I am now currently without pay. I'll fight with you." All eyes turned in his direction. Sithril laughed. "Come now, I care not who I kill, just how much their scalp is worth. I'm a merc, no different than you. You need an extra sword. I need a bounty."

Jari blew a raspberry and rubbed his temples. "I'm okay with that if the others are. While everyone discusses it, I'm going to give this trinket to Kippa, and we can go collect on Boro. We leave first thing in the morning," Jari said, storming from the room.

Walking along the cobblestone street, he peered down the alleyways he passed. There were always pickpockets loose, and if he lost the trinket, he would lose his army. He passed a stall selling armor. A thick white gambeson with wooden toggles lay in the center of the table. An old woman with arthritic fingers sat behind the stall knitting another.

Ah, just what I was looking for.

"How much for the white one?" he asked, picking it up to examine it.

"Forty coins," she said, her voice shrill.

Jari rubbed the inside of his ear. "Sorry, I thought you said forty. I was thinking of twenty."

A sharp cackle met his reply. "Protection like this will cost you no less than thirty-five."

"Meet you at thirty. No other buyers lining up."

"There's magic-infused stitching in there."

"Magic? No such thing as magic, Crone," Jari scoffed. "Sell that to a halfwit, not a real merc."

"Oh, but there *is* magic." She cackled again. "It is the

lifeblood of Labrys."

He rolled his eyes. "Thirty is the final offer."

"I'll take it. Looks like you're going to need my special shirt," she said, folding it.

Jari nodded and scanned the other items. He picked up a bone-handle comb, some soap, and handed her the coins. "I'll take these too. Where is the nearest bathhouse?"

The crone pointed across the street. "Master Dwarf," she said, "when the sun sets in one week's time, you'll be grateful you bought that from me."

Jari chuckled. "It's a padded shirt, Crone. Nothing more."

She cackled and returned to her knitting.

After bathing and combing his beard, he felt like a new dwarf. The gambeson covered him well, and when he slung his Tok mail over it, it seemed lighter. The last rays of light began to dip behind the buildings. He hurried up the incline and approached Kippa's courtyard.

With a quick nod to the guards, he strolled through the gate and watched three dwarves sparring with a large orc nearly twice the standard size. The dwarves worked well with one another, giving the orc a hard time. Two gave diversions as the other one slammed his wooden ax into his kneecaps.

Jari smiled and walked into the dark, smoky room that was Kippa's bar. Nothing had changed the previous day except that it was much more crowded. He shoved and elbowed his way through the throng of mercs to stand in front of Kippa's table. The Loxodon glanced up, monocle over one eye. She sniffed him with her trunk.

"Where's the Taur?"

"Busy. Preparing my team for the journey," Jari said curtly. "Got your trinket."

She removed the monocle and set it down, her full gaze now on him. Jari opened his palm and tossed it to her. She caught it with her trunk and stared at it for a long while. Then she dropped it into her palm, slid the lens over her eye, and turned it several times.

"So, Metalbraid didn't fight you for it?"

"No, we agreed to kill something under the mountain that was stealing his ore. Lost a few of my orcs, and my healer was nearly killed, but here is what you requested."

Kippa handed the trinket to the merc behind her. "Ah, the joys of being a merc," she said. "Now, down to business."

"Quick question, if you don't mind," Jari said.

Kippa waved a hand dismissively. "What?"

"Metalbraid said he won that fair and square." Kippa leaned forward. Jari cleared his throat. "Any truth to that?"

Her eyes narrowed, the black irises pulsating. "None of your business, Dwarf," she growled, sliding her hand to her large three-sided ax.

"You may be right, Kippa, but if my healer dies, I want to know it was more than deception from you that brought us there in our desperation for an army."

"Life is risk, Dwarf."

"Yes," he smiled. "Yes, it is. Did Metalbraid win it? It's a simple question."

Kippa placed her palms on the table and leaned in nose to nose. "You don't ask questions in this tavern. *I* do."

Before Jari could react, Kippa snatched him up by the front of his gambeson and lifted him six feet in the air with her trunk. "Maybe I should just break your neck and tell your companions you fell when they come looking for you. What say you?"

"I'd let him go, Kippa," Betha said from behind.

Kippa dropped him with a thud. "Taur, come sit with me," she said, sliding a chair back with her trunk, a coy smile on her face.

"Think I'll stand. Thanks, though." Betha helped Jari to his feet. "You all right?" she hissed.

Jari gave a quick nod.

"Take a seat," Betha told Jari, then crossed her arms over her chest. "Enough with the pleasantries, eh, Kippa? We need five hundred mercs, and we need them now." She cut her eyes at Jari. "We've already told you what we can pay you upon completion. Do you agree to those terms?"

Kippa tapped her fingers in front of her mouth. "You did bring my treasure back, and for that, I'm grateful. But without cash up front, my mercs in town won't go."

"Even if you give them your word of confirmed payment?" Betha asked.

Kippa stared at her shrewdly. "You trying to con me, Taur?"

"Nope, just want to collect on a bounty and take a real long vacation."

A few more seconds of silence.

"If you go, I can't bed you, so I'll lead the mercs to the battlefield. And if the opportunity arrives, I'll take my chances," Kippa said, standing with a huge smile.

"You will never bed me, Loxodon. I promise that'll never happen."

"Never say never, Taur," Kippa said.

Jari sat in the windowsill later that night while the others slept. What kept him awake was the information Metalbraid gave him about Mori. *No one likes a liar or a thief.*

He glanced at the dwarf pressed up against the wall, head tilted to the side. Mori snored peacefully, his beard billowing every time he exhaled.

Jari scanned the faces of his group. Kala stared back, the embers in his pipe red. He stood and walked over to Jari. "What ails you, Old Friend?" Kala asked. "Is it the toe pain like I have?"

Jari chuckled. "No, not toe pain. Trusting a companion."

Kala raised an eyebrow. "Mori, right?"

Jari sat stone-faced.

Kala elbowed him with a smile. "C'mon, Jari. We freed him under weird circumstances at best. What do you wonder about my kin?"

"What if I told you I've been told that he's a liar and a thief?"

Kala raised an eyebrow again and then puffed on his pipe. "I'd say you had my attention."

"Metalbraid told me he was Mori's brother and that they planned the ambush of their father, and then gave up the other Death Hammers themselves."

Kala sat on a table beside the window for a few long moments, his gaze on the smoke wafting up into the air. "So, why would that matter to us? He's not a Loner, only a merc."

"Don't know if I want my back watched by a traitor if that's what he is," Jari hissed. "I was thinking about proposing him for membership before we attempt to find Boro."

"Just ask him, Jari. If the Dwarven Lords shine down on you, you'll have your answer. The Lords never lie." He stretched with a deep groan. "I'm getting too old for this shit." He headed back to his spot and lay down.

"Kala?" Jari hissed.

Kala turned.

"What was the vote for Sithril?"

Kala shook his head with a sigh. "If you vote yes and Betha votes no, he still travels with us. So the decision has been made already." He turned back around and muttered, "What is the world coming too when you have to fight by an elf? Not just any elf—a Frost Cave. Dirty bastards, the lot of them," he spat. "Ack."

Jari smiled and continued staring out the window until his chin rested on his chest.

The next morning, he awoke and rubbed the back of his hand across his eye. He blinked a few times and took a long pull from his flask of gut-rot. The rest of his party was up for the most part. Sinda sat at Arnak's side, her hand resting on his. Jari watched her lips moving in a silent prayer to the Dwarven Lords. She glared at him as he walked by, but he smiled and just kept walking.

My idea is right; just wait and see.

Betha was shouldering her pack as he approached. "So, what's the plan?" she grunted.

"Wish I knew. Kippa hates dwarves and wants to bed you. Maybe you should think of a plan," Jari said, shouldering his pack.

Betha nodded. "Let's go to the compound and see what we need to do. Then we'll take it from there."

Anak'anor was busy every minute of every day, its vendors shouting above one another before the sun rose over the horizon. The Loners mounted and followed Jari and Betha to Kippa's. The sun peeked over the sharpened wooden stakes as they crested the hill. The inside was as busy as the streets . . . Mercs of all different races hustled, gathering gear and weapons.

Jari and Betha made eye contact and motioned for the others to be at the ready before walking in. Kippa stood in the center, bellowing orders. She wore a Tok plate cuirass with her trunk sheathed in Tok as well. Betha and Jari stood a few feet away until she noticed them. She trumpeted and waved them over. Her guards moved aside as Betha approached.

"Taur, have you come by to give me a taste?" Kippa asked, licking her lips with a raised eyebrow.

"We're here to find out how many warriors you can bring," Jari said, interrupting her.

She pushed her fingers together. "Betha, I hate dwarves. Send this sawed-off stump away. I only talk to you."

Betha rolled her eyes. "How many warriors can you bring, Kippa?"

"Couple'a hundred. They're still filtering in. I sent the word out last night."

"Like me or not, Loxodon, the deal was for five hundred," Jari said, attempting to push past Betha.

Kippa's ears flapped in the breeze, and her mouth twitched. "Betha, put a muzzle on your pet, or I will," she sneered.

"Muzzle, yo—"

Kippa hefted her ax. "Something you want to say, Dwarf?" she roared, causing her mercs to stop and watch.

Betha kept her hand over Jari's mouth and motioned for Kala. "I'll handle this, Jari. Leave before you screw the whole thing up," she hissed.

Kala leaned into his ear. "She's right, Brother Jari; we should go." Kippa took a step closer. "And I mean right *now*," Kala finished.

Jari left Betha to negotiate and walked over to the others. "What's the score, Jari?" Gnok asked, watching a pair of minotaurs grapple. "These bastards are the real deal."

Jari chuckled. "Seems Kippa could only call a few hundred warriors to our cause, which me—"

"Means we're screwed," Kala said, finishing his sentence.

Jari smirked. "Not in so many words, Kala. But, yes, it is less than the number I expected to have."

"And they're fighting for money we know is not in the amount you quoted, right?" Gnok asked over his shoulder without turning.

Jari paused. "That is correct."

Gnok spat and continued watching the minotaurs. "I'm in to kill him. What are you going to do when she finds out we don't have the money promised?"

"I'll . . . I'll think of something."

Gnok turned. "You better, Cousin, or I'll have Zog stick his two-foot cock up your ass."

Zog winked and blew him a kiss.

Chapter 32

Jari sat on a rock near the entrance of the compound, picking his teeth. He watched Gnok point at a merc sparing nearby and then to a practice ring. The gnome followed and yanked his blades from his belt. Gnok smiled and flipped his ax in the air and caught it by the shaft. He strode forward and swung at the gnome who shifted to the side and, with a flick of his wrist, caught Gnok in the eyes with sand.

Jari heard him curse as he wiped his eyes and swung his weapon. The gnome ducked under the wild blows and slammed his blunted knives into Gnok's chest and thighs. The groans and curses continued, louder than before.

After several more blows, a wheezing Gnok hit his knees. The merc punched him across the face with his fist around the pommel of his weapon. In the blink of an eye, Gnok was dazed and on his back. Jari and the others roared with laughter. The gnome walked into the tavern, and the others moved to pick up Gnok. Dusting him off, Jari thrust his ax into his hands.

"You're getting slow, Cousin. A gnome beat you." He roared with laughter. "A bloody gnome."

Gnok cleared his nostrils. "Piss off, Jari."

Betha approached from behind them. "What's the word, Betha?" Jari asked.

"Kippa's got as much sense as a two-headed Bohal. She says we get three hundred mercs for half a mil, which we don't have. If Boro doesn't have it, we're dead anyway, right?"

"Betha, I told—"

"You'll figure it out." She thrust an empty flask into his chest. "Get me something stronger than gut-rot. We leave in a few hours."

She eyed Gnok. "Who tore up your ass?"

Gnok spat and walked away. Betha roared with laughter. "Cat got your tongue, eh, Gnok?"

Jari handed the canteen to Kala. "Please fill this up with the rest."

Kala muttered something under his breath and shouldered Grumps aside, who bleated at him. Betha wiped her brow and checked her blades. An awkward silence filled the air around them, neither wanting to confront the situation in front of them that was spiraling out of control. The choices weren't favorable either way. Jari was the first to speak.

"So, what do you think?"

Betha shrugged. "I think if you keep putting us in unwinnable situations, I'll cast my vote to elect a new leader."

"And who would that be?" Jari spat. "And who said I was planning to get us in a pickle again?"

She rolled her eyes. "I'd vote for Kala. And that's because you repeatedly keep screwing this up," she said as Kala inched his way over with eight canteens and several jugs.

"No way, Taur. I'll never vote a dwarf out of leadership. Now, let's stop bickering like little ones and come up with a plan," Kala said.

Begrudgingly, Betha leaned against the boulder Jari was atop of and cut into a red apple. "Our options are limited. The only idea I think would work is that the seven of us sneak behind enemy lines when the battle between Kippa and Boro kicks off. When we reach the camp, we kill everyone left behind and secure the treasure," she said.

Kala pulled on his beard. "I'm in."

Jari glanced among the faces of his crew. Everyone assembled voted on the plan. A moment later, a loud whining horn blew three crisp notes. Kippa approached. "Taur, get your group together. We are moving out."

"Thought we had three hours," Betha protested.

"We did."

"What the hell happened?"

"You never want to get stuck by the Black Rock at nightfall. That's prime prisoner time."

Mori made eye contact with the others. "Then we best be going."

Sithril carried the back of Arnak's litter, his slender arms straining. Managing to navigate the tight stairwell, they finally eased him onto the street, then loaded him in the wagon. Sinda and Gnok rode up front. Mori shouldered his way past Sithril, who smiled as he passed.

"Elves can't be trusted," Mori said, mounting his Bohal next to Jari. "Can't be trusted."

"Thought you didn't ride Bohals," Jari said with a snicker.

"So, what direction does our army march, Sithril?" Jari asked with Kippa standing a few feet away, admiring Betha's form.

"Boro *should* be camped at the base of the Colorless Pinnacle by Frost Caves."

Kippa sniffed the elf with disdain and pushed him back a step. "I hate Frost Elves."

"As I hate armored Loxodons," Sithril said before walking away.

"You better have my coin, Dwarf," Kippa said, glaring at Jari.
Jari shrugged and urged Grumps forward. "Giddyap."

The army led by Kippa wound down the mountain from
Anak'anor. It stretched half a mile as it wound like a snake
through the wilderness. All matter of races were intermixed.
Dwarves walked with elves, minotaurs and centaurs moved in a
pack, and a few insects Jari couldn't readily identify chittered as
they clambered past. The Loners pulled off the road and watched
the procession march by, most paying them no attention.

"All we need is a troll, and we have the complete package,"
Kala joked.

At that moment, a massive grey troll with boils on its face and
upper chest stomped past them, his stone club dragging behind
him.

Jari smiled. "Full package it is, Brother. Full package it is."

If it was one thing about Labrian mercs Jari loved, it was their
ability to put aside their personal hatred for the ultimate
motivator—coin. And half a million coins would change a lot of
lives. It would retire most in the group. But as Jari rode alongside
the column, he knew there was no half million. The Loners rode
in silence for an hour as the sun roasted them as they passed the
shade just out of reach.

"Damn, it's hot," Gnok groaned.

Zog walked past them. "Zog no hot. You cry like little ork."

Everyone jeered Gnok as his face reddened.

They cleared the Black Rock and headed for The Expanse. An
hour later, the weather finally cooled as night approached. Kippa
trumpeted from the head of the column. The mercs came to a slow
grinding halt. "Make camp."

Fires were quickly built, and the smell of charred meat and
vegetables filtered through the night sky. The Loners found a nice,
secluded spot between a few boulders, out of the elements. Zog
and Kala drew the first watch. Jari and Betha made their way over

to Arnak while Sinda sat beside him, sharpening her knives. When Jari approached, she flipped one into her palm and flung it at his head. With a loud thud, it stuck in the post he was standing beside. He growled and stomped past it.

Arnak lay on his stomach, a large fur covering his shell. Sinda had rubbed water and mud along his limbs during the journey to keep his scales moist. She stared at Jari, her lip twitching and her palm tightening on a small knife attached to her thigh. "What do you want?" she hissed.

"How is he?"

Sinda placed her hand on his arm. "He shivers and waits for death."

"May I try to help?" Sithril asked, walking up behind Jari.

"He's fine," Sinda growled.

"Ah, I suppose he is. But if I could take a look, I could ascertain that for myself."

"Aser—what?" Jari asked.

"I see your vocabulary rivals your height." He patted Jari on the head, then leaped into the back of the wagon with catlike reflexes. He inched closer to Sinda. "May I?"

She sat still for a moment, then lamented, "If you save him, you can have my share of the loot."

Sithril smiled wide. "How kind of you to volunteer what has not yet been found. Even if you could, I wouldn't take it. I'm sworn to help those who are in need."

"I'll be damned, you're a healer," Jari said, trying to hide his shock.

Sithril prodded Arnak's wound as he hummed. He glanced at Jari's furrowed brow. "I know a few simple things; nothing like him, I'm afraid."

"Between you and Kala, he may have a chance," Jari said.

"Only the Frost Lords know his destiny. Before we go into battle, it may be a good idea to stop at my camp so we can help heal him."

"Go to Frost Elf camp? You must be insane," Gnok snorted, coming around one side of the wagon. "Cold day in The Expanse 'ore I let that happen."

Sithril gave a light chuckle. "Dwarf, I worry not about you. You can't even pee without dripping it on your trousers."

"Damn short peter," Gnok muttered, touching the wet spot.

Sithril fished around his pocket for something, then rubbed it between his fingers. He placed it behind Arnak's ear. The tortle let out a loud sigh, then began to snore. The elf gave an exaggerated bow, then leaped from the wagon. "I need a short bow and a longbow. I shall return."

"What did you do to Arnak?" Sinda demanded.

Keeping his stride, he said, "Sleep medicine. Elven secret."

Jari watched him as he walked away. *Great, a mysterious healer in our midst.*

With a loud groan, Jari sat down next to Sinda. "Look, I know you're mad as hell at me, and you have every right to be, but if Arn—"

"He won't die, and don't you curse him."

Jari held his hands up. "Look, I made a call. Time will tell whether that call was right or wrong."

"Same as the call with Toli," Sinda spat.

"This is going nowhere," Jari hissed.

"No one asked you to sit."

Jari stormed over to Grumps, mounted him, and rode out of the camp. Betha shouted to him, but he kept riding. He let Grumps take the lead. They rode along the upcoming path for several hundred yards. As Grumps slowed, Jari tugged on his beard.

I can't believe how ungrateful she is. I've done everything for her and the others. I should have just taken the elven bounties in Port Agu. It would have been less hassle.

Grumps left the path and cantered over to some thornbushes,

his favorite food. The leaves smelled like garbage, and they gave the Bohals gas, but if Grumps was happy, he was happy. The noonday sun beat down on him. His Tok mail felt like it was channeling all the heat on Labrys into his chest. He wiped his brow with a rag and took a deep breath.

I should be getting back.

He turned Grumps around. The Bohal bleated his disapproval and nipped at Jari's ankle in protest. "Oh, hush up, you pain in the ass. Those leaves aren't good for you anyway," he muttered, turning Grumps's reins to the right.

An arrow snapped by his face. He felt the heat from the feathers as they tickled his nose. A group of goblins ran out of the woods after him. With a bleat, Grumps turned to face his enemies. Jari slammed his visor down and leaned forward in the saddle. "For the Loners!" He dug his ankles into Grumps's flank. With no delay, they attacked as one. *Shitty goblins.*

As the goblins approached him, they fanned out. Jari rode straight up the middle and gored a small goblin. Grumps flipped him over Jari's head and turned for another pass.

The five goblins formed into a spear formation and charged. *What in the Dwarven Lords' name? Goblins don't organize.*

Jari stared at them as they charged. He freed his bolas, licked his thumb, and thrust it into the air. With a calculation, he made the necessary adjustments and let his bolas soar downrange. It took the two lead goblins down. The others strode over them. A black shaft flew in his direction. The arrow would have missed anyone near him due to distance. But he recklessly drove Grumps forward for a better chance with his bolas with only two left. As Jari searched his saddlebag for more bolas, a black arrow thudded into his right shoulder and threw him off. He landed with a thud. Grumps circled around and pawed the earth above Jari, who spat dirt from his mouth.

Grumps reared up, leaped over Jari, and slammed his hooves

into the closest goblin. The creature staggered back, its lungs caved in. With a quick turn, he bucked the other goblin with his back legs, crushing its skull. With a bleat, he stood over Jari protectively.

I don't feel so good. He took a deep breath and glanced at his shoulder. The black arrow shaft had snapped off, and only the head remained. *How did it make it through my Tok mail?* A sharp, penetrating pain shot through his shoulder, down his arm, and into his fingertips. He pressed two thick fingers against the wound and brought them back. Black specks were mixed in with his blood. He tasted a tiny amount of blood and spat it out.

Poison.

With an audible groan, he lay back . . . then blackness enveloped him.

Jari woke on his back, pressed up against a large boulder, a small fire nearby, warming his side. He groaned and rubbed his shoulder, the pain radiating down his back. Blinking a few times, he ran his stubby fingers across his eye, attempting to clear the crusts of sleep. The sky was pitch black, with only one star visible. His weapons lay on the other side of the fire, and his armor draped over a large boulder.

He cleared his throat, coughed, then spat. "Anyone here?" he rasped.

"Yes, we are always here," Sithril's voice answered.

Jari chuckled and lay back. "Ah, the mysterious elven healer." Sithril came into his view. "Why am I lying on my back?"

"Healing."

"From what?" Jari asked.

Sithril shook his head with a smirk. "Poison, Master Dwarf."

Jari nodded. "Tell me something I don't know, Sithril."

"That you're a sawed-off dwarf and ugly as they come," he said, sniffing a concoction in a vial. "Here, drink this."

Jari eyed it warily. "Nope, I'm good."

Sithril smiled wide. "I won't ask you again. I'll just pour it down your throat."

Jari gave a deep laugh. "Like to see—"

Before he could defend himself, Sithril held Jari's head by his ponytail, slammed his foot on his hand, and poured the mixture down his throat. Jari gagged, spat, and cursed. "You-you damn Frost Elf." He rubbed the back of his hand across his mouth. "What did you give me?"

"Antivenom, Master Dwarf. An arrow penetrated your Tok mail and gambeson. If it weren't for the gambeson sucking up most of it, you'd already be dead. The potion will take effect soon." He smiled. "I was quite shocked that a goblin arrow could break through Tok mail. When I found you, I extracted the arrowhead and analyzed it."

Jari winced. *No such thing as magic . . . guess not.*

"What did you find?" Jari asked, sitting up.

Sithril frowned. "It's no goblin weapon, mind you. Someone or something gave them the arrows and the poison with which to kill you. I watched the skirmish from a tree above you. Just like you, I've never seen a group of goblins attack with any sort of proficiency."

"So, you're the one who saved me?" Jari asked.

"Yes, but it was too late to make it back to camp. We will hole up in this enclave, then leave in the morning."

Great. I'm stuck in the wilderness with a damned Frost Elf with poison coursing through my body.

Jari and Sithril made eye contact.

Master Dwarf, please don't refer to me as a damned Frost Elf. It's insulting. My name is Sithril Frostsong. And, no, you don't have poison coursing through your veins. Don't be so dramatic.

Jari sat upright with a gasp and freed his dagger. He pointed it at Sithril. "Why were you in my head?"

Sithril shrugged, a smile tugging the corner of his mouth. "I haven't the foggiest idea what you're talking about. Are you running a fever?"

"No, I'm not running a fever," he spat. "You said your name in my head. That's how I know."

Sithril smiled again, and this time, his ivory teeth appeared. "Master Dwarf, if I did what you said I did, why am I staring at you without any clue of what you are referring to?"

Jari growled and reached for his ax. "Be in my skull again, and I'll kill you."

Sithril gave a Cheshire grin and leaned back against the rocks. "I'd like to see you try. Now, let me sleep."

Chapter 33

Jari groaned and rubbed his aching arms. The sun peeked over the horizon in front of him. *Am I alive?* The pain shot through his arm and down his fingertips. *Ugh, yup. Still breathing.*

He shed the blanket covering him, attempting to stand. With a loud grunt, he made it to one knee. After finally making it to his feet, he fell forward onto his face. He slammed his meaty fist into the ground and growled. Sithril picked him up from behind like a feather.

"Master Dwarf, please try not to ruin my meditations in the morning. They are necessary for me to attain enlightenment."

"Enligh—"

"It's something akin to peace, Master Dwarf. Don't try to understand with your limited knowledge. You'll only hurt your head."

"Ack, always the smart-ass, aren't you?"

Sithril gave a mock bow. "Ever at your service, m'lord."

Jari scoffed and freed his canteen. He took three loud gulps and belched. After a moment, he extended the canteen. "Want a taste?"

Sithril shook his head and nodded to a clay pot dangling over the fire. "No, thank you. My tea is ready." He made his way to the fire, lifted the top off the metal hook it hung from, and then poured it into his canteen.

Jari sniffed the air and gagged. "What is that smell?"

"Igaroot."

"You drink that?"

Sithril pursed his lips and blew a frosty mist on the steaming froth, then took a sip with relish. "That, I do, Master Dwarf. That, I do."

"I heard Igaroot helps those with child. Are you with child, Sithril?"

Sithril chuckled and packed his sack. Mounting his horse, he gave Jari a sad smile. "I'm not a female of my species, Master Dwarf. But, yes, once long ago, I did."

He turned and rode into the underbrush. Jari shook his head, slid on his mail, and mounted Grumps. He tapped his flanks and followed Sithril's path cut through the shrubbery. Grumps bleated several times in protest as he struggled to keep up with Sithril's mount. Jari urged him harder, lowering himself onto Grumps's neck to ease the wind resistance. The naked limbs of the trees slapped his bushy cheeks as they rode.

A few birds chirped above them, but nothing else was noticeable. Sithril's mount leaped over a hidden ditch, through the last of the tall grass, and into the clearing. Grumps slowed, found a large log, and scampered across it.

Jari picked a reed from his bright red beard and tossed it over his shoulder. He glanced up at Sithril. "You seem to know this ground pretty well."

Sithril sighed and took a deep breath. "Suppose I should. We are close to the Frost Caves."

Jari's spine stiffened, and his palm instinctively slid to his ax handle. Sithril clicked his tongue. "As long as you're with me, Master Dwarf, no harm will befall you."

Jari gulped as three distinct silhouettes appeared on the cliffs above them. "And them?" he asked.

Sithril glanced in the direction Jari pointed. "Pray I never leave your side."

"How far away is Kippa's camp?" Jari asked.

Sithril gave a head nod to the east and urged his mount forward. The pair traveled through the lush green grass, the Frost Caves off to their right a few miles away. The mountains cast a large shadow over the valley as they neared the border. Kagos could be seen atop the mountain in their clans, huddled in a circle. Sithril didn't even acknowledge them. He just kept a straight line for Kippa's. The familiar smell of roasted meat and sewage wafted into Jari's nostrils.

Sithril reined his horse in as they approached a pair of guards at their camp, lying against large boulders. The orc and the gnome held up their hands as they approached. "Help you with something?" asked the gnome in a shrill voice.

"I'm Jari Rockjaw, and I ride with the Loners. Let us through."

The gnome glanced at the orc. "Jari, who?"

The orc sneered. "Don't know Jari."

Sithril closed his eyes, his lips moving quickly.

"'Course you do, Mush, it's Jari Rockjaw. The one with half a million coins," the gnome exclaimed.

"Move aside, Little One," Jari said, urging Grumps past.

Sithril followed behind him. He placed his index finger and his thumb around his nose and blew hard. Then he groaned as he cleared his ears. His teeth chattered, and he spat. "I hate when I have to do that."

"What was that?" Jari asked.

Sithril ignored him.

"Oi, I'm talking to you."

Sithril rode straight ahead, leaving Jari by himself in the middle of the road. *Elves are the damndest creatures.* "Giddyap, Grumps. Find Betha."

We're not as mysterious as you may think.

Jari exhaled. "Stay out of my damned head."

Grumps plodded down the dirt road and followed his nose. He wound through several minicamps where mercs were gambling and drinking. Jari watched the games for a few minutes, then let Grumps lead him on. After passing another few groups, he stamped into the area Betha and the others had created. Jari dismounted and walked over to the fire.

"Where did you spend the night?" Betha asked with a snort.

"In the woods. Wanted to clear my head. How's Arnak?"

"The same," Betha said.

"So, what's our next play?" Jari asked.

No one spoke.

"Oi, did you not hear me?"

Kala blew a smoke ring. "Kippa isn't going any further."

Jari glanced across the fire at him. "Say what?"

"She won't cross over the Frost Caves until they send an emissary letting us know we have permission to cross. She said she doesn't want bad blood," Kala said with a grunt.

"Are you kidding me?" Jari roared.

"Zog deal with."

"Why does that not put my mind at ease, Zog?" Jari spat.

"Zog be back shortly." He stood and walked toward Kippa's tent.

Twenty minutes later, Kala lay against a rock, having received no word, his pipe hanging loosely from his lips. Gnok and Sinda sat off to the side with Arnak. Betha sharpened her blades a few feet away, and Mori sat eating an apple behind him.

"What's gotten into everyone?" Jari asked.

"Ready for action. I'm not one for sitting around waiting on the permission of elves," Mori mumbled as he cut another piece of apple.

Betha growled in agreement.

"I can't make her move. Zog will—"

A loud trumpeting interrupted Jari.

"What in the devil was that?" Jari hissed, freeing his ax.

Kala chuckled. "I think I know."

Jari cut his eyes at him. Kala kept chuckling. "Wait for it."

A few moments later, Zog limped back up the road. He reached the group and wiped the back of his hand across his lips. He sighed and tossed his weapon to Jari and gave a deep groan.

"What in the hell was that about?" Jari demanded.

"Zog give two feet. Clean weapon, leader," he said, rubbing his crotch. "Horny elephant now not horny. Zog need nap."

The others exploded into laughter.

Betha grinned, her septum ring rattling. "Well, now, she may leave me alone."

What in the Dwarven Lords is going on here?

Zog climbed into a nearby wagon and was snoring in a few moments. Sithril approached and knelt by Arnak.

"This is why I left," he said, handing Sinda a handful of flowers. "I rode into my kins' land to find the cure for your healer and to locate Boro."

Jari and the others crowded around him. "What you got there, Elf?"

"Watch and see," Sithril said, crushing the flowers. "You may want to step back."

"Not bloody likely," Sinda hissed, keeping a close eye on him.

A red hue lightly pulsated around Arnak, then grew brighter. The crushed flowers began to levitate. Sithril closed his eyes and started humming. He flicked his fingers in multiple directions, and the flowers danced with them. Right, left, up, and down. He continued his incantation for a few more seconds, then clapped his hands together, knocking everyone back as the red light exploded, and the flowers settled onto Arnak's shell.

The red particles sought the crack. Settling, they intertwined with one another, slowly at first, then gradually picking up speed. Sithril's eyes opened wide, and he swung his arms wide. The mesh grew wider.

"*K'atha'ra*," he shouted and slammed his palm on Arnak's shell.

The spell sank the red mass into his carapace. It was slow. Everyone held their breath. The flowers sealed, and all that remained was a half-inch scar that ran from tailbone to neck. Sithril gave a weak smile and fell back on his rear. The others stared at him in wonder. No one spoke for a long while.

Arnak gasped and then opened his eyes.

Sinda stepped around Arnak and hugged Sithril around the neck. "How in the Dwarven Lords did you manage that?"

"All in a day's work, Mistress Dwarf. All in day's work."

Jari sat next to him, speechless. "How, I mean, what, I mean how?"

Sithril smiled and lay back. "I'll take a little rest now. All your questions will be answered in a short time, my friend. Wake me when we are ready to leave."

Kala walked over to him and lay a blanket over him. Jari raised his eyebrow. "What? He saved one of us, so I gave him the benefit of the doubt," Kala said after lighting his pipe.

Jari snickered. "Changing every day, aren't you, Old Dwarf?"

"Suck it," Kala muttered over his shoulder, returning to his rock.

Sinda moved over to Jari. "I just wanted to say I understand why you made your decision. And I'm grateful you voted to bring Sithril along."

Jari grinned. "My pleasure." Sinda turned around.

"What was your vote, by the way?" Jari asked.

She stopped and glanced at Arnak. "What do you think?"

"I think you voted yes."

Sinda shrugged. "It's not important now. Excuse me. I will

return to watching Arnak."

Now we're getting back in the rhythm.

An hour later, Kippa sent a runner to Jari and his crew. The gnome wandered among them, then headed over to Jari. "Kippa wants to see you and the Loners in her tent," he squeaked.

"Tell her we will be by shortly."

The gnome headed back to Kippa.

"Loners, on me," Jari said.

The rest of the group surrounded him. Zog blinked the sleep from his eyes. Sithril swayed on his feet. Kala gripped his arm and held him up. Arnak dragged his club behind him and joined the rest of them.

"Welcome back, friend," Jari said, nudging Arnak's arm.

"Thank you. Who saved me?" he grumbled.

"The elf did," Gnok said.

"That a fact? You don't look like much," Arnak said, eyeing Sithril.

Sithril frowned. "Should have seen me this morning."

"All right, everyone, listen up. We've been called to Kippa's tent. Let's go see what this Loxodon wants. Mount up."

The group readied and followed Jari down the dirt path toward Kippa's. The mercs surrounding her area parted like the Red Sea, some nodding at Zog with a wide grin. Sinda drove the wagon behind them, jostling over the rocks in the road. Arnak kept a firm grip on the railing, occasionally swaying as they traversed the bumps. Sithril kept a steady hand on his shoulder, paying close attention to the unwashed bodies around them.

Jari held his fist in the air, and everyone stopped. Kippa stepped out of her tent with an immense grin, the likes of which made Jari cringe. She stuck her trunk in the air and sniffed loudly.

"Back for another round, Orc?"

"No, Zog crotch hurt. You big."

Kippa feigned offense. "Pity. Could use that two feet again. But all's fair in love and war." Her eyes found Jari. "So, Short-stuff, you want to take Boro head-on, eh?"

Jari gave a curt nod. "'Course, I do. But we are outnumbered two to one. He has Kagos, and we have none."

Kippa snorted. "Odds are odds, Short-stuff. I'm not gambling. If this venture weren't possible, I would have stayed in Anak'anor."

"The payday was too great for you to stay, I get it, but we don't stand a chance against a larger force. My thought is for my Loners to infiltrate their camp while you and yours distract them. We only need an hour. If you can keep them busy, we could steal the gold and bring it back to you."

Kippa tapped her chin for a long moment, then spoke. "You have a point, Loner. But what's to stop you from running once we engage Boro? I'll hunt you across Labrys, then cut you into a million pieces if you run, you know that?" She yawned. "What insurance do I have?"

"I ride with you," Zog said from behind.

Jari made to object, but Zog's glare steadied him.

Kippa grinned and rubbed her palms together. "Oh, *really*?"

"You hear Zog. I go. But when Loners go, Zog go too."

"Interesting. Will you share my tent?"

Zog paused. "If that what take."

Kippa smiled. "And to think I wasted time with the Taur." Her trunk slid toward Zog and wrapped around his broad shoulders. "So, lover, I'll let you say goodbye, and I'll meet you at the head of the column."

Chapter 34

The Loners commandeered a wagon and set about breaking camp. Betha wandered over to Zog with a frown. She stopped a few feet away.

"Why, Zog?"

Zog shrugged. "She horny, no help us." He grabbed his crotch. "But this help. Zog use it."

Betha gave a wide smile. "Watch your back in that battle, Orc. As soon as we have the coins and Boro's head, I'll find you on the field, and we'll withdraw."

Zog gave a grim nod and what appeared to be a smile. "If Zog no—"

"I'll take care of the orks with Chief Muk," she said, knowing where he was going.

Zog smiled. "We go."

And so it begins, Jari thought, mounting Grumps.

The army moved out at a snail's pace. As they entered Frost Cave lands, Sithril rode outside the column, closest to the caves. He raised his bow high in the air, and a small army rode out toward them. Sithril gave Jari a nod and rode toward the elves.

Kippa glanced at Jari, who shrugged. "Face the caves," she roared.

As one, every merc in the column faced right and took defensive positions. Jari waved his hand, and the Loners followed behind him. "Wedge formation," he said, reining in.

"What in the Dwarven Lords' name?" Sinda muttered.

Sithril rode at the head of the column and came up out of arrow range. He waved a white flag high in the air atop his bow and rode to the Loners with an elf the size of an orc in tow.

"What in the hells is going on, Sithril?" Jari demanded.

"Boro has half a million coins, correct?" he asked.

Jari stood stone-faced.

"I overheard you talking." He smiled wide. "These mercs would like a piece of the action."

"You gave me no warning," Jari hissed.

The large elf with Sithril asked, "Dwarf, you are going to battle?"

Jari bristled. "He doesn—"

"As I said, Kethil, we will pay you once the battle is over," Sithril said, winking at Jari.

"Good. I have a hundred mercs at the ready," Kethil said.

Without saying anything else, Kethil cut the white rag on Sithril's bow and tied it to his own. He pointed at Kippa. He rode past Jari on a mount that Jari had never seen before. It had the look of a horse, but with larger hooves and a lion's head.

After all the riders had ridden by, Jari turned to Sithril. "Explain."

"Had I told you my plan, Master Dwarf, you would never have agreed," Sithril said with a shrug.

"There's no loot there to my knowledge," Jari said.

"Where there is a will, there is a way," he said, turning his mount around before riding back to the army.

Jari tapped Grumps's flanks and rode after him. Sithril

returned to his place in line, and the column moved out. Kethil rode next to Kippa for a moment, then turned around with his group and rode to the front of the line.

After several hours of travel, the large army came to within a mile of the Colorless Pinnacle by the Frost Caves, where Boro's army was entrenched on the high ground. Jari and the others had ridden to the head of the column during the journey, and with Kippa standing next to him, he pulled his spyglass to his eye.

Several flags fluttered in the breeze, and four Kagos stood in a gap between the mountain pass. "Just great—Kagos," Jari muttered.

Kippa grinned. "Do you know how much a Kago's head is worth in An'kanor?"

Jari shook his head.

"Five thousand gold with the eyes attached," she said, tapping her three-sided ax. "That's twenty thousand sitting in the valley of those mountains."

"You ready to die for it, Loxodon?" Jari asked.

Kippa blew notes from her trunk to signal the column to move forward. "Take the elves. Sneak behind them when my group engages, kill Boro, and when you're finished, hit them from the back. We'll bottleneck them in the pass."

Jari took a sharp breath and glanced at the Loners, each head nodding in response. "Fine. We'll see you—"

Kippa strode forward without letting him finish and said over her shoulder. "Fuck me over on the field, and I'll kill your orc in payment, then the rest of you when I track you down."

Jari sat in the saddle and rolled his eye as the column moved out. Zog gave a wave and followed behind Kippa, rubbing his ax head. "Zog see you later."

The column passed them, and Jari rode to the east of the mountain range with the others. Sithril and Kethil caught up to him, their silver hair fluttering in the breeze.

Remember, Master Dwarf, I am with you until the end. Kethil will take us to where Boro's camp is, and then it's up to us to finish the game. Hope you brought a large enough bag for all the treasure and trophies coming.

Jari spat in response. "Stay . . . out . . . of . . . my—"

"*Head, Master Dwarf. It saves time. If you lose me in the chaos, just close your eyes and mutter my name, and I will find you.*"

Without waiting for an acknowledgment, Sithril and Kethil raised their bows high in the air, and the Frost Caves elves surrounded them in a diamond formation. Jari noticed that the short bows were used up front, and the longbows were in the back.

"Oh, goody," Jari muttered as Grumps rode across the plains.

Chapter 35

The wind blew through Jari's beard, tossing it over his shoulder. The sounds of battle had begun on the other side of the mountain. Sithril sent thirty elves to provide bow support for their flank when they finally stopped to rest their mounts.

"Loners, on me," Jari barked.

Everyone rode to him and formed a semicircle. The Bohals' breath could be seen in the cold air. As they rode across the plains, the weather grew increasingly colder. The air chilled everyone's bones as they sat saddled.

Jari rubbed his hands together and lit his pipe, savoring the smoke rolling into his lungs. Grumps bleat as they stood huddled together. Jari exhaled loudly with a sigh and touched his mount's horns.

"All right, any questions before we begin?" he asked.

Kala spat. "Ack, let's go kill this bastard and go drink."

Gnok giggled. "Ah, remember the kill—"

"Belongs to me," Sinda said, sharpening her knives.

Arnak swung his arms wide and stretched with his club behind his back. "Let's do this," he grumbled in his low baritone voice.

Kala adjusted himself in the saddle. "Let's get this over with. My ass is starting to chafe from this saddle."

Mori blew his nose without a handkerchief, spat, then adjusted his helmet. "Ready when you are."

Lastly, Betha and Jari made eye contact. "For Toli," she said. *For Toli.*

Sithril rode up with Kethil. "We are with you, Master Dwarf. Follow us up on the path. We will engage his entourage, and the rest of you can find Boro and kill him. Kethil says his headquarters are in a cave in the far back. If Kippa and her army are defeated, we will have no choice but to escape to high ground in the Spires."

"Loners," Jari roared, slamming his visor down, "form a wedge."

Kippa blew a long note from her trunk and then patted Zog on the shoulder with it. "Have that two-footer ready for me, Orc. I will ride you after this battle until the sun sets."

Zog groaned and rubbed his still-sore crotch. "Lucky Zog. Loxodon horny again."

Kippa raised her humongous three-sided ax in the air and then trumpeted. Boro's forces were stacked in rows behind the Kagos in the pass. Her mercs cheered as she strode forward.

"To riches and glory," Kippa roared. "Double time to the pass!"

The army lurched forward, the mercs with her used to unorganized combat. They made it fifty yards before arrows began to rain down upon them. One bounced off Kippa's tough hide, and she didn't pay it a single glance. The Kagos stepped forward and swung their clubs.

Zog slammed his club against his chest and charged with the rest of the army. After another few yards, Zog heard the mercs scream as they were hit by hundreds of arrows raining down.

He ducked one, then two, and then another. Kippa disappeared with her trolls and other Loxodons as they neared the Kagos. A troll appeared in front of him with the Kagos and swung its club. Zog slipped by and smacked it across the knees, crippling it.

Next to him, a Red Widow placed both pinchers on opposite sides of the troll's neck and bit in, sawing through gristle and fat. The troll's head popped off and rolled away. The widow chittered and tossed it in a bag and continued.

Three Frost Cave elves appeared in front of Zog. A gnome climbed up his back before he could blink, leaped from his shoulders, and drove two of his daggers into the elves' eyes. Zog swung his club, caving in the other one's head. The gnome smiled at him and continued up the incline.

"Gnome ruin eyes," Zog huffed as he picked one out of a head and chewed on it. He watched the Loxodons and trolls battle the Kagos, several bodies of their fellow mercs piled up at their feet. Kippa swung her mighty ax, felling a Kago in three strokes.

He watched as she engaged the last one, arrows peppering her torso and bouncing off. She bellowed as the Kago cleaved one of her wrists off, sending her ax flying. She grabbed the nub and fell back, her trunk waving in the air.

Zog sprinted to her and shouted, "Loners!"

He slammed his thick skull into the Kago's stomach, doubling it over. As it bent down, Zog swung his club up, connected with its chin, and snapped its neck. As it fell, a group of Red Widows clambered over the body and made their way toward the helpless Kippa.

Zog yanked a pair of bolas from his belt and hurtled them at the attackers. One went down, and the others turned in his direction.

He roared. "Come to Mighty Zog!"

The widows attacked, pinchers snipping pieces of his flesh. Outnumbered with numerous wounds, he fell to one knee. A pincher descended from above to finish the job, but suddenly, the limb snapped off, giving him time to retreat.

Kippa's ax lay by his feet. He snatched it off the ground and swung it with his club in the opposite hand, creating a whirlwind of death. After the widows were killed, he rushed to Kippa's side.

"Zog here, Loxodon," he said, panting.

"That's my kill," she hissed, then smiled. "Go to your friends."

He helped her up as a gnome appeared with a bandage to wrap her severed hand. Her mercs pushed by her and into the other army as they descended the high ground.

"Zog honor agreement."

Kippa chuckled and snatched her ax out of his hand and took a deep breath. "Your choice, Orc."

The pair strode behind the hungry mercs, the battle raging around them. Four Red Widows moved toward them, and as they were about to engage, thirty arrows from above slaughtered them. Zog glanced up at a mountain ledge and watched their allied Frost Elves continue to rain arrows down from above, giving Kippa's army time to reorganize.

Boro's army raised their bows and fired back. A few elves plummeted from above and on to the defenders below. Zog reorganized a line with a few trolls in the center and then slapped the one nearest him on the ass, and away they went.

The trolls killed everything in sight. When a troll fell, it would enrage the others, who would slaughter more, crushing bodies, ripping off heads. A small contingent of gnomes stood shoulder to shoulder to the left of them, engaged with a host of widows.

Zog nudged Kippa and sprinted to their aid. Nearing them, he cleaved their pincers, attempting not to step on the dying and wounded gnomes in the process. He tripped over a body and fell forward, a Red Widow close by.

He blocked one pincer and then the other. He rose to his feet and headbutted one, smashing its carapace. The other one bit him in the lower back. He pitched forward again. With him lying helpless, Kippa charged over him, wrapped the widow around the throat with her trunk, and crushed it.

She pulled Zog to his feet with her trunk and a smile. "Now, we're even."

Chapter 36

Jari peered out from behind one of the boulders where the Loners were hiding and studied the sentries. The elves had distracted most of Boro's bodyguards. He had three Kagos and nearly fifty Iron Dwarves in his private compound who chased after the Frost Cave elves. They rode in a circle around them through the mountain passes, taking heavy casualties as a price.

Jari loathed Iron Dwarves. They had no respect for life and lived alone in the mountain below them, adamantly against coexisting with the other dwarves. If Boro had recruited them, there was no telling how many were in the caverns below them.

"I despise Iron Dwarves," Gnok spat.

"There's plenty to kill if we dally any longer, Cousin," Jari hissed, scanning for the best opportunity to attack.

In front of them was an escarpment, then a six-foot stone wall that would have to be scaled. Behind that was a long hut with other smaller huts for the hired mercs.

"Damn the Dwarven Lords, this is bad," Jari muttered.

"So, what's the plan?" Betha asked.

"We'll need someone to throw us dwarves on top, then we jump off and pray to our ancestors that we make it over without catching an arrow," Jari whispered, the defeat evident in his voice.

Sithril appeared behind, sending Jari's heart thumping

through his chest. "By the Dwarven Lords, you scared the hell out of me."

Sithril grinned. "Have no fear, Master Dwarf, for I am with you."

"Cold day in hell before someone throws this fucking dwarf anywhere," Kala said, sliding his palm to his ax handle. "Unless you want to meet your ancestors sooner than later, Jari Rockjaw. I'll gladly pay your fare to the afterlife."

Jari shook his head. "You see any other way, Scalp Master?"

Sithril spoke up. "I do." All heads turned in his direction. "You probably won't be thrilled, though."

"Get on with it, Elf," Jari uttered.

"The sewage line is unguarded. If we sneak through there, we will be able to take Boro by surprise. I will ask Kethil to ride past with four others and distract them while we make a break for it."

"How do you propose that?" Betha huffed.

Sithril closed his eyes and began humming. After a moment, his eyelids flew open, and his irises were opaque. He muttered something in elvish and then closed his eyelids again. When he opened them, his irises were a cold deep blue.

"Everyone set?" he asked as if nothing had happened.

All faces turned toward Sithril.

"Wh-What did I say?"

In the next moment, five riders galloped past on their steads, the lions' heads roaring. Sithril waved them on as Kethil and his team rode past. The Loners made it a hundred feet when they heard one the mounts screech, a large spear piercing its side.

Kethil lay underneath his mount as arrows thudded into the ground around him. His team wheeled around and rode back for him, all taking several arrows, killing them instantly. Kethil groaned, and as the Loners crossed the area into the sewer, Mori held back with a growl.

Jari turned. "Mori, what are you doing? Hurry up!"

Mori stared at the stone wall, then at Kethil as he hid under his mount's body, avoiding as many arrows as he could, although he had already been hit a few times.

He turned to Jari. "The Grey Dwarves are no more, Brother. We are sworn to protect all who need our assistance, and his sacrifice was what got us in, so I go to return the favor. If we meet again, Brother Blue Dwarf, then we do." He shrugged with a grin. "And if not, I'll see you in the afterlife."

"Mori, are you insane?"

Mori snickered. "More than likely. Kept in captivity for almost one hundred years will do that to you. I betrayed my family and killed my kin. I must redeem my honor. Farewell in the coming battle, Brother Jari."

"For the Gray Dwarves," he roared, sprinting out to Kethil.

Jari nodded his head, raised his ax in salute, then turned around to follow the others. As he caught up, he saw Sithril leaning against the wall. Jari checked him over.

"Are you all right?" he asked.

Sithril lifted his head. "One hundred mercenaries rode to their deaths because I asked them to. I feel one faint heartbeat, and it is fading. All the others are silent."

"You did the best you could. Let us be done with this battle and pay their families their share. Fair?" Jari asked.

Sithril smiled. "Yes, that's fair, Master Dwarf."

"When you two are done kissing, we need to go," Betha said from the entrance. "It smells like shit in here."

"Keen observation, Mistress Minotaur," Sithril said, slipping by her and navigating the tunnel.

"Where's Mori?" Kala asked as Jari passed.

"Regaining his honor," Jari said as he strode by.

Kala gave a grim nod. "May the Dwarven Lords bless the dead. I am now the last Grey Dwarf."

"You're a Loner," Jari said over his shoulder.

The group navigated up the tunnel, each vomiting as they made their forward. Arnak fell several times in the slush, cursing each time. They kept plodding forward, their footsteps the only sound in the dark, dank, foul-smelling entrance.

"Sithril, how did you discover this disgusting path?" Jari hissed.

"Some things are best left unsaid, Master Dwarf," Sithril grunted while pressing his palm against the steel door.

His hand pulsated with light, then fizzled out. The group stared at the door, then one another. Betha and Arnak were bent at the waist. Betha's horn kept grinding against the ceiling as if she were grinding her nails on a slate board.

"Betha, can you drop your head lower? It's the most annoying sound," Kala muttered.

"I'm not as short as you, Stumpy," Betha growled. "Grow a few feet, *then* say that."

"What do we do now?" Jari hissed.

"Where there is a will, there is a way, Master Dwarf. Iron Dwarf runes protect the door. Once it's locked, it cannot be opened from the outside."

Gnok shouldered his way to the front. "Move aside."

"Cousin, didn't you hear Sithril?" Jari asked.

Gnok nodded and placed his palm against the door. He muttered an incantation, and the door creaked open. Jari stared at him open-mouthed.

"You mind telling me how you did that?" he asked.

Gnok adjusted his axes and cleaned the sewage from his beard. "Remember, Boro and I hunted together, Cousin. It's a password he taught me and said that if he ever had a permanent home, he would use it to lock everything down." He shrugged. "A lot rolls around in this brain of mine."

Jari grinned. "Who's ready to retire?"

He heard grunts of approval from the others.

He extended his hand to Sithril. "If you'd be so kind as to lead the way."

Sithril nodded and closed his eyes. His opaque orbs pulsated and then turned back to their usual color. "I have found Boro."

"Good, my daggers are thirsty," Sinda said from the back. "Now, lead the way, Sithril."

Sithril nocked his bow and proceeded through the door. The others followed him in single file until the cave opened up. Sithril made his way to the back. The Loners followed behind him, cursing the whole way. Sinda lit a torch and passed it to Jari.

"This should help."

The room illuminated, and below them were hundreds of skulls and bones. "What in the Dwarven Lords' name?" Jari hissed, picking up a femur.

"So, Boro *does* have bones in the bottom of his place," Gnok said.

"Who are they?" Betha asked.

"The dwarves whose souls he has stolen. Looks like he became a necromancer like he said he would someday," Gnok muttered with a hint of admiration in his voice. "This is worse than I thought."

Jari nodded and freed his axes. "Necromancers die just like everyone else. Let's kill him and be done with it."

"Agreed," Betha growled.

Sithril touched the wall and then walked beside it. He stopped and made a double tap with his knuckles, and immediately, a door swung open, revealing a stone staircase carved into the wall.

Sithril led them up, carefully inspecting each step for boobytraps. He tentatively stepped on one near the top, and seven crossbow quarrels snapped in front of his face, embedding in the wall across from him.

Jari gave a deep sigh. "Shit, that was close."

Sithril nodded and held up his hand. He listened for a few

moments, then said, "Seven Iron Dwarves in the room."

Betha unslung her ax, accidentally smacking Gnok on the helmet. "Oops."

Gnok shook his head and rubbed it. "Hate to be on the other side of that."

Betha growled a laugh. "Me too."

"Sithril, Betha, and Gnok with me. Kala, Sinda, and Arnak with each other. Split when we get into the room. Sithril, cover both groups with your bow. Everyone understand?"

All heads nodded.

Sithril carefully opened the door and slipped in, followed by the others. Seven Iron Dwarves stood around a campfire with their backs to them, complaining about guarding the tunnel. Sithril raised his bow and aimed. He nodded at Jari, who slid by him with his group in tow, the others moving in the opposite direction.

Jari freed his bolas and swung them above his head. The rest of the teams readied their projectiles. As one, they launched them. Most found their mark. Jari's took an Iron Dwarf from behind, knocking him into the fire. After all the projectiles had been released, two dwarves remained. Sithril ended the threat, hitting each between the eyes.

He strode over to the other groups as they scalped them. The Velcro sound of beards, hair, and ears being scalped reverberated in the cavern. Betha glanced up, sniffed, and stood up.

"More are coming," she hissed, striding forward to the next door.

"Prepare yourselves," Jari said. "Form ranks."

The door opened. Betha waited until all of them cleared the doorway, and as the last ones did, she swung her ax overhand, slaughtering three before they knew what hit them. Jari and the others charged as Sithril fired his arrows over their heads.

Twenty Iron Dwarves walked in, and by the time Betha slammed the door to muffle the screams of the dying, only ten were left standing. Betha gored one from behind and snapped another's neck. Sithril killed another two, and Sinda's knives claimed three more.

Gnok charged and was hit with a bola, leaving a large gash above his left eye. He growled and choked the dwarf who hit him. Then he slammed him against the wall and headbutted his attacker until there was nothing left but mush.

Sithril walked up behind him and placed his hand on his shoulder. "He is dead, Master Dwarf."

Gnok slammed his forehead into him one more time. "Never been injured by an Iron Dwarf," he spat, dropping the body.

Jari shook his head as he scalped. "Gnok, you need help."

Gnok grinned. "Yes . . . I believe I do. I hate the bastards."

"Shall we continue our journey?" Sithril asked.

Betha tossed him a scalp. "This one is yours."

Sithril caught it, then tossed it back. "I don't take trophies."

Betha laughed. "You're a merc. How do you make a living?"

"I'm here for a higher purpose."

"And that is?" Jari asked.

Sithril smiled. "I wasn't entirely honest when we first met."

Everyone stared at him, some holding their weapons tight. Sithril exhaled and shrugged off the looks. He tapped his chin as if deciding what to say.

"My real name is Sithril Frostsong, second son to King Frostsong. The one hundred elves with me were my personal bodyguards. My father wouldn't send an army. So, you see, I'm in no need of scalps."

Jari's eyes bulged wide. "Why the deception?"

Sithril sighed. "We were paid to block your entrance to Anak'anor."

Kala cleared his throat, spat, then raised his gory warhammer. "I say we kill this deceiving elf."

Jari placed a hand on Kala's forearm as he advanced. "That

won't be necessary, Scalp Master."

"You choosing dwarves over elves, Brother?"

"No, but he did bring his personal bodyguards as a diversion." He glanced at Sithril. "I want to know why."

"The answer to that is simpler than you would think."

"And how's that?" Jari asked.

"I was captured, true enough. But when I saw the care you showed your healer, I knew that you would be a great company one day. As a second son, I stand no chance for the throne. My life was not going to be attending dinners and kissing nobles' asses. So, instead of escaping the hundreds of times I could have, I stuck around to find out the mettle of your brotherhood. It's nice to be useful for once in my life."

"Who paid you to kill us?" Betha growled.

Sithril shrugged.

"So, that's how you knew where he was hiding."

"It is."

"So you helped because we took care of one of our own?" Kala asked.

"Yes. Few on Labrys left are like your band, Master Dwarf."

Jari smiled. "We're down a dwarf in our company. You up for the job?"

Sithril stood quietly for a moment. "I was praying you would ask that. But many of your fellow dwarves would not be thrilled with your suggestion."

"Damn right," Kala said. Then his tone softened. "But you're a great fighter and healer. You saved my brother, so I cast my vote as agreed."

"Betha?" Jari asked.

She nodded as did the others, except Gnok, who stood alone by the door. "Ack, I hate your kind. You're no real merc. You don't even take trophies." He tossed an ax to him. "So, if you don't take scalps, at least take a weapon," he said with a smile. "But we're all misfits in one way or another. Welcome to the Loners."

Sithril smiled and slid the ax in his belt, then gave Gnok a head nod. "Shall we continue?"

Chapter 37

The Loners opened the door and continued down their path. Sithril led them, his feet not making a sound. They approached another set of wooden stairs where the sounds of battle intensified.

Sinda pushed her way to the front. "I'll lead the charge. If Boro is up there, I'm going straight for him."

The others nodded as Arnak followed Sinda and placed a large scaly hand on her shoulder. "Are you ready?"

She touched the ring around her neck, then kissed it and muttered a prayer. The stairs groaned as she took the first one. With a glance over her shoulder, she grinned, then her face turned to stone. "Let's kill this bastard and get the hell out of here."

Without another word, her firm legs took the steps two at a time. She lowered her shoulder, and with a loud war cry, she burst through the wooden door, flattening the dwarf on the other side.

Arnak followed behind her, his large feet crunching the Iron Dwarf under the door. "Oops," he muttered, crossing it.

As Sinda crossed into the room, she was astonished to face forty Iron Dwarves. Then she saw him. Boro stood in front of the door, preparing to charge into the battle. He glanced at her, then the others. He sneered when he saw Gnok. Then his eyes found Sinda.

She snatched the ring from her neck and threw it across the

room. "I'm here to collect scalps," she shouted.

Boro roared with laughter. "Who the hell are you?"

"Sinda Rockgut, wife to a murdered husband."

"Rockgut?" He thought for a minute. "Doesn't ring any bells."

Sinda growled and slid her knives from her belt and pointed at him. "My knives may change your mind."

"Brother Gnok," Boro said with a frown, "you should have stayed out of this."

"I'm not your brother, and you know why," Gnok said, then spat.

Boro raised a brow. "And now you're better than me, eh?"

"When you started stealing souls to feed your dark arts is where I stopped following you. Now, I'm here to help Sinda claim your scalp."

Boro laughed again. His white beard shook, and he rubbed his palm over his bald head with a loud sigh. "You're outnumbered five to one." He made his way to the front of the group. "But we will grant your—"

Two arrows thudded into the dwarves' eyes beside him. They collapsed without a sound, except for their armor hitting the ground.

"Now you're down to thirty-eight," Sithril said, stepping up next to her.

"Kill them!" Boro shrieked.

"Loners, form a wedge," Betha and Arnak roared, kneeling beside Sinda, who formed the point of the wedge. Jari and Gnok took the right side, Kala took the left with his massive warhammer, and Sithril took the center. He fired arrow after arrow as the Iron Dwarves churned up the dirt in front of them. He killed six before they crossed the contested area.

Boro held back and watched his mercs engage. Arnak and Betha swung their weapons like two well-oiled machines. Betha fell back with a roar, a spear piercing her shoulder. Kala slew three before an ax hit him in the shoulder, crushing it and sending him reeling back.

Sithril fired an arrow into the dwarf's face attacking him. The dwarf fell on top of Kala. As Sithril turned, a bola caught him in the face, knocking his bow from his hand. Two dwarves tackled him to the ground.

Gnok shouted as Boro knocked his ax from his hand and slammed him with a headbutt, sending him into Sinda, knocking her to the ground. Jari backpedaled with Arnak, and they stood back-to-back.

As Boro advanced, Sinda grasped his ankle and slammed a knife into his groin. He shrieked in pain and clubbed her over the head. Arnak pounded his chest, sprinted forward, and then spun his shell outward, slamming Boro and three others to the ground. Jari pressed his attack, killing another two dwarves before he was taken down.

Boro rolled away and then rose to his feet. He spat on Sinda and then raised his ax to finish the job. As it swung down, an arrow hit him in the shoulder. He dropped his weapon and glanced up.

"For the Loners," Mori shouted with Kethil by his side.

The door behind Boro shook, and a loud trumpet sounded— then it shattered. The remaining Iron Dwarves turned to Boro and then faced the oncoming onslaught. Mori, with blood dripping from his bottom lip, pushed Boro to his knees, then lifted Sinda.

"Now, claim your scalp for your kin," he whispered before falling to his knees, holding his stomach. "My watch is over."

As he collapsed, Sinda shook with fury. She approached as Zog and the others collided with Boro's last line of defense. She stalked over to Boro and kicked him in the face, knocking out several of his teeth.

Everything around her disappeared in a haze of tears as she pulled her husband's dagger from her boot. "Sinda Rockgut is my name. It's the last name you will hear before I send you to the depths," she hissed, shoving her dagger into his eye to the hilt.

Boro let out a groan and didn't drop until she let go of the dagger. She turned to Zog, who tossed her an ax lying by his feet while he chewed on a juicy eyeball. Sinda caressed the head of it, then slammed it down on Boro's neck, beheading him. She pulled a pouch from her waist, shoved the head in, then tied it back to her belt.

"Loners, account for yourselves," Jari shouted, yanking his dented helmet off, blood dripping down his fingers from his wound.

"Betha?" he asked.

"I'm not dead," she roared as Zog yanked the spear from her shoulder. "Minotaurs balls, that hurt!"

Arnak approached, part of his left ear missing. He tapped Sinda on the shoulder with a wide smile. "I am alive," he grumbled.

"Gnok?"

Gnok groaned as he made it to his feet. "I told you sons 'a bitches that was a terrible idea." He spat blood and lit his pipe. "But, yeah, I'm breathing. Now, where are my coins?"

"Kala?" Jari asked.

"Damn, I hate these Iron Dwarves. They weigh as much as two Gray Dwarves," he said, shoving the bodies off himself.

"Sithril?"

Sithril spat some blood, touched his forehead with a wince, and nodded. "I'm here, Master Dwarf." He glanced at his feet. "But Kethil is dead."

Kala knelt next to Mori Greygrog and closed his eyelids. "You have regained your honor, Brother Mori. May the Dwarven Lords hold you eternally." Then he rose to his feet. "Now, the Gray Dwarves are no more."

Jari patted him on the shoulder. "Let's get our scalps."

Chapter 38

Kippa led her army into the square. She surveyed the scene with a sigh. She picked up a crushed Red Widow with her trunk and tossed the body aside. She glanced at her nub and gave a nod to herself with a smirk.

"You fight good, Loxodon," Zog said, scalping a dwarf in front of him.

"Easy for you to say, Orc." She held up her nub. "I lost a hand in this venture."

Zog glanced at her hand, then handed her a scalp. "Take all Zog loot."

Kippa smiled. "Take your loot? Why did you even fight?"

Zog stared at the Loners as they scalped. "My friends alive because you help. Zog don't have many friends."

"So, you went for your band?"

"Only friends Zog has." He wiped his brow, then snatched an eyeball from his pouch. "Zog go to see friends."

"Our deal is complete," Kippa muttered. "Ask your leader where my gold is."

Zog walked over to Jari. "Loxodon wants coin."

Jari rubbed his beard. "You know there's no treasure, right, Zog?"

Zog gripped his club. "Yes, Mighty Zog know."

Sithril emerged from the long hut where Boro lived. "I wouldn't say that too loud, Master Dwarf."

Jari turned to him. "Unless you found an escape path, I'm in no mood for your advice."

Sithril grinned. "Follow me."

Jari followed him into the hut and shrugged. "All I see are dead bodies."

"Don't be so quick to judge," Sithril said, then pointed at a small opening in the ground by the wall.

Jari took a step closer and watched Gnok and Kala lift the coins out of the hole. Gnok rubbed his arm across his forehead. "Well, don't just stand there with your cock in your hand, Cousin. Help us give this treasure to Kippa."

Jari turned to Sithril. "But how?"

Sithril patted him on the shoulder. "Some things are best left unsaid, Master Dwarf."

Kippa and some others walked into the room. "Do you have my treasure?"

"Yes," Jari said.

"Good. I'm glad we didn't have to kill you." She strode over to the hole and lifted a chest of gold coins with her trunk. "We'll take half."

Jari breathed a sigh of relief as Betha approached. "We have more than enough to retire. Where's it gonna be?" she asked.

TO BE CONTINUED....

Other Titles from
Wahida Clark Presents

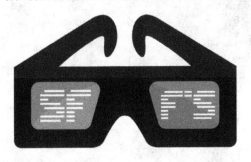

SCIENCE FICTION FANTASY
FOR THE CULTURE
W . C L A R K P U B L I S H I N G

EMPERORS

& ASSASSINS

WAHIDA CLARK

WAHIDA CLARK PRESENTS

THE ROAD OF
RESISTANCE

PART ONE

CHASE BOLLING

A SCI-FI FANTASY NOVEL